I0613796

SUZANNE COWLES

Shallow Basin

Novel One of Trilogy

▲

Pragmatic Press

Published by Pragmatic Press

First Trade Paperback Edition March 2014

Manufactured in the United States of America

For information on subsidiary rights visit:

http://pragmaticpress.wix.com/index

Follow the author at: http://suzannecowles.com

Dedicated to my loving husband, for believing in me and helping to make this artistic dream possible.

Table of Contents

Shallow Basin

CHAPTER 1

The torrid air laden with transparent liquid dripped angular secretions on the unsuspecting flora below. Powerless to defend against the onslaught, each leaf's spine contorted to the point of finally breaking under the immutable pressure. In response, the accumulated moisture wafted toward the heavens as life-giving water transformed into invisible vapor.

A lanky Blue Heron circled above guided by the swirling breeze. From its gullet, a minuscule bean crashed on the saturated mineral loam. As it rested amid an inhospitable landscape, tendrils appeared from the seed's casement digging into the sediment. Firmly rooted and fortified by nutrients over time, sapling leaves emerged forming an evergreen crown. Branches stretched up toward the porcelain iridescence of the moon. A tree shaft developed, eventually bearing multiple growth rings, standing vigil in the Atchafalaya River Delta.

Native animals wandered aimlessly, trampling the ground and killing competitive life forms. A specter for all to see, their ghostly images frolicked in the after-hours as late night sputtered onward. Nothing rested in the darkness while the void consumed the moonlight.

The sun ignited early morning with rays of fire, as beams of light barely visible through the impenetrable long-leaf pines filtered past the spindly tree trunks with extended fingers.

An opaque fog hovered above the floor plane no taller than a tombstone. Its surface boiled and churned like a witch's brew rolling in a cast-iron cauldron.

The dank air had a musty odor of sodden newspapers, while the stench of mold and mildew sashayed above the soil.

The setting was eerily tranquil except for the guttural moan of bullfrogs and field crickets. Their intermittent noises punctuated the humidity. Harmonic sound resonated longer than usual, like a canyon echo.

Drab olive boots, the kind a shrimper wore, marched in an orderly fashion. The profile of the neoprene shoes suggested that waterproof slip-ons were more important than laces in this environment. One foot lumbered in front of the other, blending with the background. The only factor noticeable was the ivory lug sole and deep treads now defiled with mud.

Twigs snapped, as a camouflaged interloper crept through Creekwoods headed for the swamp. He trudged by seasoned live oak trees draped in Spanish moss, whose massive branches twisted in odd ways as a result of being trapped in a confined space.

One tree stood out from all the others majestic in its girth with a widespread canopy. The tree was an old-timer whose mighty arms splayed out clinching the woods. It kept all residents close to protect them and forewarned strangers not to pass.

The undulating branches signified a season change to fall, a ritual of decay and a time when death preceded rebirth. Almost devoid of leaves, crooked blackened limbs remained motionless like the arms of a scarecrow.

The town folk respected the Creekwoods tree that resided near the entrance to Shallow Basin swamp. It acted as a sentry between two incompatible worlds. The only notification that wise men should not precede farther was this giant live oak restricting admission to land that had been off-limits.

Adele Crenshaw, a reclusive old woman rumored to be a witch, owned the land. The property had been in her family prior to the town's charter, when everything was part of a sprawling plantation.

She was proud to be a Crenshaw, although married she never took her late husband Earl Chaisson's surname. He tried for years to get her to move away, but she ardently refused to leave her birth land and it ceased to be a problem after his mysterious death.

The vast swamp and bottomland hardwoods that surrounded her house were uncharted; a pristine jewel any outdoor enthusiast could not wait to explore. Curious strangers that denied the posted warning signs on Route 3 ventured in never to return, possible victims of a legendary monster that protected the witch.

The legend of the Creepler was a fictitious story created by Adele, to keep the area unspoiled. It was mere coincidence that fools who wandered into Creekwoods never were seen again, victims of a freak accident or other logical explanation according to the sheriff from the adjacent town. Only the locals from Stray Oaks knew better than to trespass.

Inside the basin, topaz cattails lined the periphery of the shallows. Shallow Basin became more than a descriptive name for a southern bayou. It was the wetland home of diverse creatures, which depended on a healthy ecosystem. In this natural setting lived ten-point deer, granddaddy catfish and the largemouth bass of legends that often got away.

The hunter moved past the giant oak tree unaware of his fatal error. Glaring sunlight tumbled down casting radiance on shadows that seemed to cavort like demons on the marshy terrain. Each deliberate step met the squash of waterlogged dirt compressed beneath his boot leaving an impression. Footprints were the only evidence that someone had been there.

Brown Recluse spiders labored in the morning dew, as their wiry lace weavings girdled limbs. Quickly responding to vibrations, they attacked helpless insects stuck to their deathtraps.

Bloodsucking flies swarmed close, eager to taste fresh meat. Ravenous mosquitos buzzed his ears attracted to the dark clothing.

A reticulated serpent coiled at a tree base nestled between two root knots. Its aggressive stance was a final warning before exposing the cottony interior of its venomous mouth.

Danger was present, as the hunter slogged on determined in his quest. Stable ground turned to slippery grass, which turned to marshy muck. Live oaks replaced scrub oaks, which replaced pine trees. The landscape transformed into a bald cypress wilderness.

Advancing farther, his rubber chest waders were soon knee-high in a slimy pea soup. Tiny duckweed floated on the water's surface gently engulfing him.

A few feet away, clumps of water hyacinth bobbed as the transfixed eyes of a juvenile alligator surfaced. The young reptile floated while watching.

Baby raccoons pranced around a tree trunk, like devils chasing each other, knocking off a patch of lichens. The falling mushrooms caught the attention of one cub causing it to stop running, allowing the other to catch up. Each froze with fear when they detected the stranger's presence. The masked faces stared wide-eyed at the man.

Bubbles from the depths vanished after reaching the placid surface. A mature snapping turtle poked its snout into the air. It scuttled up a partly submerged log to get a better vantage, settling on an area of bark shrouded in moss. The gapping mouth was evidence of a fierce disposition. Its saw-toothed armor pointed toward the sun, as variegated eyeballs rotated to scrutinize.

Observers were everywhere, watching. The animals instinctively waited for something wicked to happen, like bystanders appraising a curse.

The guardian who protected the swamp inhabitants brought order to chaos. For harmony to exist, they pledged allegiance to the Creepler without questioning its methods. Nature had distilled a balance, a food chain and a circle of life. However, this creature was unnatural, an aberration malformed by witchcraft. Some called it sorcery; others knew it as pure evil. Still, all eyes waited and watched.

A Black Crow gliding overhead announced its presence to the unadulterated world with a loud repetitive squawk. The annoyance could scare off any potential deer, so the hunter took aim at the bird with his crossbow. As he set the carbide arrow in place, the crow shouted an incessant protest. The shrieks grew louder, like beats of a funeral drum.

The hunter could feel his eardrums bleed from the monotonous racket. The harpy's shrill voice caused his skin to cringe, making it difficult to sight the target. He squinted in vain.

He plucked back on the cord, while tension locked the dart in place.

Then as if the obstinate bird realized its fate, it abruptly ceased squawking. It sat motionless perched on the twisted branch above glaring down with ebony slits.

The hunter became aware of a maniacal presence. Something was behind him that had not been there before. Losing focus on the bird, he warily turned around. A terrifying misshapen figure met his apprehension.

Before his eyes could process the visual overload, a razor webbed claw thrashed through the air knocking him into the sludge. Forcefully strewn blood droplets spattered the landscape.

A flash of sinister eyes and savage jaws descended upon his paralyzed body. Brackish waves crashed in the tumultuous battle.

The Creepler made a recurring sound, like a symphony of male Cicadas hissing in the afternoon. It screamed and shrieked between going under water.

A scaly appendage knocked the crossbow from the hunter's grasp. The weapon floated for a second, then sunk into the blackness.

He gasped for air as he struggled to get his head above water, before plunging back down beneath the murk. The duckweed spread covering the stagnant water's surface, leaving no trace of a disturbance. Only silence and dead calm remained.

The crow, whose black iridescent feathers ruffled in the breeze, hesitated before flying away. The alligator, satisfied too, descended. All other witnesses quietly faded into the landscape. Serenity returned to Shallow Basin.

Eight steps and a landing, then twelve steps to the finish; each day the same narrow path taunted Beau Boudreaux. What was it that he despised so much about the concrete stairs carved into a hillside? Maybe it was the overstuffed book bag weighing heavy on his shoulders, or where the stairs led. In either case, holding the iron handrail that segregated the sides had not made the journey any easier. Some days he took his time, stopping to look around. On others, he jogged frantically up and down the steps, going nowhere. Today he chose to climb two steps at once.

His modest fan club met him at the top of the stairs, consisting of a malleable boy wearing a varsity letter jacket and a vivacious girl with red hair that worshipped his advancing steps.

Saylor Landry wrapped her arms around the back of Beau's neck briefly leaving the ground, as he returned the embrace, squeezing her furry pink jacket. She smiled a captivating grin with cerulean eyes radiating affection. Her look encapsulated their lengthy courtship since grade school. In Saylor's small universe, Beau was the massive celestial body that she chose to orbit.

Demanding less attention than most athletes do, Riley Daigle was different. He was Beau's loyal confidant and sidekick, constantly encouraging him. Riley was a humble wrestling team star, proof that one could have goals without becoming self-absorbed. Beau admired this quality about him and was proud to call them best friends.

"Is everything okay? We have been waiting here for a while," Saylor said.

"Sorry I'm late, guys. The tyrant detained me with a lecture about applying myself, so I can get into the law school of his choice," Beau said as they walked toward the crowd. "Then I was questioned about what I'm wearing."

"Bummer dude, I feel your pain. My mom complained that my hair is too long," Riley said carrying a heavy duffle bag.

Beau took Saylor's hand, clasping it tightly and smiled. "Don't worry, just another day at the Boudreaux homestead."

Groups of boys in the parking lot gathered around a new Camaro, staring intently at the engine as if it held treasures. A row of denim buttocks bent over the yellow car curves with all heads crammed under the hood. Jim Rousseau mashed the accelerator, revving the 326 horsepower engine a few times while the boys rejoiced. Some were more amazed with the rumbling sound of Cody Mouton's late model V8 GTO. The muscle car club compared notes of who had the coolest hot rod.

On the sidewalk the real muscle club, huddled members of the football team, compared statistics of professional players and discussed the upcoming strategy for Friday night's away game. They too wore school colors for the afternoon pep rally.

The quarterback Marvin Herbert; stopped talking to the linebacker Walter Guidry long enough to smile at Saylor as she walked by. He had been sweet on her since the third grade, when she lent him a sharpened pencil. As a person in a position of leadership, he respected her relationship with Beau and was content to ogle her from afar.

On the lawn, Jennifer Savoie and Meghan Bergeron whispered about who had broken up with whom over summer vacation. The cheerleading team was the in-crowd consisting of a pretty girl clique of which Saylor was the captain. However, she would have to wait until lunchtime to catch up on the latest drama rivaling reality television.

The rest of the crowd outside of Stray Oaks High School was more interested in those things that made young adolescence a forgettable time.

Amid the tripartite brick exterior, diptych castle towers loomed overhead. The garnet fortress was rich in history dating back to 1825. The walls outlined in precast concrete stored memories of generations of: Chaissons, Doucets, Crenshaws and Herberts. Those Cajun families settled the town, populated it with their lineage and kept it alive. Each clan added to the colorful legacy of the secluded backwoods, a simmering gumbo consisting of the necessary staple ingredients flavored with guarded family secrets.

As they approached the foreboding architecture, a pair of double doors caused Beau's stomach to churn. The outside of each steel slab appeared to be sturdy, but the hollow interior contained vast emptiness and the wire-mesh glass used for protection did little except to remind Beau of a prison.

Kelvin Herbert the school janitor/maintenance man; had repeatedly applied thick layers of glossy oil paint to the doors to conceal rust spots and gouges, attempting to hide the truth from surfacing.

The awful dread of confinement inside those entrance doors, in an institution that molded students into matching rectangular bricks, was more than Beau could stand.

Sensing his discomfort, Riley held the door open. "After you gents, I mean ladies."

"Cute Riley ... cute," Beau said.

"Can we stop by my locker to get my books?" Saylor said.

In the hall, the cinder block walls closed in on Beau as convex pressure bent in at the waist high dado. He felt trapped in a cage. The constriction stretched on and terminated into a final point where the other hall end seemed to vanish.

Saylor fumbled in her locker for a hairbrush with eyes glued to the magnetic mirror inside the door. She constantly worried about her appearance.

"Don't look now Beau, here comes the little brown-noser," Riley said.

Saylor ignored them, primping with a pink-glitter tube of lip-gloss.

Beau saw Jim approaching in the distance, weaving through the other teenagers who ignored his requests for safe passage.

"Hey Beau, my dad sure is ... thrilled that your dad ... will be speaking ... at the press conference. It's such an honor ... to have, I mean ... a famous fishing pro like him involved ... in the tournament," Jim said.

"Well, I'm sure he'll be thrilled at the photo op," Beau said.

Jim continued to needle. "Will you ... be there too? It's going to be ... a great event for ... my dad's reelection push."

And there it was, what Beau had been avoiding all fall, the meeting for the upcoming annual bass fishing tournament. It was time again, to stand in his dad's shadow and smile a fake grin for the cameras. Not that he would be alone. His mom Kacie would be there too. All three of them would pretend to get along, to be the perfect family and to care about one another.

The thought made Beau's stomach ache. He felt his intestines writhing and knotting from the impending doom. No one knew the truth about his idyllic family; they only saw the false façade.

Mayor Eugene Rousseau's son Jim played by the rules. His biggest offense was occasionally streaking his hot rod through town at late hours, giving Sheriff Wiley Aucoin fits. Rumor had it that the mayor paid his son's traffic fines in beer.

Otherwise harmless, Jim listened to every instruction his father dictated, with the sole intent of one day growing up to be his replacement. He had predestined job security through nepotism.

Jim did not technically stutter, but he had a strange way of pausing in his speech at all the wrong places when he got nervous. This mannerism was highly irritating to those who had to listen to him. He needed to cure the speech defect if he was going to replace such an eloquent public speaker.

Mayor Rousseau had finesse and panache, a polite way of saying he was a conman. He negotiated the sale of nutria meat to the local food bank both to feed the poor and to cut the numbers of nomadic rodents. He used public funds to purchase an eighteenth Century desk from auction, quoting its historic value. He read the Bible on

11

Sundays to the church congregation, without worrying about his own sins. That is why Jim wanted to be like his dad.

The thought of emulating one's father made Beau even sicker. *Do as I say;* that was the hidden message in every communication between father and son and Beau was determined not to grow up to be his clone.

The first warning bell rang, and students scampered throughout the stuffed hallway. Locker doors slammed, jocks tripped nerds, hall monitors yelled commands, the janitor immune to the bedlam toted a cleaning cart by and the fabulous trio slipped into first period. A new day had begun for the senior class.

Chemistry students grudgingly made their way to their assigned lab stations. A pyramid of five-gallon pails sat at the front of the classroom. Even with the lids sealed, the stench of formaldehyde reeked as it invaded every nostril leaving a taste of metal on the tongue. No one wanted to participate in dissecting a pig fetus, but it counted as thirty percent of the grade.

Saylor tied a vinyl lab apron around her waist to protect her designer clothing. She covered her freshly painted manicure with purple-surgical gloves. The fashionista glimpsed her reflection in the glass door of the wall cabinets. She was so involved in dress-up, that she forgot the purpose of today's exercise.

Riley was concerned with failing the class, due to poor scores on previous assignments. Coach Remy Doucet warned him that if he did not attain a passing grade, he would be off the team. The possibility terrified him more than he feared Coach's wrath. Riley excelled at sports, which was the only subject he lived and breathed. It coursed through his blood, and a scholarship was his one-way ticket out of small town hell.

Riley wanted something that the town could not offer. He felt compelled to search for his missing father. Growing up under the supervision of a single mother left him longing for a male perspective. According to Lin Daigle, the sperm donor was out there somewhere and Riley just needed to find him.

Saylor and Riley shared this desire, to escape the dead-end generational backwoods. The two focused heavily on their futures more than living in the present. Sharing equal ambitions, they should have been a couple, but that was impossible because Saylor was stuck on Beau.

He was the golden boy's son, a perfect combination of good looks, brains and southern charm. Beau had a sensibility for photography; an eye that perccived the details that made life interesting, coupled with a sharp intellect that noticed what others usually missed.

As the class settled into their seats, Riley fidgeted. "Hey, can you help me out? I'm not really prepared for this assignment."

"Didn't you read the chapter on porcine physiology last night?" Beau said.

"Dude come on, you're insulting me."

"Sorry, I forgot that you can't read," Beau said.

"It's not that I can't, I just don't. Besides, who has the time with practice every day? Just lean over and let me copy a bit," Riley said.

"Riley, get a life! I'm not failing because of you," Saylor said.

"Thanks a lot, Miss America."

"Don't mention it, cheater," Saylor said.

Ms. Chillingham brought the class to order in dictatorial fashion and distributed the piglets to teams of two. The timed examination commenced on the count of three. She dimmed the room's ambient lighting to add drama to the procedure.

Saylor held the pristine scalpel in her hand. Its shiny new blade reflected part of her face with stunning precision. She hesitated and then bore down as constant pressure tore the bluish-white skin in half. A citron puss escaped the surface followed by some milky plasma. The grim sight repulsed her delicate sensibilities.

Riley seated one row back whispered, "Careful that one's still breathing."

Saylor made a disapproving smirk over her shoulder. "Come on, we're trying to work here." She completed the last cut, as Beau pinned back all flaps of tissue to reveal the innards of a defunct circulatory and digestive system.

Like a spring, curly intestines shot forward spilling from the carriage. The twisted mass laced with bloody fluids and pent-up decomposition gases escaped to their freedom. The odor was offensive and nauseating. Saylor quickly turned her head away to avoid heaving her breakfast all over the table.

Beau assisted her any way he could, and followed along answering the lab questions. The two worked together not like a piston head turned by a camshaft, but like the torque created from such synchronicity. Their close association, where each worshipped the other in fervent passion would one-day lead to tragedy.

While the class worked hard on the assignment, Saylor pretended to be a doctor on a daytime soap opera. She acted the part of the principal character who glued the fabric of the slow-moving plot together with her beauty and talent. She mumbled ad libitum dialogue riddled with subtext, stressing the last dramatic word for the cliffhanger.

"Oh my God, there's an arterial blockage. I need to incise the left vertical before he croaks. Get me the forceps stat. Hurry up nurse!" Saylor said.

"Huh, oh … here you go, Dr. Landry," Beau said.

"Good work nurse, now get me a sponge."

Ever the thespian with dreams of becoming a movie star, she intended to shed Stray Oaks for New York after graduation. Saylor had a bold personality with blazing hair and her fire was not going to smolder. She would easily manifest fame and fortune with her talent and beauty, but not everything in life would be so simple.

Saylor envisioned marrying Beau and eventually having children once her career skyrocketed. She wanted him to be her director, and she would be his star actor.

"Hey you guys, a little help please," Riley said.

Beau looked back at Riley's table and saw a baby pig hog-tied by string, and laying diagonally in the dissection pan uncut. He choked back a laugh, "Wow, that's a different presentation."

"I know, it doesn't look right." Riley's bewilderment was spreading to his lab partner.

"You need to tie the legs to each corner of the dissection pan, like ours." Beau moved over so they could see. "And make two incisions; posterior to dorsal, then ventrally."

Saylor peered through the plastic lab goggles. "And hold your nose, because it's gross." While Beau continued to guide Riley in the right direction, she moved on to step five.

The pig's heart ventricles had a bulbous main coronary artery down the center, injected with a ruby compound. It stood out against the desiccated flesh.

Beau returned to assist her, forcing numbered spikes into each organ. The pig died again, stabbed to death like a pincushion. Cadaverous lungs, stomach, liver, spleen and a gallbladder overflowing with ocher bile were the culinary appetizer the class wanted before lunch break.

At the front of the room, Ms. Chillingham approached Beau's table holding a grade book in one arm. She scrutinized every detail, leaning over to get a closer look. "Hmmm, looks good. I like the clean incision. Saylor you should go into medicine with steady hands like that. Well done team."

Beau smiled, satisfied that a good grade would get his father off his back for a while. Flawless academic performance was easy for him to produce, but living up to the expectations of narcissistic perfectionism was grueling.

Riley could not resist commenting on the teacher's new pet, "Remind me never to loan you my bow knife and follow you into the woods alone."

Saylor turned around making a scowl face, "If given a chance, I can be very dangerous … you should fear me."

It was a hurried drive from Baton Rouge over Interstate Ten. The whole time Trace Morgan was fuming, not because of the deplorable weather moving to the East, but because some old woman was slowing progress.

The investors already formed a legal and binding partnership, the architect had acquired the necessary permits and the general contractor received the surety bond. Everything was in place to move forward with phase one of the most lucrative real estate development that Trace had ever concocted.

Reelman's Resort would be a fountainhead of good fortune with profits rising from the basin. Morgan Developers would transform the 12,500 acres of virginal swampland into a four-star hotel with a renowned chef, targeting clientele that could afford to forgo the typical stilted fishing lodge. For the guest, communing with nature would include a day of fishing in a luxury chauffeured bass boat with a bait boy, followed by a shiatsu massage and prime rib.

The mere thought of such decadence left Trace catching a thin string of drool before it jettisoned from his chin.

The rain poured in sheets, making it impossible for the windshield wipers to clear a path. He strained to focus on the white center markers, which seemed to pulsate.

Recent meetings with investors stressed his over-taxed brain causing his forehead to crumple. For months, Trace had tried unsuccessfully to reach Ms. Adele Crenshaw, while proceeding forward with the project. As the company chairperson, he could not figure out why there had been no response to such a generous offer.

Maybe she had passed away. His lips pursed a smile at the possibility, before anger returned. *On the other hand, she was holding out for more money. That was it. The biddy was playing hardball.*

Trace drove on as the weather changed.

Gray wisps of fibrous threads rolled by ragged cloud shadows to reveal streaks of sunlight. The sultry wavelengths caused the brumous ground to sizzle, as heat seared off the Earth's crust. Serpentine steam rose high enough to deplete a set curl.

Vernon Crenshaw sat up in bed scratching his chest, and stared at the clock. It was time to get moving. He picked up a small framed photograph of a younger version of himself hugging the love of his life. Then he swallowed the first of five prescriptions, a daily regimen of schizophrenia medications starting with lithium. The rest of the drugs professed to cure his depression, anxiety and psychosis. The pills dulled the pain, but they could not silence the voices in his head.

He was on his way out of the door to the family home that he had lived in for thirty-five years. He wore ordinary blue jeans and a plaid buttoned-down shirt as he scooted downstairs. His face was rough, unshaven and haggard. While buttoning his shirt, he dropped a sock on the stairs. Along the wall were photographs of the family, mostly of Vernon and his twin brother Chester.

In the living room on a tapestry wing chair, Adele studied a book of spells. For a witch she was morally neutral, neither standing for good nor conjuring evil. Her intention alone created the desired effect in accordance with the cult's plan.

She wore a blue dress with long-fitted sleeves, buttoned up to the chin and a skirt dusting the floor. The color was so dark, it blended with the night concealing who she was, a mysterious force that interfered with other's affairs, orchestrating each event that affected something else. In addition, she wore a 24k gold Egyptian ankh covering her heart.

Adele peered over the rim of her bifocals, as the worn oak steps screeched. "Going somewhere?"

Vernon stopped at the newel post to put on his boots. He was a natural outdoorsman. As a child, he and his brother explored every inch of the rustic land. He loved to be in the secluded woods, hunting and fishing, where he could forget about the voices.

Next to the stairs, odd stacks of unopened envelopes and various sized cardboard mailers sent from MD Incorporated covered a console table.

"Maw, when are you going to deal with this?" Vernon said.

"In due time dear." She rested the book face down on her lap. "I asked you a question."

Vernon hedged, "I've got to run into town." He bent to kiss her wrinkled cheek, which smelled of cloves.

"And for what this time?" Adele said.

"I need some tackle."

Adele squinted at him and smiled. "Or should I say for whom?"

Vernon backed out of the screen door causing it to shudder against the frame. "I'll be back soon." He raced to the pickup truck concerned about time.

In such a rush, Vernon failed to notice the expensive German sedan coming from the other direction down the county road. As he exited the gravel driveway, rocks flew into the air ejected from an angry tire tread.

Adele stood by the window ready to address the developing situation. She returned the handmade lace curtain to its stationary position. Like any southerner living in a remote area, she grabbed her double-aught shotgun to welcome the uninvited guest.

The two-story Crenshaw ancestral home was antebellum clapboard with an upper balcony over the porch. Tall fluted columns supported the cedar shake roof in need of repair. The paint blistered from years of neglect. Its color was dingy white no longer pure, but not buttery enough to pass for cream. Leafless vines twisted around a tormented porch railing.

The interior filled with antiques was the same, dusty and abused. Tattered upholstery loafed on worn-out furniture, stuffed with duck feathers from hunting kills. Family mementos covered in cobwebs lined the shelves amid knickknacks. The cat took care of intruding varmints, which Adele used in her poisonous brew.

A pair of men's dress shoes stepped out of the car into a sticky condition. The pristine black soles touched down on moist clover and dollar weed. Trace fumbled for documents and stowed his cell phone in his side pocket. The sweltering humidity slapped him awake faster than an expensive cup of coffee. He wrangled with his tie, loosening the restriction.

As he walked up the porch steps, Adele was already standing in the doorway. She held the shotgun diagonally in front of her chest without speaking.

"Ms. Crenshaw, sorry to disturb you. I'm—," Trace said.

"I know who you are, Mr. Morgan," Adele said.

"Yes well, won't you please invite me in? It's awfully humid today."

"I don't see that we have anything to discuss, unless you've come to fetch all this paper you sent," Adele said.

"I can see I've caught you at a bad time. I would have called first, but you don't seem to have a telephone," Trace said.

"Don't need one out here."

Trace did his best to be polite, while sweat caused his shirt to cling to his backside. He felt his confidence waning with each drop of perspiration.

"Ma'am the matter at hand is that my company, Morgan Developers, wants to purchase your land for a sizable amount."

"It's not for sale," Adele said.

"I can assure you that based on the appraisal; our offer is more than generous."

Adele stared at him in uncomfortable silence.

Trace squirmed mustering the courage to lay down his trump card. "If you're holding out for more money, this offer is final."

Adele forced the screen door open, hitting him in the nose. She walked toward him raising the shotgun. "Let me give you an appraisal of the situation. You have until the count of three to get in your fancy car and scurry back to the North."

"Well Madame, you're leaving me with no choice." Trace ran down the steps and tripped over a curious black cat, then dashed into his car.

"One … two …" Before she could say *three*, the car backed down the driveway.

A large fur ball with almond eyes pounced onto the porch, stopping to rub against Adele's shins.

She reached down to scoop up Midnight, her cat of thirteen years. She held the minx in front of her with its legs dangling. "When will they learn not to bother me?"

CHAPTER 2

Late morning sunlight illuminated the room's interior with warmth. The walls bore testament to decades of informal chats, bantering and holy blessings over meals. The family gathered day after day around an old walnut slab passed down through the years. The antique table exhibited the markings from domestic experience.

In this room, Kacie Boudreaux cooked each meal with love to nurture and sustain her family. When Beau was a baby, she wiped up spilled bowls of applesauce that he felt more comfortable wearing, while finger painting cryptic symbols in the mess. Other times during a storm when the electricity was out, the family gathered around the table and played card games indicating that Buck Boudreaux was the champion.

Those were special times, but Kacie cherished the ordinary minutes that flowed seamlessly into the next most of all. A grounded person, she recognized the beauty in simplicity.

From the table she dispensed money from the checkbook, rifled through endless grocery bags and labored countless hours over the family scrapbook, documenting those precious moments in life that the men never perceived.

The lemons were ripe, teetering between puckering lips and saccharine sweetness. As Kacie squeezed them into the crystal pitcher, she gazed out of the kitchen window noticing three squirrels darting around an oak tree with their claws biting into the crusted bark. It was another beautiful Louisiana day in the *Sportsman's*

Paradise, a nice place for a preacher's daughter to call home.

Kacie placed the spent rinds into the compost bin next to the recycling container. Ardent about protecting the environment, she did everything she could to leave a minimal carbon footprint.

Physically, she resembled an invigorating tonic on a tepid summer's day. Kacie was tall and cool, like a southern drink. Lemonade summed her up with its natural ingredients, the liquid of life mixed with cane sugar balanced by citric acid. More than a glass of refreshment, she was nurturing.

As a teenager, Kacie planned to go to college and become a middle school teacher. Instead, she married and started a family at a young age, then focusing on Buck's career left no time for her aspirations so she remained a homemaker.

Once Beau was old enough, Kacie started working a few days a week at the library to get out of the house. On Saturdays, she read to the children while they sat in toddler chairs. They easily connected with her motherly nature. She was attentive, understanding and sympathetic to their needs.

In the kitchen, the almond cookies made from scratch filled the room with the fresh smells of goodness. Kacie frequently baked deserts to hand out at the library, rewarding young children for finishing a book.

A ringing phone intruded on her solitude. She glanced at the caller ID, not recognizing the number. "Boudreaux residence, Kacie speaking."

"This is Dean Stanton calling from State University, to welcome Beau into the freshman class next fall. We have reserved his seat in the English department. I understand that he will also pursue a juris doctor after completing his undergraduate degree."

"Do you call all the parents personally?" Kacie said.

The dean chuckled, "Only the ones that donate a wing to the law library."

"That would be my husband's doing, but we are both very excited about Beau's admission nonetheless."

"And may I add that we look forward to a long relationship with the Boudreaux family, as there are plenty of opportunities for future support of campus expansion," Dean Stanton said.

"Yes sir, I'm sure there are. I will let Buck know you called. "

In the corner, was a built-in desk area that Kacie used for making arts and crafts. A dry erase marker board hung over the worksurface fashioned into a calendar. Colored sticky notes covered it, to remind her of all the responsibilities she shared for others. Signs filled each space leaving no time left for herself.

Kacie went back to work on the scrapbook. This one was to commemorate Beau's high school years. She picked up the hot-glue gun, and set it back down again before squeezing the trigger. Her lower back ached and she felt warm moisture under her thigh. Lately, she visited the bathroom too frequently.

In the powder room, she discovered additional menstrual spotting. She grabbed a sanitary napkin from the sink cabinet, and realized she was almost out of pads. She was not overly concerned about the schedule change from her regular time of the month, just annoyed at the inconvenience of constant stained clothes.

As a home remedy, she swallowed extra vitamin B tablets, hoping to get an energy boost. She also ingested herbal supplements, extra minerals and was on a cleansing juice diet. Before she could give it another thought, the phone rang again.

It was Haley LeBlanc, Buck's publicist. She began their partnership as his agent negotiating deals for public appearances and sponsorships. Then she advanced to controlling press releases, scheduling interviews and selling merchandise. Her aggressive personality could sell garbage, spin scandal and charm a monk with grace. The marketing duo thought alike, got along with ease and communicated well as a team, a powerhouse for a non-contact sport.

"Good morning Haley," Kacie said.

"Kacie darling, I have good news. The publisher is printing 100,000 copies of Buck's auto. Would you be a doll and tell him?" Haley said.

"We're going to eat at Fourchette's tonight. Would you and Amber like to join us for dinner around six o'clock? We can discuss the details then, and the kids can chat."

"Fabulous darling, you know I'd love to marry those two off one day, but I've got to run for now … kisses."

The stove buzzer sounded, alerting Kacie that the cookies had finished baking. She pulled the cookie sheet from the oven rack, as a wave of hot air slapped her face. She set them down on top of the stove when the phone rang yet again.

"Hello Dad, I was going to call you later," Kacie said.

"Honey, there's a crisis and I need your help," Pastor Louis Foret said.

"You sound awfully stressed. What's the matter?"

"It's Ms. Guidry; Betty's dropped out of the bake sale on the count of the flu. We really need her pecan, apple and peach pies. Would you be a dear and fill in?"

"Sure, in addition to my tray of bread pudding, not a problem."

"Oh, you're my favorite daughter."

"I'm your only daughter."

"Yes, we broke the mold with you sweet Kacie."

"I've got to go dad, the bakery waits."

Tending to the congregation required most of Pastor Foret's time. Almost everyone in the town was a member of his church. Only a handful of people were other denominations, and he knew who they were.

Caring for the salvation of those who needed saving was a fulltime calling. In addition to managing church business, he provided Sunday sermons, baptisms, marriages, funerals, graduation convocations, tended to the infirm and absolved sins. He was a strong man, proud leader and thought his daughter was a vision of saintliness, as did Buck.

On the back porch of the historic Victorian, Buck perched on the edge of a cushioned wicker chair tying a lure. Compressed so many times, the seat stuffing congregated in the periphery leaving prickly wicker sticking him in the tailbone.

His trusted companion Sampson the bloodhound, rested in the corner with one eye opened curled into a black-and-tan ball. Sampson was always alert, especially his olfactory glands to the scent of food. He excelled at finding dead things in the woods by way of his nose, a superb hunting machine when needed.

Lure making was an art passed down through generations, but Buck thought of it as a chore. Designing his custom signature lure series, which was a big hit sold exclusively at Fishermen's World, demanded all his free time. The manufacturer eagerly awaited submission of his latest prototype. They had a production deadline to meet.

Concentrating, Buck used a straight-edged razor to cut a shallow slit into a tiny bottle cork. He glued a fishing hook in the slit with the hook point facing the narrowest part of the cork and set it aside with the others for painting.

Buck locked one hook shank into the fly-tying vise and worked the round-bend pliers around the shaft as if he could breathe life into the bronze-mallard shoulder feathers. He used prewaxed monochord thread to dress the hook, adding short rubber bug legs and holographic stranded plastic fibers. Satisfied with the outcome, he tied a half-hitch knot and glued on doll eyes. He worked diligently on the new cork popper design.

Buck was a habitual creature limited by routine and devoid of spontaneity. Regimented tasks set at specific times controlled his day. A tight schedule existed in his mind with little room for deviation.

Buck worked hard to expand his stardom, while Kacie worked even harder to please him. Their lingering marriage was a last concern on his agenda, a comfortable arrangement made for convenience. In their long relationship they still loved each other deeply, but without burning passion. The present situation was a result of a crucial life decision made in high school that changed their lives forever.

Languishing in the background of Buck's shadow was not objectionable to Kacie. He was a famous professional angler with a huge contingent of fans. Because of his winnings, they had plenty of money, enough to be eternally wealthy in Stray Oaks.

As she walked through the screen door, it creaked. The noise was another reminder of the growing maintenance list that Buck would never address. She landed the sparkling elixir on the glass tabletop without him noticing her presence.

He focused on the proper tension of the bobbin, though the stainless-steel hook did all the damage to the fish. It was customary for the obvious to escape him. His clouded vision seldom achieved clear sight.

Kacie waited patiently for an acknowledgement, while fiddling with the gold crucifix hanging from her neck. Unsurprisingly, Buck remained engrossed with his task. She gently massaged the tension out of his shoulders, though the physical contact seemed to annoy him more than communicate her affection. He looked up at her tersely to stop.

"Anybody in there?" Kacie said.

"Sorry baby, you know how I get under a deadline," Buck said.

"I invited the LeBlanc's to dinner. Haley wants to discuss your book deal."

"Is Amber coming too? She would be such a great girlfriend for Beau. "

"Yes, I hope we can get them together." Kacie acted playfully, relaxing on his lap. "May I interest you in anything else?"

That is why Buck married her seventeen years ago. She was a raving beauty and the warmest soul he had ever met. Her grounded demeanor tempered his driven supremacy. He needed her as a bee needed a flower, together they flourished.

Buck ignored the question. "By the way, what are you wearing to the press conference?"

"I was thinking about the little black dress with the ruffles."

"Um, that would be nice, but why don't you wear the red one I gave you for Christmas? Yeah, that would be perfect. You look hot in red." Buck held the vision in his head for a moment. "Maybe I'll take you up on that offer later."

Kacie crumpled her nose. "You're no fun, besides who says there will be a later?"

"I do, we have all the time in the world when my schedule permits."

"We'll see. I've got some errands to run in town, for now I'll settle for a kiss." Kacie pressed her velvet skin against Buck's shaved cheek, gently caressing it with her lips. She turned toward him nestling her nose under his, Eskimo style. He could taste the cinnamon and vanilla scent she wore as her sable hair fell away from her neck. She lingered for a moment, long enough for Buck to reevaluate his decision.

Then she rose in orderly fashion and started to walk away.

Buck abruptly clenched her wrist. "Wait."

She looked down at him puzzled. "Yes?"

"What are we going to do about that boy?"

"You want to talk about this now? Can't it wait?" Kacie said.

"Not really."

"Well, he's got his spot in college and you've ordered his birthday car. What more is there?"

"He's always moping around here and scowling at me as if he hates me," Buck said.

"He's a hormonal teenage boy. What do you expect?" Kacie said.

"Why can't he be more appreciative and show some respect? We buy him everything he wants and I do not need him sulking at the press conference. It sends the wrong message to my fans."

"I'm sure his moodiness has something to do with that girl he sees. Don't worry, I'll talk to him."

Kacie flashed an insincere expression, the one she used occasionally to mask concern. The friction between her husband and son was approaching disaster levels. She routinely acted as a buffer between them, but felt powerless to stop their growing interpersonal conflict.

The two did not get along or relate well to each other, constantly arguing like a debate team of point-counterpoint, but now was not the time to worry about their problems for Kacie had a few of her own.

Raised sidewalks fenced by conjoined masonry flanked the modest cobblestone roadway. The eclectic downtown architecture rambled on in either direction of

Main Street. The jagged tops of the rusticated building faces cut into the sky like a serrated knife.

Kacie parked the hybrid subcompact parallel to the curb, in an opening between two automobiles down from the grocery store. She could afford a luxury vehicle, but she worried more about the environment; carbon monoxide emissions contributed to climate change. She felt better about herself saving the world, rather than riding around in style.

Her foot landed in a depressed pocket of bricks that had retreated from eroded soil. Louisiana was sinking due to a high-water table. In the early 1800's, the dirt road was riddled with potholes. Once paved it took on the charm of a quaint little town, each brick rose and fell perfectly at the corners. The newness did not last, each year more bricks succumbed to the sinkhole.

After gathering her things, Kacie stepped up to the curb. She searched inside her purse for a shopping list. As she walked blindly forward, a man slammed into her shoulder nearly knocking her down. She did not recognize him, but could tell from his dress and manner that he was from out-of-town.

"Pardon me," Kacie said.

"Why don't you watch out? Eyes only work when pointed forward," Trace said. His anger was evident from the shade of his complexion.

"I said I'm sorry sir." Kacie accepted blame willingly, even when it was not her fault. She learned to keep the peace, while her father dispensed the sacred word high on a sermon mount. She mostly feared his wrath, rather than having a propensity for forgiving others. The pastor could be an intimidating man with God on his side.

Trace continued to mutter to himself as the two parted ways, headed for a grey-stucco Spanish Revival styled building displaying a bronze plaque with engraved letters that read: *Town Hall.*

He ripped open the door so hard; the cut glass rattled inside the lead came. The hinges squealed in complaint. Trace grappled for the handle quickly escaping from his force. Crossing the threshold with continuous forward motion, he slammed the door shut.

The icy chill of air conditioning sent a shiver up his spine, making him aware of how damp his clothes had become from the humidity.

Trace was born in Stray Oaks but his parents divorced at an early age, forcing his mother to find work in Baton Rouge. She was involved in a profession older than religion, and specialized in state politicians as clients.

Because Jolene Morgan was attractive, many of her patrons became long-standing regulars. One fashioned himself as her pseudo-boyfriend, though his name remained anonymous.

Mr. Feelgood hung around their home too often. He unofficially adopted Trace as a son, mentoring him as a surrogate white-collar crime trainee. The master taught his young progeny the fine art of swindling, and helped Trace land his first major real estate deal.

Together they formed a development group with laundered capital generated from silent partners. They reaped the benefits of a depressed real estate market, bottom feeding on desperate sellers and then flipped the property for a profit. That worked for a while until they became bored with their conquests, and moved up to the liquidity of exploiting the legal loopholes in governmental laws.

The reception area of Town Hall was a ghost town. Stately furniture sat vacant while instrumental music played in a loop overhead. The gatekeeper, Lin Daigle, was not at her desk.

Without stopping, Trace steam rolled to Mayor Eugene Rousseau's private office. The door was slightly ajar, enough to see their surprised faces when he finally put on the brakes. Eugene and Lin were both wearing *Vote for Rousseau* buttons.

"Sorry, you can't—," Lin said.

"It's all right Lin, we know each other," Eugene said. "Let's pick this up after lunch. Looks like Mr. Morgan has a problem."

As Lin exited the room, she gave Trace the *Asian stare of death*, the same look she frequently gave her son Riley when he misbehaved. She closed the door with a professional thud to reinforce her bad attitude.

"You're damn right I have a problem. No, we have a problem," Trace said.

"Cut to the chase please."

"I just came from the Crenshaws."

"And how did it go?" Eugene said.

"Well, she waved me off with a shotgun, that's how it went."

"From the looks of it no bullet holes, so I'd say it went well." The mayor had developed a tolerance to people barging into his office for a scream session.

"Look Eugene, don't play with me. You need this development just as much as I do if you want this town to grow." Trace plopped down in a comfortable guest chair after flinging rolled construction drawings on the desk.

"Don't get snippy." Eugene unrolled the scrolls and looked at the map. "What do you want from me?"

Trace pointed to the blue markings. "You're going to commandeer this land here for the town through eminent domain."

Eugene scoffed and leaned back in his leather chair nearly tipping. "Why would I do that? The Crenshaws are nice folks."

Trace stood up canted forward, depressing white knuckles into the mahogany. "Let me show you." He pointed to the various resort structures on the drawings, while giving a rehearsed sales pitch.

"It sounds really nice but—," Eugene said.

"I knew you would say that, ever pandering to your constituents." Trace pulled out a thick envelope from inside his coat pocket, dropping it on the plans.

Eugene picked it up and fanned through the contents, causing the corner of his mouth to slightly foam. "Lots of Grover Clevelands, I see." Then his scruples tried to force his hand to return the envelope. "What kind of a person do you think I am? I can't accept this."

"Call it a campaign contribution. Go on, smell it, smell the victory."

"And what about the Crenshaws?"

"Don't tell me you're afraid of her?" Trace said.

"Well, they say she's a witch," Eugene said.

"Oh come on, next you'll tell me the monster is real too."

"It is strange that people go missing all the time."

"That urban legend is just a story made up by adults to keep the kids from necking in the woods. So don't let a little old lady stop us from making millions."

"I guess you are right," Eugene said.

"Tell you what; I don't need all 12,500 acres. They can keep an acre with that dumpy house."

Eugene had the facial expression of losing at a poker game. "Your generosity is very underwhelming."

"And just because I'm a nice guy, I'll let you hold the fishing tournament there to prove nothing bad will happen. It will be good advertisement for the project."

Eugene sighed. "As you wish. I'll have Julian Dixon draw up the papers."

Trace extended a skeletal palm to seal the deal. "Nice doing business with you Mayor. Keep up the good work. You're worth every penny."

The plastic banner stretched across both sides of Main Street, tied between two wrought iron lampposts. It billowed in the wind like a fragmented parachute. The message printed in standard block letters advertised the fiftieth annual fishing tournament. A blue graphic of a bass fish jumping out of the water, looked happy tethered to a hook. It was just a sign.

Kacie did not feel good, deducing her illness was from the stress of an overloaded schedule with the upcoming fishing tournament, Buck's numerous public appearances, Beau in his senior high school year and the onset of the busy fall reading season at the library.

However, this symptom differed from typical anxiety; a persistent lingering fatigue sapped her energy.

36

The home remedies garnered from an Internet medical site had not helped. She knew the problem could not be depression; it was too early for empty nester's syndrome.

There was a sidewalk sale at Lillian's Bookstore, and one day she would be selling Buck's autobiography book. Lillian Charbonneau, Kacie's best friend from high school, was displaying the mayor's reelection poster in the window. She waved for Kacie to come inside.

Lillian was going through difficult times in her two-year marriage. She recently learned that her husband, Wilbur Charbonneau the local emergency medical technician, was cheating.

Devastated by the revelation, she did not know how to proceed. In a state of shock, she kicked him out of the house sending him back into the arms of his male lover.

When Lillian and Wilbur married as virgins, their honeymoon produced a son. Fortunately, Eddie was barely old enough to speak and could not understand the dilemma his mother now faced. Competing for Wilbur's affections with another woman would be difficult enough, but going up against another man was almost impossible.

Each day the forced separation drained their meager savings with Wilbur living in a motel, while the town gossiped about the affair. Embarrassed by the events, Lillian would not discuss the salacious details in marriage counseling, so their problem festered.

Wilbur was dismayed at the new realization that he could not lead a heterosexual lifestyle, no matter how hard he tried. He loved Lillian, just not in the same physical way. It broke his heart to see her self-confidence as a woman destroyed by the reality of his sexual orientation.

Kacie stuck her head in the door and smiled. The familiar smell of old paper lingered in the air. It was the same as the library. "I hate to bring it up, but what's the latest in the family saga?"

"No change. Wilbur is convinced we made a mistake marrying, and I'm sitting at home alone with my son."

"How is little Eddie in all this?"

"He doesn't understand what's going on, but he misses his father."

"Oh honey, I'm so sorry," Kacie said.

Lillian stepped down from the ladder. "How are you? You look worse than I feel."

"I'm still having that problem, plus now I'm bloated with gas."

"Please go to the doctor. It could turn out to be something very serious."

Kacie took the good advice on the way out the door, and filed it away in her mind under denial. Mouton's Pack and Save would have what she needed.

Posters of food products and sale prices littered the storefront windows. The corporate graffiti were just more signs next to a white vinyl banner hung below the awning that read: *Vote Rousseau for Mayor*.

Standing by the cash register, Francine Mouton installed a new roll of receipt tape. "Morning Kacie, Kenny is putting out some fresh merlitons in the produce section."

"Thanks Francine, but I only need a few things." Kacie bypassed the shopping carts, and headed for the pharmacy area. She read the overhead sign: *Feminine Hygiene*. This was the aisle she needed.

Suddenly, a thick ball of phlegm building in the back of her throat choked her. The checkerboard black-and-white floor tile reflected the glaring lights. She felt flush, as warm heat brewed under her shirt collar. The room started to kink and snarl in slow motion. The black tiles seemed to transform into vacant black holes, while the white tiles floated on the air. Kacie fell backward in a semiconscious state.

A sturdy arm reached around her waist. Kenny Mouton broke the fall. "Are you okay?"

Kacie looked dazed. Her voice cracked trying to speak. "Yes, I'm fine."

"Let me get you some water." Kenny ran to an open-air cooler and grabbed a bottle of spring water, then offered it to her. "This one's on the house."

"Thanks Kenny. I think I got a case of vertigo from skipping breakfast." She tortured the truth. "You know, I don't feel very good right now, maybe I should just head home."

"Okay, you take care now. We'll be here when you return." Kenny smiled from a distance, nursing an old high school crush.

Kacie waved goodbye to Francine, who was tagging soup cans on sale.

With her head down focused on the floor, which was still gyrating, she exited the store.

When she came out of the automatic doors, she collided with Vernon who was trying to enter. He had been waiting for her on the curb.

"Oh dear, please forgive me," Kacie said.

Vernon gripped her arms to keep her upright. "You okay Sunshine?"

"Not really, you're the second person I've run into today, literally." Kacie straightened her posture and slipped free from his grasp, while still looking down. She could not look directly at him; his piercing malachite eyes haunted her.

Vernon did more than look at her, he saw through to her soul. She felt naked and vulnerable in his gaze.

She was uncomfortable being close to him; too much history perhaps. History she desperately tried to suffocate under her innermost desires, hiding it from the rest of the world.

Kacie thought that time would cure it, the feelings would die or she would forget him. Eighteen years has passed and nothing had changed. She nervously twisted the base of the crucifix necklace.

"You look uncomfortable. Is it me?" Vernon asked a self-deprecating question because he wanted validation for feeling rejected by her. He used her rejection to squelch the guilt he carried for abandoning her in high school.

"I think it's better for everyone if we don't speak." Kacie focused more on the welfare of others, at the expense of her own personal needs. This strategy did not diminish her pain; it just made her feel like a martyr.

"I remember a time when you wanted to be near me. In fact, you hated to be apart." Vernon played the sympathy card; it was the last one he held.

"That was a long time ago, so long I can hardly remember."

Vernon bent down to the side of her cheek, and whispered in her ear. "Remember when you would sneak out of your bedroom window late at night and we would lie on the ground looking up at the stars?"

Kacie pulled away. "I remember a lot of things, which is why we are where we are today. Now if you'll excuse me." Kacie started to walk toward her car.

"You know, I've always wondered, why did you hook up with that corporate sellout?" Vernon said.

Kacie ever defensive about her family, turned around to address the question squarely. "Who Buck?"

"Yeah, the loser."

"Well Vernon, if you are asking me why I chose Buck over you, the answer should be obvious."

"I thought you wanted to be somebody? Are you really happy as a housewife eating the scraps he throws?" Vernon said.

Kacie walked up to him and articulated her words. "I love my family, and that's all that matters." Feeling vindicated, she started to walk away again. However, she could not let it go. She felt the need to provoke him. "Just curious, if the big city is so great, then why are you still here?"

Vernon sensed her weakness. Fighting was just another form of love. He approached her, closing the distance between them. He stared straight into her eyes, and spoke in a sensual voice. "Because I'm mighty fond of the scenery around here."

Kacie hesitated, lingering for a moment under his warm scrutiny.

He peered into her soul, and he could feel the truth.

On the opposite side of the street was a building people avoided by following the law. Those whom did not received a personal tour of the interior with complimentary lodging.

Inside was a steel desk from the 1950's. The walnut laminate top had chips around the edges caused from things colliding with it: metal chairs, flying objects and occasionally human bones. The battleship-grey body had scratches, scuffmarks and some offensive words etched into the paint. Most of the chrome finish had rubbed off the steel legs. The drawer-lock keys vanished decades ago. Still, Officer Wiley Aucoin worked at his desk every day; ignoring the violence that took place inside these four walls.

Each stick of wood he pressed inside the electric pencil sharpener came out transformed into a writing device bearing the proper point. The machine ground away thin veneers of wood, layer after layer, until the lead core emerged. Wiley lined then up uniformly in a row on top of his desk, carefully placing each to the left of the last.

The rest of his desk items were: a pencil cup, nameplate, stapler, tape dispenser, phone and an empty letter tray. Each item had a specific placement on the surface. If anything moved out of alignment, he quickly returned it to its home. Wiley found comfort in order, which masked the ugliness of his life.

Dixie Savoie, his part-time secretary chatted on the phone with Lin Daigle. They gossiped about who Jessica Blaze, the local news reporter was allegedly seeing.

"I heard he's from out-of-town, and over the weekend, I saw the two of them driving down Route 3 together," Dixie said.

"No doubt they were headed for Motel Haven in Bakersfield," Lin said.

"I know she's such a tart. They probably have a room just for her."

Bring, bring, bring went the second phone line. Wiley gave Dixie a look of displeasure.

"I'll get it Dixie, never mind with troubling yourself." Wiley picked up the receiver. "Stray Oaks Sheriff's Office, Officer Aucoin speaking. How may I help you?"

On the other end of the line was an investigative officer from the Lafayette Police Department who needed assistance. A hunter's wife found some global position satellite coordinates for Creekwoods scribbled on paper in their garage. The hunter had not returned yet or called home. It had been several days since the couple last spoke, and she was concerned.

Wiley recognized the numbers without looking at the wall map. "Yes, I know where that is. Let me go check it out, and I will get back to you. I'm sure it's nothing."

In the 5'x5' holding cell, known by his stage name, Mr. Stumpy was sleeping off a drunken stupor from last night. He was not under arrest; he just did not have anywhere else to go. Wiley occasionally drank with him at Fourchette's Bar & Grill, commiserating together in their misery.

Mr. Stumpy was a diminutive homeless man who occasionally worked as a freelance party clown. As a little person he could do all the things typical clowns did, like

43

tie fancy balloon animals, but his stunted size made him especially scary during Halloween. With a sadistic nature, he loved to scare young children and make them cry, running to their parents for protection.

Wiley drank too often, with or without Mr. Stumpy around. Unmarried and childless, he could afford to throw away his entire paycheck, and he did.

He routinely drank beer to numb the internal pain. The hops and malt warmed him, while the yeast caused him feel full, but inside he remained hollow as an oak barrel.

Beer was an easy choice to disguise his suffering. It was a social drink, and the one winners often chose, something slightly less than hard liquor. An aged ale did not require acceptance into the alcoholism club. Although failure was his excuse to drink, the booze was to blame for his defeat. He wallowed each day in mediocrity as a functional drunk.

Wiley had a younger brother by a few years. Growing up he tried to set a good example for him, but the brother was indifferent to his intentions. The harder that Wiley strove for perfection, the more his mother seemed to favor the other brother. His reward for righteousness was her maternal rejection.

The younger brother had a kind heart, but was unmotivated to succeed at anything difficult. The low bar of his goals kept him in favor with their mother, who coddled him. She treated him like a baby so he would never grow up. She secured her own dependence by keeping him feeble. Today, they still lived together in the same two-bedroom house where Wiley grew up.

Emotionally abandoned by his family, Wiley pursued his career goals for admission to an elite male club, but the judges who held his fate in their hands crushed his dreams. Their repudiation devastated him, undermining his confidence.

Being a prideful man, he stuffed his emotions behind a stern façade. On the outside, he seemed tough and in control, but on the inside his soul was screaming for justice.

Alcohol lessened the sting of not making it onto the state-trooper force. The official rejection letter stated that Wiley did not meet the qualifications. Although he passed the written examination, he failed the psychological evaluation, too obsessive-compulsive for their close fraternity.

Stuck in his current position, he reveled in the town's acceptance of him. They adored him, while he slowly disintegrated into a discontented heap of bottle caps.

Each day he awoke, and went to work trying to survive the recurring nightly demons. He prayed that an angel would come bearing mercy on his soul, before the final resort would be swallowing the barrel of his gun.

He strained to suppress the constant urge that controlled him by drowning in a pool of amber liquid. He lied to himself to cope with life, existing in a perpetual cycle of denial, guilt and begging for forgiveness.

At nights, he acted as an unofficial bar bouncer for Clovis Fourchette, his long time high school friend. The two watched over each other in a mutual guardianship. Also alone, Clovis lost his wife to another man, years ago.

Emotionally cut off for a different reason, Clovis gave it all to Lorelei. He married her, and devoted himself to making the restaurant a financial success. Still, providing for his family was not enough to please her. No matter what he did, she was repeatedly unfaithful.

He felt like a failure too, although his only error was thinking he could control her wandering tendencies. She was a free spirit and a troubled child. Her own desires trumped the needs of others, especially dependents. Lorelei left Mabel alone crying in the crib to entertain her boyfriends. Meanwhile, Clovis slaved at the family business overlooking her moral transgressions.

Marriage was not the problem; she had needs Clovis could not fulfill. The decision to look elsewhere was elemental to her, one and one equaled two, nothing more.

Lorelei played wild and loose with life, and tigers could not change their stripes. She was honest about who she was from the start, but Clovis felt his love and attention could tame the beast inside her. Marrying her did not corral her carnal desires. The white picket fence that enclosed their front yard was too low to contain her. Adding the adult responsibility of raising a child to her plate made her run farther from commitment. Instead of forcing her to conform, she rebelled even more becoming vindictive with her male conquests and flaunting the spoils of war.

She could only be what she was, and one day she packed a small suitcase and left. The note she wrote read: *Sorry it is better this way for all of us.*

Mabel was the reason that Clovis kept going. He took comfort in his baby girl. At the end of every long day she was there welcoming his presence home. She grew up in the back room while he worked the bar. He brought her out to the dining area periodically, and the patrons basked in her cuteness. She smiled, gurgled and wiggled her fingers to their delight.

As time rolled on, she helped seat patrons and wait on tables. She was a quick study and charmer; the right amount of compassion and business etiquette. Customers praised her demeanor, a product of an eclectic rearing.

She needed her father, and he depended on her help. Now as a young adult woman, she was concerned with one thing, being there for him as he had been there for her.

Lorelei did not exist in her world. In fact, Mabel had forgotten her name, eternally erased from her memory. There was no explanation needed for the abandonment, and no words from her former mother could fill the chasm that existed between them. More than passing strangers, they were now estranged.

Rather than wallow in sadness from the loss of such an important figure, Mabel was a bright shining vision of happiness. She greeted their guests with undying exuberance, and pretended that Lorelei was dead.

Wiley passed the houseguest on his way to the kitchen area. A countertop lined with black coffee, pink antacid liquid and a jumbo aspirin bottle held his breakfast. He mixed the substances in a travel mug and gulped them down. The clock read six more hours until relief.

Wiley grabbed his pistol and keys from the desk drawer. He flipped the *Open* sign hanging on the glass entrance door to: *Be Back Soon*. It was customary that he would come and go all day long. He flipped the sign because Dixie did not really do any work while she was there, and absolutely none while he was gone. She volunteered her time even though Wiley wrote her a paycheck on Fridays.

Working alone was not difficult for him. The workload was usually light and the town respected him enough to remain civilized. He enjoyed the solitude and was content with doing enough to scrape by.

Wiley headed for the official pickup truck. He saw Vernon across the street and waved for him to come over. "I was just going to your place."

Vernon scratched at his cheek. "Why? I already checked in with my parole officer this week."

"It's not about you this time."

"What's the matter?" Vernon twitched, a side effect of the drugs.

"There's an all-points bulletin for a hunter who's probably on your land," Wiley said.

"Someone local?"

"Is it ever? No, a parrish over."

Vernon blinked several times. "What do you want from me?"

"Have you seen or heard anything unusual?" Wiley spoke in the inquisitive tone that made Vernon nervous.

"No, not really."

Wiley breathed a deep sigh. "I'm going to check the road for abandoned vehicles."

"Good idea."

"Then later, I might stop by to speak with Adele."

Vernon heard voices in his head saying: *kill him when he comes to the house.* "Why? I mean, she hasn't said anything to me about it and you know she would." The Crenshaws preferred to keep to themselves, and did not entertain many houseguests.

"You're right. I don't want to trouble her." Wiley opened the truck door. "There's probably a simple explanation, like the guy is on a drinking binge somewhere." Wiley understood this excuse because he had used it before.

Vernon offered an olive branch. "Let us know if we can help." The mental voices turned to *screams.*

"All right and Vernon, stay out of trouble."

"Sure thing Sheriff."

Eugene was troubled by midday, the time when half the day was behind him, which soon ushered in the pressures of tomorrow. Like dominos falling in slow motion, he could see the erected monoliths waiting in a precarious path, but was powerless to halt the contagion. Each crashed into the next tumbling down, taking his future away by the hour. Each stole precious minutes and pushed him one-step closer to the end. Unlike in winning a race, the finish line was the end of the road without fanfare or trophies. He knew what was waiting for him. He dreaded that day. It was coming soon.

Sadie's Boutique was what he needed to calm his nerves. He stopped by the salon for some pampering. "Can I get a quickie?"

Sadie Bergeron popped up from behind the checkout counter. "Oh Mayor, anything for you." She wore a tight low-cut sweater that advertised her best feature, endless cleavage.

"I need a little hair trimmed off the sides for the press conference." He sat in the chair, as she swaddled him in a vinyl poncho.

"Must be an exciting time for you with the tournament and election coming up so soon." She unintentionally bounced as she spoke. She had a bodacious frame ever since her teens. Now her chest required a heavy harness for support.

"May I ask, what did you think of the Crenshaw boy's when we were in high school?"

"Oh gosh, that was a long time ago. Well, it was tragic for Adele to lose two sons at once with the car accident and prison." Sadie worked the scissors around his ear, rubbing against his shoulder with her buxom figure. "More tragic for Kacie, but I guess she did all right ending up with Buck. It's so great to live amid a real celebrity." Sadie tilted his head to the front. "So how's that boy of yours? You know, you really should start dating again. He needs a mom at his age."

"I've never found anyone quite like Judith."

Sadie helped him out of the chair once the haircut was finished. "I know, hun."

Eugene's wife had died a slow and painful death wasting away from cancer, a rare kind affecting the nasal passages. Judith was happy being a homemaker until one day when her nose started to bleed. Compress pressure and head elevation could not stop the constant flow. She thought that maybe the aspirin she was taking for chronic headaches was thinning her blood too much. Therefore, she stopped taking it. She also cut out of her diet any green leafy vegetables. However, over time the headaches and nosebleeds grew worse. Later she developed coughing fits because of phlegm dripping down the back of her throat.

At home, she suffered in silence, as Eugene spent his free time perusing the Internet. He said he had to do work research, since his days were full with town administration and solving other people's civic problems.

Actually, he was shutting out the world to escape into a perverse world of child pornography to commit felony voyeurism. He thought that no one would get hurt if no one knew about it.

One day while dusting, Judith bumped into the computer keyboard and the hibernating monitor awoke. Plastered before her were images of naked preteen boys with user names like: *EyeCandy10* and *BoyToy12*. They posed in stances too offensive to describe. Some of the boys were around their son's age at the time. Judith was horrified. Not only was her husband engaging in illegal activities, he was possibly a homosexual and a pedophile.

Concerned, she went on to check his email account; something she had never done before. In it were communications with other men about trading photographs. They described the pictures with subject lines like: *cute redhead wishing for man in the moon.*

There was a repetitive entry from someone named *Passionfruit.* Judith's fingers quivered as she hit the enter key to open the email. The message was from a teenage boy naming a time and place to meet at a motel in Bakersfield. In the attached photograph, he wore Wolverine High School colors. The message read: *I cannot wait to feel your manly embrace.* Then he went on to lay out his expectations in graphic detail.

Judith's nose started to bleed, dripping blood on the keyboard in between the "D" and "F" keys. She felt sick to her stomach. She confronted Eugene when he got home from work, but because of the cancer they stayed together.

Maybe that was why Eugene married her. Somehow cosmically he knew that she would protect his secret and she did.

He pondered this as he walked down the block to Fourchette's Bar & Grill. Along the way, unconsciously his penny loafers avoided the concrete spalls. An old wives tale or a habit, either way he did not need more bad luck.

The restaurant was busy for lunchtime, although tonight it would entertain a different bustling crowd. This was the place where Eugene mostly conducted secret business. The kind he did not want anyone else to know about, especially Lin. For an administrative assistant she was average, but it was her uncanny efficiency at spreading news faster than a live feed that Eugene feared the most.

Mabel Fourchette greeted him with the youthful vigor of a nineteen-year-old. "Welcome Mayor, I've got your favorite table ready."

"Thanks Mabel, I'm meeting with Julian. Here, have a campaign button to show your support."

"All right then, two sweet teas for now and the usual?"

"You got it, keep it flowing." Eugene removed his suit coat revealing slim paisley suspenders. The fabric matched the clip-on bow tie. He looked professional without working at it, always taking the easy way out.

The four-seat table was secluded in the rear between a structural column and the wall containing the kitchen. It was so noisy back there; no one wanted to sit close to the swinging doors. It was not the kind of ambiance for couples, and it was too far from the restrooms for families. It became a private conference room for the Mayor's Office, which suited everyone just fine.

Clovis was behind the bar stocking longneck bottles in the deep freeze bin under the counter. He was careful not to bust any while placing them in the ice. He kept to himself, a good listener and the perfect bartender.

Julian Dixon strolled in from Baton Rouge fifteen minutes late. By then, Eugene was working on consuming the second basket of sticky buns. The ice cubes in the amber plastic glasses had melted long ago, leaving behind a pool of perspiration on the beverage napkins.

He walked up to the table and sat down. "I got here as fast as I could. Hope you haven't waited long."

"I didn't give you much notice." Eugene offered him the orphaned roll from the plastic tray.

"So what's the emergency?"

"I need some legal counsel on eminent domain. What's the procedure?"

"It's called expropriation, under Titles 19 & 48 of the Louisiana Constitution. It allows the government to take land for civic use," Julian said.

"Can it be given to a private entity?" Eugene nervously stirred his tea with the jumbo straw.

"Maybe, if it were for public use under the takings clause."

"Laymen's terms please," Eugene said.

"The Fifth Amendment of the Constitution protects landowners by limiting the use to a public purpose, and the owner must be compensated fair market value."

"Could this third party use it for a profit producing enterprise?"

"Yes, economic development could be considered a public use," Julian said.

"Can the owner contest?"

"They have ten days from notification to challenge, but they also have the burden of proof to show that the government acted in bad faith."

"Like a personal vendetta?" Eugene said.

"Yes maybe. What's this about?"

"I need you to draw up documents to expropriate the Crenshaw's land minus one acre with their house."

"Do you have a current appraisal based on the best and highest use for the land?" Julian said.

"I have a number in mind."

Julian leaned back in the wooden chair, sipping on his tea. He did not say anything for a few minutes, staring into space. He was going over the details of a mental checklist. "You know I practice criminal law. Why are you asking me to do this?"

"Because you're the only district attorney I'm friends with. Besides you don't ask a lot of questions, so don't start now."

"In my line of business, dangerous questions are what I do best."

Mabel delivered two plates of steaming fried catfish. The cornmeal was still sizzling from the peanut oil. "There you go gentlemen." She pulled a bottle of ketchup from her apron pocket. "Enjoy." Then she abruptly left to answer the phone.

"When do you need this completed by?"

"Yesterday." Eugene pulled the channel cat in two. "But wait, there's more."

Julian made a grimace while beating the condiment bottle over his plate.

"There's going to be a small public area; a park with fishing, some picnic tables and barbecue pits."

Julian swirled a cornbread hushpuppy in the paper cup of tartar sauce. "That sounds nice. Maybe it will get the town on your side, because you know this is political suicide. Aren't you up for reelection soon?"

"Yes, I know. I'm concerned about that so I'm moving the fishing tournament from Devil's Hole to the swamp."

"You can't be serious. What about the legend?" Julian said.

"Come on, that's not real. It's like Santa Claus, just fiction," Eugene said.

"Are you sure about that Eugene? Because if you move the event there, and something bad happens, it's all coming back on you."

"Julian, you worry too much. No one is going to get hurt."

CHAPTER 3

Route 3 was a two-lane highway that ran between Stray Oaks and the adjacent town of Bakersfield. The original Creekwood plantation had a dirt road carved through live oak trees, and it became the only way in and out of town. A portion of the road later paved went from the town limits to Devil's Hole Lake, past the Crenshaw's house surrounded by Creekwoods and Shallow Basin, toward Bakersfield. Bordered by slender pine trees, the tail of the escape route symbolized freedom, but was also the location of many fatal car accidents.

During the ride, Wiley contemplated the possibilities for the hunter's delay in returning home. People who disappeared often had a rational explanation, but it was his duty as sheriff to entertain the likelihood of foul play.

Pine needles fell, leaving a thick umber carpet on top of the dying grass. Squirrels frantically darted everywhere searching for nuts to prepare for winter. The truck's muddy tires screeched, as Wiley swerved to avoid hitting one rodent on the road.

In the distant sky, Wiley observed a kettle of turkey vultures circling. The six-foot blackish-grey wings of the birds stretched in a V-formation and floated on thermal drafts maintaining stability by teetering from side-to-side. Their presence was a sign of nearby death. Enticed by an acute sense of smell from up to a mile away, the carrion scavengers fed on the remains of dead animals.

As Wiley got closer to the area in question, he scanned the trees on the side of the road. The truck crept along in the single lane of the highway. His sweaty palms gripped the steering wheel, feeling uneasy about the unknown.

Leaving the overhead light bar illuminated without the siren, he pulled the truck over to the shoulder and grabbed his tactical flashlight to investigate. His immediate concern as the first responder was to secure the area.

A single tire track in the grass led from the road on a diagonal line into the woods.

He flashed the light around, which reflected on chrome handlebars behind a tree trunk. The dirt bike was leaning up against the tree, hidden from view by palmetto bushes.

Wiley methodically approached the bike, being careful of where he stepped to preserve the scene with minimal contamination.

He listened, but it was quiet. "Hello, is anybody there?" There was no response only silence, except for the sporadic turbulence of swirling tree limbs above.

Remaining alert, Wiley walked in straight-line patterns searching for evidence.

A metal button on a tattered piece of shirt reflected the focused spotlight. Stretched between two branches, the fabric was moist with a burgundy substance and dripping. There were also scattered droplets with thick chunks of fleshy goo.

The odor was pungent and offensive, adding to his hangover nausea. Recoiling, he covered his nose with his hand to stall gagging.

Wiley drew his .45 pistol with a shaky hand and reached for a shrub. As he moved it out of the way, a wake of ugly vultures perched on a corpse screeched.

From the intrusion, some vomited the ingested flesh on the ground before flying off.

A bald headed vulture with a red beak thrust inside the man's rotting skull cavity. The crater was devoid of brains, already eaten. The bird spread its wings to fly off and Wiley jumped back as the tip of the wing clipped him in the face.

The scavengers left the remains of a middle-aged man sitting upright, with his back against an oak tree. The tips of the rubber boots pointed toward the sky. A chunk was missing out of the left boot, with toes partially eaten.

His arms draped at his sides. One hand was completely absent, severed clean at the wrist bone. The chest cavity seemed torn open by a sharp object. Horse flies swarmed around the body in a frenzy. White maggots slithered aimlessly, consuming the remains.

Concerned, Wiley keyed the radio. He became irritated when Dixie did not respond to his call. "Dixie, we've got a situation. Get the coroner out here before the sun goes down please. I'm near mile marker twenty-three."

Wiley then called the Lafayette investigative officer to relay the bad news; the hunter was dead. The officer listened as Wiley rambled emotionless through procedures. "I'll process the scene and send the completed report. The medical examiner is on his way, though my initial walk-through shows no signs of a perpetrator. The dirt bike is still here. It appears to be functional, but there's too much damage to the body to know for sure what happened."

Wiley returned to his truck for the evidence kit and camera. He strung police barricade tape between two trees so that the physical evidence remained undisturbed.

He jotted down the dirt bike license plate number on his steno pad with the location, date and time, then noted the weather conditions and sketched the area in a diagram taking measurements.

Wiley snapped photographs of the crime scene, from wide-angle to close-up shots and used the video camera to record a survey of the area focusing on the four Cardinal points starting from the road. He was obsessive about documenting the minute details step by step, without really processing the entire scene.

Wiley pulled rubber gloves from his rear pocket. He collected liquid blood picked up with a gauze pad, placing the evidence in a zipper-closure envelope. He dusted the bike for fingerprints and measured blood-spatter marks, then walked around taking more notes trying to stay busy to keep his mind off the growing compulsion to drink.

Coroner Andre Chaisson arrived to the scene shortly after and walked around the dead body. He looked at the injuries and poked a few portions of the corpse with his gloved fingers. "Is this all there is?"

"I reckon, there are some globs of stuff here and there, but I don't see anything of significance for cause of death," Wiley said.

"Does anybody else know about this?" Andre said.

"Just the Lafayette detective and Dixie," Wiley said.

"So basically, all of Stray Oaks?" Andre said.

Wiley laughed. "I hear you."

"Well, let's try and keep it contained until the autopsy is complete."

Wiley thought for a moment. "Isn't it odd the way the body is sitting up against a tree? It looks staged to me."

"Nothing to be concerned about, this time of year it's likely a black bear attack."

Wiley looked at his watch feeling the pangs of alcohol withdrawal. He did not argue with Andre though he disagreed. It was too close to quitting time.

They loaded the bike onto the back of Wiley's truck and slid the body bag into the black van. Then they parted ways without discussing the matter further.

The sun was setting, ready for the night watchmen to take over. Motionless shadows prevailed, elongated below the tree canopy, but one shadow was roving around. It searched through the woods, periodically glancing down to observe its own silhouette, which was distended and protracted.

The Creepler moved through Creekwoods, shuffling red maple leaves attracted to the audio sensations of human voices nearby. Flaxen skin covered in scales on webbed feet approached them. It moved closer hidden from view, while slinking through the trees. The creature stopped a short distance away from the couple.

Saylor and Beau sat next to the creek on a fallen log, its massive top eroded long ago from the constant rapids. As the tree crown bent over to kiss the water's surface, exposed roots grappled for oxygen. The twosome was unaware that something watched them.

Beau had the face of a young knight, cherub-like and his skin radiated with luminance. His succulent lips had a pomegranate hue. He had his mother's nose, slender and graceful. Dimples framed an infectious smile, while his faint freckles masqueraded until flushed. His laughter was a resonant sound striking chords of a symphony. Smoky-black bangs touched his eyebrows, sweeping down like an ocean crest.

Saylor had the face of a china doll with alabaster skin, plump lips and exaggerated eyes. She tucked her chin under gracefully like a swan. She was a temptress that preyed on boys, and the beguiling vixen that tugged at his heart.

Each facile word she spoke danced in wickedness aboard her pointed tongue. Declarations contorted in swirled visages of languid poison, throwing him off his game.

For all of her good traits, she could only progress in one direction as defined by a vision of herself she created. Her façade was tenuous, a thin veil covering secrets.

On the exterior, Saylor was a driven individual and a natural leader. She was the one students followed because her internal light was so dazzling. She drew them to her like a magnetic force. Without questioning, they willingly followed her.

Saylor acted as their social coordinator, organizing pep rallies, dispensing cheer and maintaining a positive attitude. She portrayed an image of the perfect girl, the one everyone wanted to emulate. Though her classmates assumed she was just another pretty face, someone who did not have to work like the others, they were wrong.

Beau understood Saylor, her ambition for star power and the desire to abandon her heritage and run away from an internal monster. What he did not know was what would latter happen to her if she stayed in Stray Oaks. No one could know that.

Together they formed an intimate connection without ever having physical relations. The cosmic electricity they felt was a natural chemical reaction, a fusion of pure energy. The word *love* was too minuscule to describe the sensation they felt and the passion elicited from such a feeling. They were soul mates, opposite sides of the same sphere, a void and a flood. Together the two pulsated as one luminary. Searching for infinity, their arms reached for the extents becoming lost in pure feeling while devoid of thought.

When Beau held her in his arms, she felt safe. When Saylor cuddled with him, he felt loved. They thrived because of this perfect amalgamation. She surrendered what he craved, and he stole enough energy to persist in her company.

In each other's presence, they ebbed and flowed in happiness. At other times there was tranquility, unlike what they witnessed by adults, especially their parents. Marriage on paper was not what they desired. However, external forces who thought they knew better conspired to destroy them.

When they were younger teenagers, it was acceptable for them to date. However, now that they approached adulthood, things needed to change. The outside interference was damaging their relationship, ripping them asunder.

Despite this, Beau recognized that their lives were not on the same path anymore and that bothered him. During the summer, he felt compelled to tear away from her plans and journey into the secluded woods alone. The attraction to freedom was pervasive. Something invisible pulled him to get out of town fast, unaware of the truth at the core of a buried family secret.

Saylor challenged Beau to flee from the monster that was hiding deep within, while a real monster hid in the shadows waiting for the right opportunity to make its presence known. The beast inside tore him left and she pulled him right, which made it insufferable to move.

However, Saylor did not hold the power to control his destiny, only he could change the course of his predetermined fate. If Beau ran away with her, it would not be because of her, but in spite of her actions.

He simply could not live an ordinary life as defined by typical happiness in a square box. There had to be more to life than just working to attain material possessions.

His parents had all the money in the world and still could not experience true joy. Beau saw firsthand what acquisitions had done to their souls. Their reality became clouded, losing touch with what was important. He vowed to be different.

To leave the fold meant great personal risk, to be vulnerable to attack and receive possible banishment. Expressing his true feelings would upset them. Nevertheless, pretending to be happy was living a lie, which would eventually crush his spirit. All these things weighed heavily on his mind.

Beau accepted that Saylor deserved better than his conflicted emotions. He loved her enough to let her go, to walk away freeing her, allowing her to be who she wanted. Beau knew that just pretending the situation was okay would not make it so. That made thoughts of the forthcoming breakup even more excruciating.

Saylor sensed his emotional withdrawal and feared for their future together. She pretended everything was normal, lied about what was going on inside her own head and stuffed away dark visions of her future, while acting the part of head cheerleader, preordained senior prom queen and upcoming Oscar winning actor.

Then Saylor smiled at him. In that moment, electron collages sparked magic and angels sang. She made him forget about the burdens, time paused and their unison glowed. He got her and she had him.

Beau worked the scenery into the camera's viewfinder, perfectly framing each composition. He observed electric spikes of energy with cataclysmic eruptions and the quakes and moans of time setting rhythmic heartbeats against the wind.

"Why don't you ever want to hang out with the others afterschool at Devil's Hole?" Saylor said.

"I don't know. I like it better here in the woods, it feels more like home." Beau adjusted the camera settings. "Plus, we have all this privacy to make out."

"Yes, there is that." Saylor made a sexy pose, puckering her lips for each click of the shutter. "Some day when I'm rich and famous, you can be my paparazzo and follow me around."

"Don't I deserve some exclusivity?" Beau focused the lens, zooming close onto her right eye. "I should be your official photographer, like the Queen has."

"That's only if you come with me to New York." Saylor hesitated to reveal the good news, afraid of his reaction. "I was accepted to Juilliard." She dramatically jumped up on her knees pleading with him with puppy dog eyes. "Please, please, please come with me?"

Beau knew the answer to her question was negative, but tried not to hurt her feelings. "You know that I want nothing more than to marry you one day someday soon."

The Creepler continued to watch from a distance breathing heavily. The girl mesmerized it, and something about the boy stopped it from attacking.

"And start a family?" Saylor threw several stones into the creek, apprehensive about his responses.

"Maybe one day. I'm not sure how I feel about having a clone. That would be a bit creepy. And being an only child, I don't really have any experience with caring for kids."

"I have an adopted little brother, and he's a royal pain. You can have him anytime. I'm not sure why you think having a sibling is all that great," Saylor said.

"After knowing about my twin, I always wanted a brother but my parents never had the time for another one. It's hard to explain. I just feel like something is missing with him gone," Beau said.

Saylor moved off the log onto the bank pouting. She leaned back on the ground looking up at the afternoon sunlight, filtering through the swaying treetops. "I guess it doesn't matter right now. To hear your mother talk though, sounds like you're staying here after graduation."

"No way, I'm not going to State. I don't care what they want." Beau joined her on the grass. "So why are your parents cool with you moving away?"

Saylor laughed. "My dad can't wait to spend my money when I'm rich and famous." She hugged him, nestling close under his arm. She radiated an aura that amplified his energy, two strong magnets in harmony. "So, why don't you stand up to your parents for once?"

Beau did not answer. He held her tight, momentarily forgetting all his problems. For a while, they were both silent looking at the sky. He laid there holding her and being too in his head instead of enjoying their closeness. He worried, but knew time would work everything out.

He just could not play the part that everyone else wanted. They all had plans for him, and he was tired of being their puppet. The dilemma was crushing his creativity like shackles binding his infinite ability. He could follow his parent's decree and lose his soul in the process. However, in his mind there was not any middle ground. Living a lie was simply not worth doing.

A wolf spider quietly crawled onto Saylor's forearm. Eight fuzzy tarsus delicately pricked the skin, tickling her flesh. Saylor glanced down to see multiple black eyeballs staring back at her. She jumped to her feet and violently brushed the creature off. "Oh my God, gross. I hate spiders!"

Beau sat up too, the sun was almost gone. He glanced at his watch. "I've got to get home anyway. We're eating out with Ms. LeBlanc so that I can be bored to tears by her daughter."

Saylor stalled and crouched beside him, "I'm really looking forward to your birthday. Maybe you'd like to have your present now." She pulled the waistline of her jeans down past her hipbone to reveal a petite tattoo of two entwined hearts.

"Oh my God, that's awesome! You're the best." Beau leaned over to kiss her.

"You know, I've been meaning to ask, why doesn't your mom like me?"

"I don't know, maybe because you have a tramp stamp. I'm just kidding. She has never said anything to me about it. Why, what makes you think that?" Beau said.

"Oh, she's very polite to me, but it's just a strange feeling I get when I'm around her."

"Don't worry about it. My parents have never really liked any of my friends, including Riley."

"Well that I can understand," Saylor said.

Beau offered his hand to help her get up. "It's getting late and we need to go before dark."

Saylor tried to postpone their departure again. "Let's get back to your birthday."

"What's the fuss? It's not that big of a deal, just a day like any other."

"What are you talking about? Eighteen is a rite of passage. Besides, I'm already an adult, how does it feel to date an older woman?" Saylor said.

"Like you are corrupting me, oh temptress with the tattoo," Beau hugged her. "Anyway, I thought the thirteenth was supposed to be an unlucky day, especially in October."

Saylor kissed him on the cheek. "Come on, you know you're the chosen one."

Clovis Fourchette angled the glass just right under the tap to get the perfect amount of head. The chalky white foam cascaded down the side of the beer mug destroying the winter frost in its path.

Anticipating a chemical fix, Wiley rested on his favorite barstool. Worn at the seams, the burgundy faux leather padded cushion scrunched while the low-back bucket seat cupped his spine perfectly. He had a love affair with this stool in particular. It welcomed him after a long day of hard work, embracing him. Then as the night rolled on, it supported him keeping his body upright. It gave whatever he needed, ever alert and just for him.

Seated next to him was Mr. Stumpy, who reeked of cheap cologne that he had borrowed from the men's restroom to cover up his body odor.

Clovis looked at Wiley, "Long day, buddy?"

"Yeah, you're right! Hit me up." Wiley said.

He deposited the overflowing mug on a fresh beverage napkin that had an imprint: *Fourchette's For Sure*. Clovis wiped around the bar area with a moist towel, which left streaks of sudsy water on the resin top. He stood there in front of Wiley on the other side of the bar, waiting.

Wiley took the first sip leaving a partial suds mustache on his face. He could feel the headache instantly receding. "There was an accident today in the woods."

"You don't say." Clovis looked at Jessica Blaze seated two stools over. She nursed a sour apple martini, while pretending not to eavesdrop on their conversation.

Blaze was the local news reporter at Station 3. She aspired to be an anchor for a national television network. Her strategy to reach that goal was to engage in sensational entertainment news, so controversial that the big executives would have to notice her talents. The plan was already set in motion, as she steadily made a name for herself as a quote twister. She even had a reel of footage ready, compiling her best highlights for when she got the audition call.

Her fingers ran through her long-blonde hair pretending to wait for a date, and she periodically checked her watch. She was dating someone well-connected, a wealthy individual from the city, yet another business arrangement to bolster her career.

Wiley's cell phone rang. He fumbled in the side pocket of his uniform pants trying to reach under the baton hanging from his belt. "Officer Aucoin, always on duty and ready to serve."

On the other end of the phone was the coroner. "I'm just about finished with the autopsy; but I wanted to let you know all indications point to a young black bear."

Wiley took a sip of his beer, slurping. "Let me get this straight, you're saying that the mutilated body is consistent with an animal attack, though it looked staged?"

"Yes, the vultures could have done that trying to drag off the body," Andre said.

Wiley did not agree with the scientific assessment; something did not add up, but it was already after hours. "And the time of death?"

"From rigor I'd say three days ago. It will all be in my report. You'll have a copy by tomorrow."

"All right, evening Coroner." Wiley sat the phone down on the bar and stared at his beer.

Blaze placed some cash on the bar for payment and got up to leave. She passed by Wiley, then stopped and turned around. "Excuse me; did I hear you say mutilated body?"

Wiley rolled his eyes at Clovis. "Can I get you a drink Blaze?"

"No thanks, I'm on my way out. What kind of animal was it?" Blaze said.

"The Coroner says it's a bear attack."

"Where was this exactly?" Blaze said.

"Are we on the record?" Wiley took a sip of the beer hoping she would go away.

"Yes, you know I have to report this," Blaze said.

"Creekwoods off Route 3, down from the Crenshaw's place."

"And the victim, a local?"

"No, of course not, one parish over," Wiley said.

In the dining area, Mabel sat the Boudreauxs at an eight-seat table by the window. Buck pulled out a chair for Kacie to sit down. Beau sat at the opposite end of the oblong table as a sign of defiance.

Haley and Amber LeBlanc entered to join them for dinner.

"Oh great, just perfect." Beau mumbled to himself.

Kacie scolded him, "Mind your manners son."

Haley sat by Buck and Kacie after air kissing them on the cheeks. "Hello darlings, good to see you all."

Amber zeroed in on Beau's location with the look of a golden retriever waiting to fetch a ball.

"Is this everyone folks?" Mabel said.

"Yes, can we get a round of sweet tea?" Buck said.

"You got it, and some sticky buns, coming right up."

Beau looked around the crowded restaurant. Riley was sitting across the room in a booth with his mother. He wore his wrestling singlet with some sweat pants. Beau acknowledged him with a nod.

Riley nodded back, while his mother continued to lecture. Ignoring her, he took out his smartphone so they could communicate without speaking.

"So Beau, are you going to Marvin's lake party?" Amber said.

He looked at her, pausing to study her face. She was average on a scale from one to ten, a few pimples, straight teeth from previous braces and visible colored eye contacts, but nothing worthy of capturing on film. "Yeah I guess. Why are you?" After Beau asked the question, he thought about how stupid it was. They both attended the same school, and Marvin had invited the entire senior class.

"Absolutely, want to ride together?" She eagerly awaited his reply.

"Actually I'm already going with Saylor, you know, my girlfriend." Beau made sure he spoke loud enough for the adults at the other end of the table to hear.

Haley and Buck were enthralled in a discussion about the details of the book deal.

72

Kacie sat in silence, half listening to their conversation though she was bored with the subject. Manipulating her son's love life was more interesting. "Beau, maybe you all wouldn't mind giving Amber a ride," Kacie said.

"Thanks Mom, but you know Saylor's roadster sports car only holds two."

"Then you can borrow my car."

"The hybrid skate? No thanks. Do you want me to be the laughing stock of the entire school?" Beau said.

"What's wrong with caring about the environment?" Kacie said.

Beau's smartphone dingled with a text message from Riley that read: *step away from the gun dude.*

"You know my rules, no phones at dinner. Put it away," Buck said.

Beau mumbled, "Yes sir, sergeant sir."

"Beau, don't talk back to your—," Kacie said.

"It's all right dear; it's just an age thing. It will pass in time." Haley dumped three sugar packets into the sweet tea glass. "So Buck, are we settled on the $10,000 advance? I'll have more information in a few weeks about the book tour."

"That's fine, but what about reviews in the big publishing magazines?" Buck said.

Blaze barged up to the table and interrupted them, standing over Kacie while looking directly at Buck. "Pardon me; I just wanted to confirm my exclusive interview with you for the fishing tournament tomorrow."

"Of course, as usual I'll come down to the station early. Would you reserve hair and makeup for when I arrive?" Buck said.

"Anything for you, Buck." Blaze was so enamored with him she did not even acknowledge the other women sitting at the table.

Blaze, an attractive girl, sat behind Buck in high school. She had a major crush on him, and was sure one day he would ask her out on a second date. Then toward the end of senior year, something bad happened. Buck remained an available bachelor happily playing the field, until the preacher's daughter hooked him. Shortly thereafter, they announced their engagement. The news devastated Blaze. She did not know why it happened or how it could, but she vowed to get him back one day. Her solution was to focus on her career and outshine Kacie with success.

Little Eddie Charbonneau sauntered over to the table. The young boy held a paper placemat and blue crayon in his hands. He offered it to Buck, while his mother Lillian watched.

"Howdy partner, would you like my signature little man?" Buck said.

The boy smiled with flushed cheeks, then quickly retrieved the autograph and ran back to his mother's arms.

Mabel carried a large oval platter on one shoulder, slamming it down on an open folding stand. She pulled out her order pad from her apron pocket to confirm the meal placement.

"Looks like your food's here, sorry to interrupt. Buck I'll see you at the station tomorrow morning," Blaze said before leaving.

Mabel distributed the hot china plates to each patron.

Beau held the cell phone under the table and sent a text message to Riley: *just shoot me.*

Riley texted back: *YOLO.* (You only live once.)

"Please, let us bow our heads in prayer…," Buck said.

Everyone stopped what they were doing, while the food steamed on the table.

Amber reached out to hold Beau's hand.

"Bless us Lord, for these gifts through Christ's bounty. Amen," Buck said.

As the Boudreauxs commenced to eating, Riley sat uncomfortably in the booth stirring his salad with the fork.

"How did you do in chemistry today?" Lin said.

"Mom, do we have to talk about school right now? I'm trying to eat," Riley said.

"Looks like you're playing with it more than eating."

"I've got weigh-in tomorrow, and you know how Coach gets before a match game."

"Okay wise guy, a little lettuce is not going kill you. Eat it." Lin signaled Mabel for another order of fried shrimp. She planned to get every penny's worth of *all you can eat* night. "So, what do we know about his situation?"

Riley breathed a heavy sigh. "Mom, I don't want to talk about it."

"Come on; tell me what's happening at school."

Riley whispered, "Ms. Charbonneau came by practice today and handed Coach Doucet a fancy box with a red ribbon."

"Go on, what was in the box?" Lin said.

"Brownies, I think. I went to his office to ask him something and they were acting all goofy."

"I knew she was seeing someone even though she's still married. But I can't blame her for wanting a real man." Lin laughed, "Apparently her husband wants one too."

"Mom please be quiet. She'll hear us," Riley said.

Lin pointed her fork in his face. "Don't you ever act a fool like that or I'll disown you. Do you hear me?"

Buck stood up and beat his spoon against the plastic cup. "Excuse me; may I have everyone's attention please?"

The noisy restaurant simmered down to a dull murmur.

"As all of you know my son is graduating from high school this year and taking his first steps toward becoming a professional lawyer. I'm happy to announce that he was recently accepted to State University."

Beau's intestines started to twist into a knot. He set his fork down feeling the onset of nausea. The news alarmed him.

"We are also honored to have the new law library wing named after our family," Buck said.

The crowd clapped and people mumbled to themselves about Buck's generous philanthropy.

"Dad, please sit down. You're embarrassing me," Beau said.

Buck returned to his seat. "Well boy, aren't you happy now?"

"Ecstatic Dad. Thanks for the awesome news."

"You know, sometimes it pays to have connections," Buck said.

"Or to be able to buy them," Beau mumbled.

The Crenshaw's basement was a cramped room that smelled of mothballs. In the corner, an elaborate sacrificial altar held ritually cleansed objects, consecrated for casting practical magic spells.

Draped across the stone top was a crimson cloth with embroidered Egyptian hieroglyphics. The gold metallic threads wove through the satin fabric tying symbols to substrate. Each pictorial character called to action specific requests for the spirits in an forgotten ancient language.

On the left side rested a golden pillar candle, which represented the male sun. On the right side rested a silver candle representing the female moon. The male and female aspects of nature functioned together holding a balance to the spirit realm.

Adele had no time to waste. Tonight was the October full moon and she was the mistress of ceremonies. An evergreen robe swathed on a mannequin with the hood covering its head stood before her. She retrieved the garment, and dressed in front of a floor-length mirror.

She pulled the gold ankh out from under the heavy cloak. A symbol for life, the male cross and female oval represented the sacred union of Sun and Moon at the river Nile. Used as an amulet to ward off evil spirits, Adele wore it as a reminder that the cult was responsible for guarding the family's secrets, confining the Creepler in the woods and ultimately protecting the town.

On the wall above the altar were framed headshots of Vernon and Kacie. There was a tall red glass novena candle in the center of the altar next to a red voodoo doll made from beeswax. A thin red ribbon tied around the doll aimed to bind the two subjects together in love.

Adele lit patchouli incense and cleared her mind, focusing on her intentions. Standing before the altar with her arms stretched out palms open; staring at the doll, she spoke an incantation aloud.

"Oh great one, I call on thee to invoke this spell for love. By the power of three, I will later sacrifice a white dove. Accept the offering, hear my prayer, bind Kacie and Vernon again as a pair." She clasped her hands together, and bowed solemnly. "The charm is made this night under the moon."

The love spell needed time to work its magic. Even with Adele's years of experience as a witch, she could not control everything or completely guarantee a spell's outcome.

Sterling silver candelabras illuminated the dim room. Several candlesticks burned down close to the wicks. The dripped wax of many colors formed stalactites and grotesque sculptures frozen in time.

On an adjacent wall, a bookshelf lined with small glass jars contained ingredients not found at the grocer. A large leather-bound grimoire, old and tattered, held incantations from generations before. Adele frequently modified the spells with her best practices, keeping a record of successes and failures for future reference.

Dead animal heads decorated the rest of the walls silently witnessing the torture that occurred in the chair, which sat in the middle of the room over a pentacle inscribed on the wooden floorboards.

The hallowed symbol safeguarded the victim from annihilation by evil forces. A circle offered protection acting as a boundary between dimensions. The five points of the pentagram star were; spirit, air, earth, fire and water. These forces of nature together with the flow of seasons and moon cycles were the tools of the enchanter.

Adele received a call on the handheld two-way radio. She purchased the 900 MHz band service to communicate over a private channel by way of its secure frequency hopping. The caller ID on the display panel read: *Annie*.

"W5, delta, lima, echo, zulu, listening," Annie said.

"W5, foxtrot, alpha, victor, sierra, back at you," Adele said.

"Did I call at a bad time?"

"I was just on my way to the ceremony."

"So, when will our family be reunited?" Annie said.

"I'm working on it. Kacie is very stubborn, even with the love spell and Vernon pining for her all the time," Adele said.

"Everything is riding on you to bring her back into the fold. We also need Beau to continue the family bloodline."

"Once Kacie and Vernon are back together, the truth will naturally come out about Beau," Adele said.

"Then you can teach Kacie our ways," Annie said.

"Yes, and everything will be back to normal."

"What's going on with that annoying developer?"

"Consider it over. I do not think he will be bothering us again. Look, I have to get going. Talk to you soon, over and out."

Upstairs, Vernon lit the kerosene lantern. The match ignited fiery sparks, as the flame rumbled and fluttered. He lowered the intensity and set the lantern on the back porch table.

Adele's cloak barely touched the floor. The Monk's robe with splayed sleeves drew tightly at her waist. She raised the hood to cover her head, while Vernon watched in silence, a ritual he participated in since birth. He held something important that she needed in his shaking hands.

She reached out for the device, and placed the mask over her face. Made from colorless bone china, it was smooth and glossy. The mask had walnut sized eyeholes and tiny openings to breathe and speak, but was expressionless.

The winds howled as Adele walked from the porch down the path that led to the woods. It was a chilly night with rolling clouds backlit by the moon. She held the lantern to guide the way to the special place, setting it down at the entrance after arriving.

Inside the subterranean cave, a fire burned in the center of a salt ring. The nine-foot circle had four equidistant points facing the Cardinal directions. Inside the circle three people facing outward dressed the same as Adele, knelt in front of the points demarcated by different colored candles: yellow for east, red for north, green for west and blue for south. Adele's position was the east, the beginning and the end of the circle.

The interior of the cave was dome shaped and riddled with irregular holes that led to various tube chambers, dug by mysterious creatures long before man walked the earth.

Next to the magic circle was a stone altar made from boulders with a massive granite slab. Previous blood sacrifices stained the rock a deep crimson. On one end was a gold metal crucifix, the opposite end held a silver pentagram. In the center, a white dove waited under a woven basket next to a double-edged ritual athame.

Adele reverently approached the altar. She held the leather wrapped dagger handle with both elbows out. The blade pointed downward, as she cut the air's energy to open a doorway for the magic to enter. She walked toward the eastern point of the circle and paused. "We call you, oh Great One to cast this magic circle using the powers of the air."

The group said, "Exaudi orationem nostrum." (Hear our prayer.)

Then Adele moved to the north point. "We call you, oh Great One to cast this magic circle using the powers of fire."

"Exaudi orationem nostrum," the group said.

Adele moved to the west point. "We call you, oh Great One to cast this magic circle using the powers of the earth."

"Exaudi orationem nostrum," the group said.

Lastly, Adele moved to the south point. "We call you, oh Great One to cast this magic circle using the powers of water."

"Exaudi orationem nostrum," the group said.

After the protective circle was prepared, she approached the altar and rang a brass bell. She held her arms out, palms toward the heavens. "Accipe sacrificium Deo O, sumus tecum." (Accept this sacrifice oh God, we are one with you.)

The hooded person representing the earth, turned toward the fire while kneeling and cast salt granules into the blaze. The sulfur caused the raging fire to crackle and pop, sizzling with delight.

The group chanted in a low deep tone, slowly reaching a crescendo.

Adele removed the basket, and held the dove still with one hand. She could feel its heart rapidly beating through her fingers. She stroked it gently a few times to soothe it before twisting its neck. The eyes bulged out of the tiny black orifices. The dove kicked and twitched one last time. She continued to pull its body apart, ripping bones and muscles with bloody tendons trailing behind.

Dark liquid squirted across the altar. She poured the rest into a chalice, raising it high to toast the Spirit. She drank through the mask, as blood escaped the corner of her mouth. She walked around the circle and each person drank from the sacred chalice. She set the cup on the altar and joined the others, taking refuge inside the protection of the ring.

After a few minutes of chanting, the sound of chirping Cicadas moved closer to the cave's entrance. The noise added to the fervor of the group.

In the corner, a white lamb tied to a wooden stake waited anxiously. It cried for its mother, deep painful sounds of agony.

A gruesome figure approached the lamb. Cast by the fire, the shadow grew larger on the rock wall. It shrieked high-pitched noises moving closer to the offering until darkness engulfed the baby lamb.

The coven chanted repeatedly, "Accipe sacrificium, accipe sacrificium."

The lamb screamed one final time before the Creepler assuaged its fears forever.

CHAPTER 4

The stockpot boiled above the gas flame occasionally bubbling greenish foam over the sides. As the broth rolled, indiscernible objects appeared for a second on the surface before going under. The witch's brew did not require a taste test, the rank smell alone indicated completion.

Next to it, another stockpot filled with fresh vegetables and a turkey neck simmered for dinner. The sweet stench of cabbage and carrots lingered in the air.

Adele wore her navy-blue nightgown and robe, seated at the kitchen table reviewing a monthly calendar. Unlike a preprinted one purchased at a store, this handwritten one denoted special occasions rather than holidays. Keeping track of time was one of her most important functions as caretaker to her land; recording moon phases, spells, offerings and cult meetings.

It was imperative that the Creepler received an offering on each full moon. The animal sacrifice ensured a treaty between the cult and the monster, so it would remain on Crenshaw property. Without it, the town of Stray Oaks was at risk.

Vernon came downstairs and brushed the cat out of his chair. Midnight grudgingly jumped down, hissing on the way. The two barely tolerated each other.

"I didn't hear you come in last night. How'd it go?" Vernon said.

"As it always does." Adele leaned back in the chair, pulling the reading glasses from her nose. "Any progress with Kacie?"

"Not enough to my liking. She's still rather hostile toward me, which I understand." Vernon picked up the *Stray Oaks Gazette*.

"If you want to win her affections back, maybe you should spend some time with the boy?" Adele retrieved a talisman from her pocket, and handed it to him. "Wear this all the time. It should help your efforts."

Vernon looked at her astonished, but accepted the magic necklace. "Is this really necessary?"

"Let me remind you, we wouldn't be in this situation if it wasn't for your screw up and Chester would still be alive."

"Maw, it was an accident. I'd gladly trade places with him … you know I would," Vernon said.

"You're right; it's not your fault. It's that damn brain disorder you've got. The one where you're not supposed to drink alcohol, since you already hallucinate."

"What are you talking about? I don't drink."

"Sure you don't."

Vernon tried to read the newspaper. Voices in his head screamed: *kill the witch … she does not love you like she loved Chester … end the torture.*

The front-page headline read: *Monster or Myth. Man Slaughtered by Mysterious Creature.* "Did you see this?"

"No. Read it to me," Adele said.

"Hunter trespassed on Crenshaw land looking for deer; the predator became the prey. Desperate wife alerted officials about missing man, gone for days. They discovered his mutilated corpse in Creekwoods off Route 3. Some body parts found detached with scavenger damage. Suspicious autopsy claims black bear attack, although hunter had crossbow for protection. There were no witnesses."

"We can always count on Blaze to keep the legend alive." Adele arose to check on the culinary delights. She added some cloves to one pot.

"That really smells bad. What are you cooking?" Vernon said.

"Nothing you'd be interested in, dear." Adele stirred the pot. "What are you up to today anyway?"

"I've got to work on the boat, something is wrong with the motor—," Vernon heard tires approaching through the screened door. "We've got company."

"Stay where you are, I'll get it." Adele walked toward the door wiping her hands on a dishtowel.

"Morning, Ms. Adele Crenshaw?" Wiley said.

"Uh huh."

Wiley handed her a manila envelope, "I'm sorry to have to do this Adele, but it's my job." He held out a clipboard. "Please sign here."

"What's this about Officer?" Adele said.

"I don't know Ma'am, but you've been served." Then he headed toward his truck.

Adele tore the envelope open, which contained legal documents stapled to blue paper. She put on her reading glasses and studied the documents.

"What is it Maw?"

"Looks like a summons to a hearing for expropriation. That damn Mayor, how dare he get involved in this." Adele fanned through the pages as her blood pressure steadily increased. "Don't worry; I'll take care of it." She went back to stirring the big pot. "Good thing I started this brew today. I know just what I'll do with it."

Hand-painted red and black letters covered white banners for the pep rally, stretched across the walls of the gymnasium. Coach Ducet's ancestors selected the school colors because they represented transformation of the soul. The panthers were going through their own transformation from reigning under dogs working toward the state championship title.

Saylor stretched her hamstrings, while the other cheerleaders dressed for practice. Ten petite girls and two strapping boys rounded out the team. She led the small squad with effective leadership and sass.

Besides acting as varsity captain Saylor was a flier, which meant she had the hardest job of all. Only super thin girls could soar into the air. Performing required a trust in others, and a will to risk personal safety. Each time she went up high, she prayed that gentle hands would catch her before her bones cracked on the hard surface.

She hated being in the air, afraid of heights since infancy. Up there everyone else looked small. Up there the only thing keeping her from hitting the floor was a steady ankle and faith. She hated relying on someone else to keep her safe. She hated being out of control.

One slip-up could paralyze her forever, effectively killing her future. Eager to please and appear confident, she pushed through the fear. Today the expectation was that she would practice her bird basket for the field goal flyover formation.

Last practice the corrections she remembered were to pull with her ankles to continue the rotation forward, tucking harder with her chest. While in the pike position on her way to catch the cradle, she needed to point her toes more. It was just minor details, but vital in her desire for perfection.

Cheerleading was extremely important to her. She loved being in front of the crowd as they chanted together at games, but inspiring others with team spirit had a price. There were lots of sore muscles, bruises, blisters and strained vocal chords. Still she made it look easy, a natural at hiding the truth.

During the warm up, she anticipated the upcoming inquisition. Her girlfriends were relentless in their voracious appetite for gossip, of which sometimes she was the target.

Jennifer and Megan discussed Marvin's party as they dressed.

"Does Beau know about the cake?" Megan said.

"No, it's a surprise," Saylor said.

"I can't believe you're really going to jump out of that thing," Jennifer said.

Megan tied her sneakers. "What are you going to wear?"

"Whip cream over a bathing suit," Saylor said.

"Truly, you have no shame," Jennifer said.

"Girls, did you see the latest cover of *Bridal Magazine*?" Megan put a scrunchie in her hair forming a ponytail.

"I know; that scalloped chiffon dress is to die for. I love the soft hint of pink," Saylor said.

"So if you're looking at bridal gowns, when is Beau popping the big question?" Megan said.

Saylor looked down at the floor and hesitated to answer. "We've talked about it often, maybe at prom." The lie slipped easily off her tongue. "Enough about me, let's get to work. I want to see straight arms, tight abdomens and clean formations ladies."

In the corner, Marvin pitched footballs into a basket exercising his throwing arm.

Kelvin entered the gym with a large rolling garbage can, motioning for his son to come over while he emptied the trash.

"Is everything set for the party?" Kelvin said.

"Yes dad, everyone's been invited," Marvin said.

"Are you sure Beau is going to attend?"

"I know Saylor is, and I'm sure he'll be with her."

"Good, I've got the truck loaded with empty pallets for the bonfire. You can break them down tonight, so don't wear out your arm," Kelvin said.

"Great, just what I want to do after practice."

"And there's an extra little something in a bag. Sprinkle the ashes on top of the boards once the pyramid is formed."

In the bleachers, Beau and Riley focused on homework. They discussed the antics of dinner, as Beau pulled out an admissions application to Savannah School of Art.

"So you're really going to do it?" Riley said.

"What choice do I have after last night?" Beau said.

"This is true." Riley set the calculator down in the middle of the algebra textbook. "Look, I think it's great that you want to pursue your passion, but your dad is going to be really pissed."

"He'll get over it. They both will."

"How are you going to pay for it? That place isn't cheap," Riley said.

"I don't know yet. First thing's first."

"Where'd you guys go yesterday afterschool? We all went down to the lake."

"To the creek," Beau said.

"Well, all right you dog, getting busy?"

"It's not like that, I just prefer the solitude."

"With that killer on the loose? The monster is going to get you one of these days," Riley said.

"Please, aren't we a little old for that?" Beau said.

"In the moonlight, you're in his sight. Better stay out of the swamp at night. Hear the Cicadas, feel the fright. The Creepler is coming with all of his might!"

"Nursery rhymes, really, grow up."

Riley burst into laughter, dropping his pencil between the bleachers.

Jim walked up carrying a stack of folded bath towels for the locker room. "Riley … Coach Doucet … wants to … see you."

"Fabulous." Riley rolled his eyes and gathered his things. "Catch you later dude." He walked on top the bleacher seats, stepping down to the floor. The maple wood was slippery, freshly buffed the night before. Kelvin made sure they were shinny for the press conference.

As Riley trudged the long walk around the basketball court he wondered what Coach wanted. The numerous possibilities swam in his cranium, as he passed by the empty locker room.

Coach's office door was partially open. The tiny room filled with extra sports equipment was just large enough for Coach Doucet and his burgeoning ego. He sat behind the steel desk, feet propped on top with folded arms. "Glad you could make it."

"What's up Coach?"

"How are your grades doing?"

"Better I think since we talked last," Riley said.

"Good, get on the scale," Coach said.

"Man!" Riley kicked off his high tops, and started peeling away layers of garments. "Can I pee first? I've really got to go."

"No."

Riley stepped on the digital scale, looking ahead silently praying to himself.

"What's it say?" Coach repeatedly tossed a baseball in the air, catching it with one hand.

"One hundred eighteen," Riley said.

"Don't lie to me boy," Coach said.

"No really, that's what it says."

"Good job then."

Riley eagerly stepped off the scale. "Coach, I'm really concerned about the Wolverines. That guy Brad is tough, and I don't know—,"

"Hush, you'll win." He hummed the ball at Riley.

Reacting quickly, Riley caught it. "How do you know that?" Riley tossed it back.

"Let's just say it's in the hands of a higher power." Coach rummaged through a cardboard box and tossed him a new school sweatshirt still in the plastic wrapping. "Leave the old one here and put this one on."

"Cool, thanks!" Riley started to dress again.

"You can go for now," Coach said.

Riley grabbed the rest of his stuff, and got out of there fast before Coach changed his mind.

Coach took the dirty sweatshirt, and opened a locked cabinet that had various items; Riley's photograph, a monkey skull, an eagle feather and a doll made from cornhusks. He placed the folded garment on a shelf next to a hanging evergreen robe and closed the door.

The slender concrete path ended in three wooden steps that led to the porch of the Twyla Fay Chaisson Library. The path was as difficult to traverse as parting the Red Sea by waving a wand. Blaze took a deep breath, and swallowed the lump formed in the back of her throat. She knew who would be waiting on the other side of the door, a face she could not erase from memory, the preacher's daughter.

Armed with her trusty journal, a half fleshed theory and a whole lot of gumption, she twisted the crystal knob causing the antique door to scrape as it dragged across the wooden floor. A tiny brass bell on top clanked, alerting the attendant that someone had arrived.

As fresh as morning dew, there stood Kacie ready and waiting to assist. "Didn't expect to have company so soon this morning. I just started coffee brewing."

"That's okay, don't trouble yourself. I know it's early." Blaze walked toward the computer carrels.

"Let me know if you need anything," Kacie said.

"Sure thing." Blaze pulled out the Mission-style oak chair, taking a seat. She opened the journal, which contained Internet search information and print outs of newspaper clippings. The library catalog database was slow to respond as she pecked at bulbous letters on a large computer keyboard. She had acclimated to the tactile ease of her smooth surfaced laptop back at the office.

The database query search listed no entries prior to 1825 for the *Stray Oaks Gazette*. She jotted down some numbers and went to the Microfiche flat-film drawer. Then she sat down at the scanner inserting the first 6"x8" card.

Entry: *10/13/1720.*

Headline: *Hooray for Twin Boys.*

Story: *Local Baron Anton Von Crenshaw names heirs to Creekwood Manor Plantation fortune, Simon and Ezra. Wealthy German immigrant, largest sugarcane producer in territory is proud father. Indigenous mother, LeCretia is well.*

Blaze scanned through the rest of the film, whizzing past frames. Then she stopped.

Entry: *10/31/1727.*

Headline: *Animals Disappear.*

Story: *For years, the week culminating in Halloween is a time for ranchers to mind their flocks. Horses, sheep, pigs and chickens disappear for no reason. No signs of foul play.*

Blaze thought this was odd. She scanned some more.

Entry: *10/13/1729.*

Headline: *Beating the Odds and Losing.*

Story: *Baron Von Crenshaw beat opponents in wager, amassing a fortune in winnings. When asked if he had psychic abilities he denied, stating that 'Luck was always on his side.'*

Blaze changed slides.

Entry: *10/31/1730.*

Headline: *Shock as Tragedy Strikes Plantation.*

Story: *A family in ruins as fortune goes up in flames. Everything burns except giant live oak. Baron Von Crenshaw beat to death in front yard by cane pole. Vladimir Chekov, Russian immigrant, arrested. When asked why he did it he stated, 'He took everything from me, so I returned the favor.' Heirs survive. Vow to rebuild. LeCretia paralyzed jumping from window.*

The articles intrigued Blaze, but this was not helping to prove that the urban legend was real. She found Kacie down a row of bookcases with a rolling cart, filling some books away.

"Excuse me; do you have any historical records?" Blaze said.

"Sure, they're in the back room. What specifically are you looking for?"

"I don't know maybe family lineage, property tax records or town council papers."

"You're in luck, follow me. I can't let you check them out, but you can view what we've got," Kacie said.

They walked to the small office behind the desk. Kacie put on cotton gloves and handed a matching pair to Blaze. Then she shuffled through leather accordion folders on a shelf.

"Ah, here it is." Kacie pulled one down releasing the elastic band. Inside was a small burgundy ledger book. "This one is sort of a town census record. It has lineage, birth dates and marriages by last name." She carefully eased the rest of the contents onto the desk. "There is also a crude hand drawn map showing tax parcels." Kacie pulled out an odd shaped document in a cellophane sleeve. "Oh, and this is very special. Please be extra careful." The parchment paper had aged turning ocher colored, but the black script ink was still legible. "This is our original town charter from 1825. It's priceless."

"Perfect, just what I need." Blaze thumbed through the ledger.

"If you don't mind me asking, why the sudden interest in our town's history?"

"I'm doing research for a possible commemorative piece to coincide with the mayoral election," Blaze said.

"That sounds very interesting. I'll leave you to it."

Blaze stared at Kacie's face for a minute. "Do you feel okay?"

"Why is everyone asking me that?" Kacie said.

"Well honestly, your skin looks kind of yellow."

Kacie smirked and started to walk away. "I'm fine, but thanks for the concern."

Blaze found a page in the journal for Crenshaw.

Von Crenshaw, Simon – Molly (Spouse), Gideon & Josiah born 10/13/1797.

Von Crenshaw, Gideon – Jobeth (Spouse), Jebadiah & Ephriam born 10/13/1847.

Von Crenshaw, Jebadiah – Gerta (Spouse), Nathanial & Miles born 10/13/1897.

Crenshaw, Nathanial – Velma (Spouse), Adelaide & Annabeth born 10/13/1947.

There were no more entries.

Blaze knew that it was common for immigrants to shorten their surnames to help conceal their nation of origin. That was normal, but bearing twins born on October thirteenth was bizarre. She took a photograph of the page with her cell phone. Then she carefully examined the Town Charter.

Grants of Louisiana Territory by the government of Stray Oaks. George, the third, by the grace of God, of Great Britain, Ireland, King, Defender of Faith.

To all persons to whom these presents shall come, greeting.

Know ye, that we of our special grace, certain knowledge and mere motion, for the due encouragement of settling a new plantation within our said Provence.

We divide two equal shares of 25,000 acres: 12,500 acres to Von Crenshaw, and 12,500 acres to Doucet, Herbert and Chaisson.

Names of grantees:
Simon Von Crenshaw
Ezra Von Crenshaw
Ismael Doucet
Saul Chaisson
Noah Herbert

In testimony whereof we have caused the seal of our said Provence to be hereunto affixed. The thirty-first day of October in the year of our Lord Christ, 1825 in the first year of our reign.

Witness Benjamin Westworth Esquire our Governor and Commander in Chief of our said Provence.

Blaze took a photograph before returning the document to its sleeve. It was late morning now, and her boss was less than understanding about hunches and assumptions. To him all that mattered were the facts, the ratings and how good Blaze looked on camera. She returned the contents to the envelope and left the gloves behind.

Kacie was at the reception counter placing checkout cards inside the book jacket pockets.

"Say, you're pretty good friends with Adele aren't you?"

"We're not as close as we used to be before the accident, but we still try to stay in touch," Kacie said.

"Did you know she had a twin sister?"

"Yes, Annie. She lives in Bakersfield," Kacie said.

"If she's one town over, how come I've never seen her?"

"I don't know. Adele usually goes there to visit."

"Sorry for all the questions, but how do you know about her?" Blaze said.

"Adele talks about her often. They're very close."

Blaze could not get the pieces to fit in her head, but noticed that Kacie was standing next to a roll of birthday wrapping paper. "Isn't Beau's birthday coming up soon?"

"Yes, October thirteenth," Kacie said.

"That's an odd date. Did you know it's also Adele's birthday?"

"As a matter of fact, yes. We used to laugh about it all the time. And strangely enough, it's also Vernon's birthday."

"You don't say? How old will Beau be?" Blaze said.

"My boy is growing up so fast; he'll be eighteen and off to college soon."

The phone rang interrupting their conversation.

"Time does fly, speaking of which. I have to run. Thanks for the info." Blaze scooted out the door, as Kacie answered the phone.

"Library ... Yes Dad, I'm feeling the same ... I will, I'll make an appointment today ... I promise."

The interior of Station 3 News was modest but housed all the necessary equipment for an affiliate television channel. Blaze hurried to her desk, rocketing past the station manager's office. The door was open, but he was on the phone talking to the parent company.

Wiley stood in front of her cubicle angrily scribbling a note. He crumpled it with one fist when he saw her approaching, and threw it on the carpet intentionally missing the trashcan.

"Where the hell do you get off?" Wiley said.

Blaze scraped by him through the narrow panel opening and deposited her things on the worksurface. "Look, don't get upset. Let me explain."

"I know the drill with you, and I'm not going to let you stir the pot that doesn't exist just to make a name for yourself."

"Calm down Officer. Here, look at these newspaper articles. I'm compiling a list of disappearances as far back as I can find that have occurred on Crenshaw land." She displayed her pile of collected artifacts across the desk.

Wiley shuffled through them without really looking. "Okay, so the swamp is a dangerous place. Big deal." He continued to invalidate her. "They don't call it wildlife for nothing. You should know that."

"Now you're making me angry. Pay attention to what I am saying. There is a pattern here worth investigating," Blaze said.

"Maybe, but I can't have folks all riled up before the tournament. The town depends too much on the revenue."

"So you'd rather put people's lives in danger than do your job? Remember the oath you swore to protect and serve?"

"Look cupcake, you do your job and I'll do mine," Wiley said.

"I am! I'm reporting to you the truth that something weird is going on."

Wiley was still unconvinced. Taking her seriously would require energy and focus that he did not have.

Blaze pressed on while she had the opportunity. "So what did the autopsy report say?"

"Not that it's any of your business, but exactly like I told you before, a bear attack."

"Really, says who?" Blaze said.

"Coroner Andre Chaisson, but you already knew that."

"Bet you did not know that his family is one of the original town founders along with the Crenshaws?"

"Yeah, so what's clandestine about that?"

"Nothing at the moment, but get back to me." Blaze leaned on the worksurface. "All I'm asking is can you really trust him?"

Wiley scoffed. "Andre is as square as Kooter Brown."

"Okay then just humor me, please get a second opinion. What about my friend Odillia Trahan?"

"She's a Micro-Biologist. I don't see how—,"

"Please, I'm begging you. I know she'll be unbiased," Blaze said.

"Fine, but the hunter's body has already been shipped to the funeral home in Lafayette at the request of his family."

"Just send her a copy of the file. She'll be discreet."

"Fine on one condition, no more sensational stories or the Mayor is going to have my head."

Blaze placed her palm over her heart. "I promise."

As Wiley left, Buck arrived for his interview. Blaze was so involved in playing detective that she forgot today was the big day. She handed Buck off to her assistant for hair and makeup. Then she dashed to the restroom to freshen her own face. After fifteen minutes of vamping, she came out to escort him to a set that looked like a small living room.

"This will be taped and edited, so don't worry if we stop filming." She sat on a lounge chair, perching on the edge of the seat. "That's my camera operator Ed. Pretend he's not here."

Buck straightened his tie. "Do I look all right?"

"You look very nice." Blaze exhaled rolling her shoulders back. "In three, two, one." She faced the camera. "Welcome to a special segment of *At Home with Blaze*. I'm your host, Jessica Blaze. Joining me is the legendary Bassmaster Buck Boudreaux." Then she turned toward her guest. "Welcome to the show Buck."

"Thanks for having me Blaze."

"Buck, I understand you are a nine-time winner of the annual Stray Oaks Fishing Tournament. What will it take to earn your tenth victory?"

"Well, I really think more of myself as a fish psychologist, rather than an angler. I mean, you can't catch fish without first understanding how they think."

"And what exactly do fish think?" Blaze said.

"Well, they're just like us. They want to eat, sleep and reproduce."

Blaze started laughing. "Maybe some of us want to do that, but not in that exact order, ha, ha, ha. Cut!" She leaned in toward Buck caressing his knee, "I'm just kidding with you." She sat upright again, "Ed, pick it up at and what do fish think?"

Buck was confused, "I'll tell you what they want. They want the most attractive bug. That's why my signature lures outsell everything else on the market. They're available exclusively at Fishermen's World."

"I understand the competition is fierce this year," Blaze said.

"Yeah, we've got the usual seasoned pros and some new young talent."

"One of those seasoned pros is your arch nemesis, Vernon Crenshaw?"

"Well, I wouldn't call him that. It is true, we go back a long way. He's a tough competitor, nothing more," Buck said.

"So you guys are friends now?"

"I guess you could say that."

"And isn't it true that Vernon dated your wife Kacie?" Blaze said.

Buck jumped up from the couch. "Now wait a minute. Ed cut! What's going on here?"

Blaze reached up and took Buck's wrist. "I'm sorry; I don't know what's gotten into me today. Too much coffee maybe. Please sit down." Blaze readjusted her skirt. "Ed take it from so you guys are friends?"

Buck was now gruff, "No, we are lovers of the same thing, that's all."

"Well there you have it folks, straight from the mouth of a professional. Tune in next week for our live coverage of the tournament. This is Jessica Blaze; covering the stories you want to hear … Cut!"

Blaze leaned over exposing the valley of her cleavage to remove Buck's microphone. She took her time gently rubbing her fingers under his shirt. In a seductive voice she spoke, lingering the words. "Good job. Thanks for doing this. It's always great to see you."

Town Hall was abuzz as the mayor left for lunch with a hand-full of volunteers. They just returned from door-to-door canvassing, handing out fliers, buttons and signs for the election. Eugene was careful not to mix his reelection efforts with taxpayer time.

Before he could leave, Lin handed him the phone. "It's Mr. Morgan."

Eugene grumbled under his breath as he took the call. "Yes Trace, she's been served. As far as I know, everything is in order." He motioned for the volunteers to give him one minute. "Okay, will do. I'll see you at the press conference."

Kenny arrived to meet with Lin to go over aspects of the tournament. Eugene was confident that his secretary could handle all the event planning. She had a nose for details and was good at ordering people around.

Kenny volunteered to do the grunt work out in the field. He enjoyed being outdoors in the humidity away from Francine, whom he left in charge of the grocery store. They got along fine working together, except for when she was cycling between hot and cold moods.

"Thanks for coming on such short notice. Let's go sit in the conference room. I have all the stuff laid out on the table," Lin said.

Kenny followed blindly without speaking, a little intimidated.

"There has been a slight change in venue, and you need to keep it to yourself."

"Yeah, Eugene mentioned something about the swamp?" Kenny said.

"Yes, he thought Devil's Hole was a bit overdone. So to spice things up...." She flipped open the map. "We are moving the fishing grounds to virgin territory."

"Ouch, that's going to piss off our reigning champ. Don't you think?" Kenny said.

"Oh well, so sorry for him. Since you're a marshal, the Mayor wants you to scout the areas highlighted on this map for the boat launch site."

Kenny had a difficult time getting oriented. "So where are we exactly?"

"Are you sure you can do this, because if not I have plenty of people lined up?" Lin said.

"Just give me a minute...," Kenny said.

The phone rang a few times. Lin abruptly snatched the receiver. "Mayor's Office."

The caller was a clerk with the aquarium vendor. He tried to explain that the acrylic tank arrived damaged in freight, and that there was not enough time to order a new one.

"That's your problem and not my concern right now. If you know what's good for you, just deliver what I ordered or else." Lin hung up the phone. "Where were we?"

"Okay, so you want the boats to launch around this part of Shallow Basin?"

"Bingo, you got it."

"What about the base camp?" Kenny said.

"That's still at Devil's Hole."

"And the RV sleeping quarters?"

"Yes, that too, just like usual, campfire, media … the whole nine yards," Lin said.

"Okeydokey, is there someone who can maybe go with me?"

"Why do you ask?" Lin said.

"I just don't feel real comfortable going out there by myself with the murderer on the loose." Kenny scratched his head. "The paper says it ain't no bear, and Francine has been harping on me."

"Do you believe everything you read? Besides we know what a loose cannon Blaze can be, among other things."

Kenny still looked befuddled.

"Here are the GPS coordinates, so you can't get lost. Just make sure the boats will fit through the clearing. That is all. It's very simple. Can you do that?"

"Well I don't know, I guess so," Kenny said.

"Fine, now maybe I can get back to actual work." Lin rolled up the map and handed it to Kenny. "Oh and be careful. If the Creepler attacks you, don't forget to dial 9-1-1."

In the basement, Adele retrieved a black-silk bag closed by a gold threaded drawstring. Inside was an ornate hand mirror, the kind used by royalty. Instead of foiled glass, the frame surrounded a piece of Obsidian. The ebony volcanic rock reflected a void, a visible darkness filled with nothingness.

This special one was decades old, passed down through generations and from where it originated even Adele did not know. Some of her sorcery tools were gifts from LeCretia, as well as the knowledge the Crenshaws protected.

LeCretia was a domestic slave of Baron Anton Von Crenshaw, but he served her needs more. She traveled with him from the age of thirteen doing all the things a nursemaid would do. In exchange, he taught her the wonders of other cultures. While traveling she secretly collected items from Egypt, Mexico and the Far East to use in her black magic.

Her Choctaw Indian ancestry was rich with medicine men and seers. She was born with psychic abilities to predict the future. Because she was special, the tribe hid her from others. As she aged, her powers grew to match her beauty. The chief did what any loving father would do; he sent her away for her own protection, to a small group of Choctaw derivatives the Bayougoula, who lived by the Mississippi River in a marshy area.

On her thirteenth birthday, All Hallows' Eve, the tribe celebrated summer's end dancing around a fire. The Great Horned Serpent God came to rule winter, while the Mother Earth Goddess rested. The change of seasons was customary as crop fields turned to decay, and the air became frigid as the days shortened.

LeCretia could see the Serpent Spirit, and it could see her. So the tribe named her *Guardian* and handed her *The Book of Shadows*, which contained rituals, incantations and symbols. LeCretia quickly learned the ancient ways and worshipped the Spirit that held the secret knowledge of the balance between the dark matter and the primordial life force.

Then the Carolina Traders came to the village. The white men snatched her away at midnight, and sold her to the Baron. She brought her elk-skin pouch, which contained ritual objects, but she left the book, the contents etched in her memory. LeCretia never returned to her native peoples in physical form.

She and the Baron became very close in every way and through the years, their love flourished, as did his love for gambling. In practicing her religion, she came to know future events. She gave this knowledge to him, and he profited holding five cards close to his chest at a table.

One day he wagered against the wrong person; a man who could not let things go. Vladimir Chekov knew Anton was somehow cheating; such a long winning streak defied the statistical probabilities of good luck. The Russian immigrant was a Godless man, who believed in retaliation. He murdered Anton, and it broke LeCretia's heart.

Her psychic aura was never the same color.

Many years later before she died, she taught the ways to her daughter-in-law, who then taught her daughter-in-law, and so on. That is how the Crenshaws became enlightened.

Vernon had the top cover off the bow-mounted trolling motor. He stood in front of the twenty-two-foot bass boat, which rested on its trailer. He had a wrench in one hand and an oil spray can in the other, with a shop rag draped over his shoulder.

Adele ran out the back door of the house. She nailed a poppet doll fashioned out of cornhusks upside down through the heart to a pine tree. Across its chest inscribed in black marker was: *Eugene*. "I'm going to town to take care of this mess once and for all." She yelled in Vernon's general direction.

"Do you need me to help with anything?" Vernon said.

"Never you mind, I can handle my affairs." She started to walk away then turned around. "Need anything while I'm there?"

Vernon was perplexed about the broken motor. "Could use some parts, but I don't know what yet. You go on, and I'll get them later."

Adele hurried toward the truck, taking her whirlwind energy with her.

Vernon went back to tinkering in peace.

A short distance away, Kenny walked in circles around the sports utility vehicle. He had the map and a handheld GPS receiver, but he could not visualize the drawing in three-dimensional space. The receiver said he was in the correct place, but it did not look like what was drawn on the map.

Something watched from behind the evergreen shrubs.

Kenny laid the items on the hood, and fished around the floorboards for his trusty baseball cap embroidered: *Got Bubba?* Then he slid into a long sleeve flannel shirt to ward off the gnats. He grabbed the items, and marched toward the tree line by the water.

The map noted a spot for the boats to launch. He looked for a clearing, but there was none. They would have to hack through the dense brush with a machete to clear a path.

The crickets chirped, but it was otherwise quiet. Kenny felt very uneasy. He stepped lightly while listening. He heard footsteps behind him. Quickly, he turned around only to find stationary trees standing before him. He stared in the same direction so long, his mind started to play tricks.

"God Kenny, man up already!" He shook the anxiety off.

In the backyard, the motor was not fixing itself. Fed up, Vernon ripped open a can tab top, and enjoyed the sensation of suds rolling down his chin. He was not supposed to mix his medications with alcohol, but Adele was not around to see. Besides, one beer could not hurt.

He strolled down the meandering path that led toward the woods and veered left to the family cemetery. Sixteen plots in all, but one held special importance to him. He meticulously cared for the grounds around his father Earl's headstone. Engraved words on the onyx granite monument cut deep into his heart:

Earl Edward Chaisson
1945–1995
Here lies Earl, lost to this world.
Better known as Paw, killed by a saw.

Vernon sat for a while on the mound, running grass through his fingers. The blades were cold and damp.

He missed his father; the times they went fishing and everything Earl taught him about how to treat a woman. The memories of their time together lingered in his mind.

It had been sixteen years since his tragic death and in each year that crept by, Vernon felt more sorrow and pain. The ache was growing like metastasized cancer.

Adele never talked much about what happened that day. Vernon and Chester came home from school and found her crying on the front porch swing, while various officials did their jobs scurrying around.

They told the boys Earl was trimming an oak that had grown too close to the house and lost his footing on the eighteen-foot ladder. He fell off holding the live chain saw and hit the corner of the roof. Luckily, it broke his fall, but he rolled off and in the process sliced his thigh before hitting the ground. The laceration severed his artery, though not being the injury to kill him.

When he landed on his back, his spine contorted snapping his neck and rendering his limbs uncontrollable. The arm still gripping the live chain saw fell back diagonally toward his chest causing the metal teeth to tear through his neck. It did enough damage to be the fatal blow. Adele found him in a pool of blood with the motor of the executioner still idling in a cloud of black smoke. At least that is how her version of the story went.

Next to Earl's grave was Chester, another family tragedy occurring two years later, but this one was Vernon's fault. He spent twelve years of his young adult life thinking about the fatal mistake in prison, serving a sentence for vehicular homicide.

Vernon did not tend to Chester's gravesite. Adele always took care of it. He spent most days trying to forget he ever had a twin, and Adele spent the rest of the time reminding him.

Back in the woods, a crow squawked as a warning to the others. Vernon recognized the siren and reached in his back pocket for his pistol. After dodging through bushes a short distance, he came upon Kenny sitting upright against a tree. Vernon let off two rounds into the air and the bird scattered from the loud noise.

Nearby a strange shadow moved about. The Creepler's vacant eyes glared at Vernon. It trampled away leaving a flurry of rumbled foliage.

Kenny had his hand compressed around his neck trying to stem the bleeding. His wide-eyes froze with a look of horror. He gasped for air, making a strange gurgling sound trying to breathe.

Vernon took off his shirt and tied it tightly around Kenny's neck. "Keep pressure here. Just hang on buddy." He hit a speed dial number for emergency services. "I need an ambulance at Creek Lane. Hurry!" Then he stowed the phone and lifted Kenny to his feet. "Lean on me, we've got to walk toward the house." They took deliberate steps, as drops of crimson soiled the evergreens in a trail behind.

Part of the way they hopped along, but after a few minutes Vernon got nervous. He did not want people nosing around their property, and he did not need any more trouble with the law.

Internal voices clamored for his attention and most of the time, Vernon could ignore them. They were not real and he knew it, but under certain conditions, they made their presence known. This was one of those times. *They're going to think you did it boy. Kill him. Ditch the body.* Vernon fought the voices by humming a lullaby aloud.

Once they made it out of the woods, he picked Kenny up carrying him draped over his shoulder. This caused blood to gush out of the deep holes in his neck. Vernon charged as fast as he could up the hill to the back porch, as the warm fluid dripped down his back.

Red and white lights pulsated, as the ambulance drove up. The emergency technicians laid Kenny on a stretcher, strapping him down. Vernon compressed the lacerations with his hands, now bloodied.

In the back of the ambulance, Wilbur Charbonneau applied large gauze bandages to the wounds. Kenny received a facemask of oxygen and all four raced to the hospital a few miles away. The siren screamed down an empty Route 3.

Blessed Heart was a modest hospital with limited resources, but still the administrator managed to provide decent health care to the community. Andre practiced double-duty as the administrator and chief medical examiner. His hands probed in everything, especially obstetrics. His specialty was delivering life in transition, either birth or death.

Dr. Babette Comeau was on duty for twenty-six hours straight when the ambulance arrived. She ingested the usual stimulants in overdose quantities, caffeine and nicotine gum plus one little blue pill. A few milligrams cut the fatigue jitters, too many made the room gyrate.

The buildup of chemicals in her bloodstream had a cumulative effect numbing her senses. In her head, visions

112

of smooth corners collided with radial intersections aborting logic. Her body moved robotically through repetition, independent of thought.

No one was watching her, and no one cared what she did. Every day she slipped one-step closer toward final self-destruction, feeding her addiction while in a white labcoat.

The medical technicians rushed Kenny's gurney into the Emergency Room as Vernon pressed on the cabernet garments saturated with lifeblood. Each seeping ounce lightened Kenny's load. The weight of day-to-day concerns eroded, as he embraced the lighted tunnel beckoning him. His soul took flight, while his physical form tingled; electrons cascaded as mass converted to energy. The trauma team was rapidly losing him.

"We need to stabilize him guys. Get me 1mg of Atropine." Dr. Comeau depressed on Kenny's abdomen and he screamed. "Um, that's not good." She calmly looked at Vernon's horrified face and found her own reflection in his fright.

"Will he make it Doc?" Vernon said.

"Too soon to tell. Let's get him prepped for surgery, so I can close these wounds."

As the medical staff wheeled the gurney away, Vernon held on until the last possible second, finally standing alone covered in blood. He hated hospitals, especially this one. Everyone he loved died here.

Officer Aucoin entered the Emergency Room and approached Vernon with a certain disdain. As a law enforcement expert, he had grown untrusting of ex-convicts especially murderers. Vernon experienced the same mistrust for authority, as the victim of prejudice.

"What's the story?" Wiley said as he flipped open his steno pad.

"I was in the yard working on the boat, when I heard screams," Vernon said.

"Were you alone?"

"Yes."

"Go on, what happened next?" Wiley said.

"So, I ran into the woods and found Kenny bleeding by a tree."

"Was anyone else there?"

"No, I mean, I don't know. I didn't look. I was focused on getting him out of there," Vernon said.

"Okay, calm down. Can you take me to the spot?"

"I guess so. May I wash up first?"

"I'll meet you back here later; I've got to drop in on someone," Wiley said.

Down the hall and around the corner was the modest laboratory of Dr. Odillia Trahan. At Wiley's request, Dixie sent her the case file on the murdered hunter.

"Knock, knock." Wiley pushed the door open.

Odillia sat on a lab stool peering into a microscope. She fiddled with her long russet hair wrapped in a bun secured by a pencil. She wore studious glasses that made her look intelligent. The labcoat combined with her title fashioned a hot commodity. Wiley had sweet eyes for her.

Odillia smiled in that way a woman does when she knows a man is interested. "I was going to call you about that case file."

Wiley casually leaned against some low-storage cabinets, intently listening to the way her voice sounded.

"Careful officer, you might catch something. I was working with Bubonic Plague over there."

Wiley smirked, "A little microbiology humor?" He moved away from the furniture anyway, just to be safe.

Odillia arose to wash her hands. "Is something wrong?"

"Unfortunately, there's been another attack. This time it's Kenny Mouton."

"Oh no, is he all right?"

"He's in surgery right now; multiple neck lacerations, but he's still kicking. That old dog."

"I hate to give you more bad news but, I disagree with the coroner's assessment. Understand that he is my boss, and I'm only risking this since Blaze is my friend."

"Don't worry, this is just between us. So if it's not a bear what is it then?" Wiley said.

"Definitely animal, but I can't match the wound patterns to anything from around here, at least not from my sources," Odillia said.

"What do you need?"

"Recent tissue samples, preferably something with a bite mark."

"I believe the hunter is already buried. What about a sample from Kenny?"

"Dr. Comeau will have cleaned and sutured the wounds by now." She paced across the floor. "But I could grab the tissue she excises before it's incinerated."

"Won't she ask questions?" Wiley said.

Odillia chuckled, "She already thinks I'm crazy for loving bugs, I mean infectious diseases. Besides, if it's a typical day, she'll be zoned out on drugs. Oops, did I say that out loud?"

In the opposite wing was Andre's office, the largest one with the best view of the dedicated angel garden. He liked to collect federal duck stamps from the U. S. Fish and Wildlife Service. Each year's medallion editions covered his walls fitting together like puzzle pieces. The artist signed and limited number prints served as both artwork and migratory bird hunting licenses. The program had been in place since 1934, raising millions with the majority going to fund wetland conservation. Many endangered species lived in those protected habitats.

Each fall the artist chosen as contest winner had their stamp design produced by the U. S. Mint, available for sale to the public the following summer. Andre was on a preferred buyer's list with automatic new edition reservation.

He had quite a collection, constantly searching the Internet for missing years. He spent many nights bidding at online auctions. Price was not a barrier; all he had to do was enter the last bid before time expired.

Kelvin sometimes did odd jobs for Andre to earn extra money. The high school did not pay him a large salary, but he enjoyed being around the students. He also kept an eye on them, while he was there for other purposes.

As an odd job, he was responsible for rearranging the wall each time Andre added to the collection. All the frames had to fit together just right, hiding as much wall surface as possible. This was a daunting task because Andre wanted them arranged in chronological order by year. Paid by the hour, Kelvin did not mind the task or how long it took. He also subscribed to the notion of perfect order.

Andre heard the ambulance arrive. He set the new addition back in the shipping box, and left his office to make rounds with curiosity piqued.

Dr. Comeau finished surgery and changed into fresh medical scrubs, already smacking nicotine gum. Andre caught her in the hall by the waiting area as she spoke with Francine.

"What's all the commotion about?" Andre said.

"Hemorrhaging caused by penetrating trauma, from what I don't know. The damage was so extensive; I had to seal the blood vessels with electrical current."

"What happens to him now?" Francine said.

"We need to keep him overnight to monitor his blood pressure, but the prognosis is very good. He received three units of blood during surgery and is stable now."

"When can I see him?" Francine said.

"When he's moved to a patient room, he's still in post-operative recovery."

"Great work Doctor." Andre said. "Francine, if there is anything you need please let me know."

Dr. Comeau headed to her office. Odillia approached with a strange request for tissue. Babette agreed, too tired to care why she wanted it. Her shift was finally over.

In post-op, Wiley leaned over Kenny asking questions, but he could not respond. His open throat exposed swollen vocal cords, preventing vibration. Wiley offered his notepad and pencil, so they could communicate.

"Do you remember anything?"

A half-conscious Kenny scribbled: *no*.

"Did you see anyone?" Wiley said.

Kenny pointed to *no* with the pencil point.

"Why were you there?"

Kenny drew a question mark.

"You don't remember?"

Kenny raised his thumb to signify: *yes*.

Dr. Comeau drew back the privacy curtain with a screech. "Officer, please! The patient needs to rest. You're not supposed to be in here anyway."

"Sorry, I'll come back later." Wiley patted Kenny on the thigh. "Glad you're okay old friend, you get better now."

When he exited the post-operative area, Odillia was waiting in the hall. "Follow me." As they walked down the corridor, Odillia looked around trying to be inconspicuous. They slipped into her lab undetected. Then she locked the door behind them. "Whatever bit him is reptile. I found mucous containing neurotoxic chemicals in the tissue samples."

"What does that do?"

"It's a combination of proteins that immobilize muscle impulses and enzymes that digest the prey."

"So it's a big snake?" Wiley said.

"Not exactly, snake venom is a type of saliva which can be secreted at high pressures. Some rattlesnakes can spit eight feet, but they usually aim for the victim's eyes."

"Kenny's wounds are different."

"I know, and there were toxic bacteria present; staphylococcus and E. coli like found in monitor lizard saliva."

"So there are a giant snake and lizard tag-team attacking people in the woods?"

"I'm suggesting something entirely different … a Cryptomorph."

"What in Hell's bells is that?" Wiley said.

"Something mysterious, like Big Foot or Nelly. It's an animal that hides from man," Odillia said.

"What kind of animal?" Wiley said.

"An unknown mutated species."

"Well that just leaves one question. Mutated from what?"

CHAPTER 5

Lin relaxed at her desk scanning the online celebrity tabloids for the latest tidbits of scandalous hearsay, when Eugene approached. He worried about the press conference specifics in the back of his mind, while rehearsing his speech aloud.

"Did they deliver the visuals yet?" Eugene said.

Lin pointed to the oversized maps affixed to foam board leaning against the wall, without looking away from the computer screen.

He picked one up studying the base camp layout around Devil's Hole and muttered to himself.

Lin ignored him. They had a standing rule that if Eugene was not going to use his words, she was not required to listen.

"Good, I think we've covered everything possible. I hope so anyway," Eugene said.

"It's exactly what you asked for, after I factored in the things you forgot," Lin said.

The phone rang. Lin let it ring two more times before answering. Another standing rule she attributed too *Asian superstition*, but the truth was she never answered before the third ring because she was not willing to drop what she was doing for the needs of other citizens.

Eugene picked up the second board, a higher aerial photograph of the fishing area with demarcated off-limits boundaries. He grew concerned when Lin did not say anything to the caller. She rarely held her tongue for anyone.

"I'm so sorry. Yes, I will let him know. Keep us posted. Take care," Lin said.

"What now?" Eugene set the board down crumpling his forehead.

"Kenny has been in an accident. Something attacked him in the woods. He is in the hospital. Don't worry, I'll send flowers."

"Oh no, did he get to check the launch area out?" Eugene said.

Lin gave him the evil eye. "He's fine, Francine thanks you for asking. Officer Aucoin is investigating what happened."

"You mean who … *Who* refers to people."

"Mayor, my English is correct. In this case, it's a what!"

Suddenly, Eugene felt flush. He grabbed the tie that he thought was the culprit, loosening the silken knot. Then he embedded his fist between his pectoral muscles pushing on his heart. He anchored himself to Lin's credenza with his free arm for support.

"Is something wrong?" Lin said.

"My chest feels very heavy, like someone just drove a spike through it."

"Do you need me to reserve a hospital room next to Kenny's?"

Before Eugene could respond, a visibly angry Adele ripped open the entry door. She aimed for Eugene and moved toward him pushing furniture out of the way. The sweeping dress trailed behind her, as if she were floating above the floor plane. She approached in a continuous movement like a butcher's knife drawing through a rotten tomato.

"Why are you doing this?" Adele said.

"Calm down Adele. Let's go into my office and talk," Eugene said.

Adele changed her course without stopping, boomeranging off his psyche.

Eugene shut the door, so Lin could not hear the complaints Adele was about to register.

"How much is he paying you?" Adele held up the legal documents crumpling them in one hand.

"I don't know what you're talking about—,"

"Oh come now Mayor, we both know the kinds of company you keep."

"This is an economic decision based on the prosperity of the town."

"Like the economic prosperity that funded your classic Cobra sports car?"

Eugene could feel a constriction around his neck, but he had already removed the tie and unbuttoned his shirt collar.

"Exactly how did you acquire that car anyway?" Adele said.

An invisible force was grappling his throat, making it difficult to breathe or speak.

"And where is little Johnny these days?" Adele said.

Eugene started wheezing. Sweat balls formed on the crown of his widow's peak.

"Cat got your tongue? That would be my feline Midnight, she is playful like that. And since you are speechless, I can fill in the blanks of what happened. You threw his carcass into the lake around 3:00 a.m. It was a bit chilly that night, but not quite as cold as your heart."

Eugene stumbled backward, landing on the credenza. "How do you know about that?"

"I know a lot of things about you. Like the kiddie porn you've grown accustomed to late at night, alone in your room, when you think no one is watching." Adele stepped closer. "Isn't that what got you in trouble in the first place? All the boys like poor little Johnny." Adele was so close to his face, she could smell the stale odor of cigarettes on his clothes.

"It was an accident." Eugene perspired. "And the harvest moon burned scarlet, like an eyeball glaring at me."

"How did it feel in the bucket seats of his car, when you had your belt fastened around his neck? Was he gasping for air, as you are now, because you clicked the belt one notch too many?

Eugene could not speak. He tried, but nothing came out.

"When did you realize he was dead, before or after you finished?"

"It was dark and I couldn't see his face."

"So you took advantage of a teenage boy from Bakersfield, dumped his body in the lake and stole his car." Adele laid the documents on his desk. As soon as she did, they burst into flames. "And you covet that car like a trophy. Does the Sandalwood air freshener remind you of his cologne? Is that why you relive the experience repeatedly, fondling yourself in the car late at night in your garage?"

"How can you possibly know all of this?" Eugene massaged his throat.

Adele laughed a bellowing sound ushered from something other than herself, a deep sinister sound rising to a crescendo. "I'm a witch, remember?"

"That's just a silly rumor. No one really believes it, least of all me," Eugene said.

"Maybe, maybe not. All I know is that this land has been in my family since my great-great-great-grandfather planted sugarcane."

"So why do you need all of it anymore? Just think of all the money you'll save on property taxes," Eugene said.

"The tax man cometh one way or another to get his due. Mark my words Eugene, you'll be sorry."

Kacie arranged the lace napkins on one side of the Queen Anne coffee table. The china teapot seemed orphaned with all the cups cloistered together. Something was missing in the presentation.

An antique silver platter hung on the wall in the foyer of the library. It had an etched surface with curvilinear designs reminiscent of the Baroque Period. It was an elaborate ornament for such a simple Craftsman-style house. Every day, it hung on the wall silently like a cross, a background object no one noticed, perpetually shinny without polishing, reflecting scrambled images as people passed.

The platter had been there since Twyla Fay died. Her family left it behind when they donated the historic house to the town, the only personal property of hers that conveyed. It remained the way she wanted it, undisturbed.

Kacie placed both hands firmly around the scalloped edges, feeling the cold metal. Anchored with magic, she removed it effortlessly. The tea set had a new home resting comfortably inside a silver fence. She was satisfied that the coffee table displayed the proper arrangement of southern etiquette.

Adele entered the library with casual ease, looking forward to visiting with an old friend. "It's a lovely day dear, come sit with me on the porch."

Kacie had not yet enjoyed the dry crisp air of fall, her favorite time of year when the humidity and mosquitos retreated farther south. Maybe the fresh air would make her feel better.

Adele's old bones settled into the plump cushions of the cedar swing.

Kacie joined by her side.

"How are you doing?" Adele said.

"I just came back from the doctor's office. It's probably nothing."

"You can talk to me dear."

"They did some tests, but I won't know for a while. Pardon my candor, but it's my cycle," Kacie said.

"Yes, go on. What's the problem?"

"It's hanging around too long. Plus, I'm tired all the time. The doctor says I'm anemic."

Adele chuckled. "That's treatable, just become a carnivore. Vegetables are for rabbits."

Kacie grinned. "You know I'm a vegetarian, besides he gave me some iron supplements so that Bambi could live."

Adele had her ankle boots planted into the floor, gently rocking them. "I'm really concerned about you. Do you remember when Beau was born?"

"Bits and pieces, but mostly I just wonder why it happened. The pregnancy was going fine until that night. Then there was all that blood."

"And that terrible accident that Dr. Blaze had. Poor girl," Adele said.

"It was awful, and right when I needed her the most. I have to tell you, I feel somewhat responsible for that whole thing."

"How so dear?" Adele said.

"Well, if the hospital wouldn't have called her to come in, then maybe she wouldn't have stepped one foot out of the tub to reach for the pager, accidentally touching the curling iron."

"Oh honey, it's not your fault that she was electrocuted. It was an unfortunate accident in an old house. That is why new houses have protection against that sort of thing. No one blames you for her death."

"Blaze does. Every time she looks at me, I feel her hatred for killing her big sister," Kacie said.

Adele put her arm around Kacie like a mother to console her. "There now dear, at least Dr. Chaisson was there to assist you."

"Yes and Beau. I just wish Andre could have saved his twin brother too."

"I don't mean to dwell, but do you remember any of the delivery?"

"It's a blur. I was so weak and lightheaded from bleeding. They knocked me out for the Cesarean Section because of the pain. Seems like I slept for a week afterward."

"Do you remember when I brought you homemade soup in the hospital?" Adele said.

"Yes, it was really good, almost like a magic pill. I felt so much better afterward."

"Well, I brought you some more today to remove this latest affliction."

"Oh, you're so nice. How'd you know?" Kacie said.

Pastor Louis Foret parked his champagne sedan in the driveway. It sparkled as it floated past the porch railing. "Morning, sorry to keep you ladies waiting."

"That's all right Dad, we're just catching up," Kacie said.

The three retired to the parlor where the perfected tea service rested. Kacie and her father sat side-by-side on the loveseat. A reckless coil straining to break free from the strapping poked Kacie in the bottom.

Strange things often happened in the house, when Kacie felt Twyla Fay's presence. Alone in the library when it was very quiet, books flew off the shelves. Occasionally, a book fell on the floor opened to a certain page. Kacie took the time to read the passage before returning it. The book subjects often were self-help, but lately there were many romance novels.

Sometimes Kacie arrived to find all the toddler chairs arranged in rows in the area where she read stories aloud to the children. Twyla's ghost desperately tried to communicate, but so far, Kacie had not been able to decipher the messages.

Adele sat stoically on the edge of the adjacent chair. "Thank you for meeting with me on such short notice,

Pastor. Let us cut to the chase. I wish to donate my land to the church, with a few stipulations, of course." She revealed a document handwritten in black ink from an eagle-feather quill inscribing the parchment paper, creating romantic lines of various thicknesses. Written in calligraphy, Louis understood the meaning as he examined the paper.

"I don't know what to say. This is most generous and unexpected," Louis said.

"May I ask, why you want to do this?" Kacie said.

"There are some evil people in this town with selfish intentions, and this will stop them," Adele said.

"What are the conditions?" Louis said.

"First, I'll keep the acres indicated on the map, and you can have the rest. Second, the land is to remain as-is infinitum."

"No disrespect, but if we can't build on it, then what good is it to the church?" Louis said.

"Dad!" Kacie was embarrassed. "I can think of lots of things. You can hold retreats there; summer youth camp and baptize people in the creek."

"You're right, I hadn't thought of all that. You know, come to think of it, Devil's Hole is a strange place for baptisms."

"So are we in agreement then?" Adele said.

"Absolutely, Ms. Crenshaw. Where do I sign?" Louis said.

"Let me go get my notary stamp." Kacie went to the desk.

Adele grinned with slanted eyes fixed on Louis as he scrolled the fountain pen, the tip scratching on the parchment grooves.

Kacie added the official seal, and signed as a witness.

Louis sandwiched Adele's wrinkled hands between his. "The church congregation thanks you very much."

"Don't mention it, Pastor. You are doing me a favor, just think of all the property taxes I will save. Hope the Mayor can afford to lose the revenue."

After time, steel touching steel exposed to the elements forms a molecular bond like aggregate and limestone. The lock wrench was not able to move the nut. It only left striations in the hex-nut head. Vernon struggled to force the bolt free. He tried spray lubricant, rubber straps and tapping gently with a hammer. Still, nothing coaxed the screw threads to turn.

Vernon knelt in the bow of the boat, trying to focus on something other than what had happened earlier in the woods, when four icy digits touched his shoulder. They firmly pressed down with familiarity. He turned expecting to greet Adele, but he was still alone.

Paranoia was his closest friend, a symptom of the mental disorder. He took a pharmaceutical to combat it, but the other drugs he took listed it as a side effect. He tried to ignore the feeling, as his imagination screamed for attention. He resumed tugging with brute force.

A bullfrog croaked notes in succession amplified under a log. The wind kicked up to a constant breeze. Leaves rustled, hopped and tumbled on the ground. A voice buried in the wind called his name. He tried to discount it, but intuitively understood the voice was not in his head. It sounded different. It sounded real. *Verrrrrrr*

130

... *nonnnnnn*. He looked around but no one was there. He leaned into the wrench, white knuckles squeezing.

Then like the sun peeking through storm clouds, the nut turned. Vernon applied so much force, when the bolt finally budged the wrench jammed his finger. "Ouch!" He rubbed his injured hand and sat up, sensing eyes on his back. When he turned around, Beau was there.

"Afternoon, Mr. Crenshaw," Beau said.

"Boy, you startled me. We don't get many visitors out here," Vernon said.

"Sorry, I was wondering if you could help me with something."

"What you got?"

"We hardly know each other Mr. Crenshaw, but I need help with a school project."

"Please call me Vern. Maybe you could help me too. I could use a hand."

"What are you doing?" Beau said.

"Trying to get ready for the tournament and this trolling motor is on the fritz. You want to come up here?"

Beau climbed onto the deck. "I'll gladly do whatever I can, but I have got to warn you, I don't know much about boats."

"I'd think you'd be an expert by now with your Paw being who he is."

"Actually, we don't spend a lot of time together."

"That's a real shame," Vernon said.

"No, it's better this way, we don't really see eye-to-eye on much."

Vernon removed all four bolts allowing the motor to be free. "Can you open that box over there?"

Beau sliced the tape on the cardboard box with a screwdriver. Inside was a brand-new motor wrapped in clear plastic. "So did you get along with yours?"

"Paw was my best friend. He took Chester and me fishing all the time." Vernon placed the motor over the mounting plate. "Can you hold it steady here?"

Beau placed his hands where they needed to be before Vernon could finish asking. He instinctively knew what he needed.

"So what do kids your age do for fun these days?" Vernon said.

"I don't really hang around with other kids much. I have friends, but I prefer to be alone in the woods."

"So what do you do for fun?"

"I love landscape photography. It's what I want to do after high school, but my parents don't agree. Instead, they want me to be a blood-sucking leech."

Vernon laughed. "Yeah well, law is a respectable field and highly lucrative, I hear."

"What's your experience with attorneys?" Beau said.

"I give them more respect than they probably deserve."

Vernon and Beau worked on the motor for a while in silence.

"Why don't you just tell your parents how you feel?" Vernon said.

"Um, do you know my dad?"

Vernon looked up from the motor, "Yep, we were in the same class. And so was your mother, but I can see your point."

"I want to do something creative. I have an eye for capturing on film what others miss and force them to see the truth. And that's why I'm here. I really want to go to art school, and I need references for the application." Beau pulled out a folded paper from his back pocket. "Would you mind taking a look at this?"

Kacie's son needed him. Surprised by the irony, Vernon accepted. "Be honored to, and with discretion of course."

"Our little secret, that'd be great." Beau felt relieved and welcomed, as if he were at home.

"So tell me about your girlfriend?" Vernon said.

"Saylor's awesome, but…"

"But what?"

"I don't know how much longer we'll be together. It's senior year and we'll be in different states soon. I don't know how to tell her that I'm not going with her to New York. It's complicated."

"Trust me, women are very complicated. I know all about it."

"Do you have somebody special?" Beau said.

"Not anymore. I still have feelings for her, but she's moved on with her life. It's complicated too." Vernon fastened the last screw. The job was complete. "All I have left is memories, and this boat named after her."

Beau hopped down and read the black vinyl letters. "Miss Sunshine?"

"Yeah, she shines like the sun."

Beau looked at his watch, realizing how late it was. "Oh no! The stupid press conference. I forgot all about it. They're going to be pissed at me."

"Oh crap kid, I'm late too."

In the corner of the gym, Eugene and Trace congregated next to the refreshments. The foldout table was beat up from years of use, but covered with a white tablecloth to hide the damage. Jim filled miniature wax cups with fruit punch, placing them in rows. Eugene nervously drank them down, almost as fast as Jim could pour.

A large turnout of people sat on the home-side bleachers. On the guest side, ten professional contestants and their amateur coanglers were holding a meet-and-greet. A national sports reporter interviewed Buck with Haley standing by his side, intentionally blocking Skeeter from view. She was determined to get a promotional word in about Buck's upcoming autobiography release.

To the left of Buck's table sat Phil, next to an empty chair for Vernon, who was absent.

On the right, Blaze interviewed Morty Vance who lived in Bakersfield. He came from a long line of commercial shrimpers, but his family could not understand why he was wasting his time on a vacation hobby. Morty sat with his nephew Doug.

Blaze hoped an opportunity would present itself to engage with the national reporter. She spoke halfheartedly with Morty, who was too dumb to realize she was just biding time. He blathered on while she kept one eye on Buck's table. She thought of purposefully tripping on her microphone cord and stumbling into them. Her talent needed national discovery, even if it required a desperate move to get attention.

Pastor Foret sat in the bleachers next to Kacie when Beau arrived.

"You're late. Where were you?" Kacie said.

"I had to stay after school for something," Beau said.

"I called your cell phone many times and even sent a text. Didn't you get my messages?"

"Sorry, I must still have the ringer turned off from algebra."

"When I couldn't reach you, I called Riley. He said you had already left school. So which is it?"

"What's with the inquisition mom?"

"This event is very important to your father and his sponsors."

"I know, but I'm here now so chill out." Beau scanned the room looking for his friends, but no one was there.

Kacie could not let it go. "You better not be spending time with that girl in the woods. I promise I'll start checking your GPS."

"Mom, give it a rest. If you must know, I was at the Crenshaws."

Kacie looked puzzled, "For what?"

Beau hesitated to answer truthfully. "I was helping Vern."

"Vern, really? Since when did you get on a first name basis with him?" Kacie wrenched his bicep and whispered in his ear. "Listen to me carefully; I do not want you hanging around him period. So help me, I'll tell your father."

Beau jerked his arm free. "Fine!"

Across the court, Vernon took his seat slightly out of breath from hurrying. He waved to Adele across the way, who sat in the bleachers. She signaled back with her cold eyes, stoic as ever.

Eugene approached the lectern standing at the edge of the basketball court. He was five feet from the crowd, but still spoke through the humming microphone. "Excuse me, if we can get started."

The crowd noise settled down to a low murmur and then quieted.

"I want to thank everyone for coming out today, as we prepare to kick off the fiftieth annual Stray Oaks Fishing Tournament, part of the hunt for the Southern Trail. As Mayor, it's an honor to welcome our out-of-town contestants and the national media."

Behind Eugene were two easels that had black fabric draped over the display-board faces. Lin started removing the covers while he spoke.

"This year we are going to move the fishing venue to a new location." He pointed to the aerial view of the fishing grounds. Instead of Devil's Hole, we will be fishing in Shallow Basin."

The crowd rumbled.

"The limits are roughly three square miles. Contestants will carry a GPS receiver that will sound a warning signal when breaching the boundary. The receiver will also mark each landed catch, transmitting the coordinates back to the judging marshals."

Clovis stood up to speak. "With all due respect Mayor, the vendors always set up in the parking lot around the lake. As one of them, what are we supposed to do for electricity in the woods?"

"Good question Clovis. The base camp will still set up as usual around the lake: contestant RVs, vendors, weigh-in officials, medical, refueling and the media." Eugene pointed to the board with the lake map. "Only the contestants will be allowed to enter the swamp." He pointed to the other display board.

"Isn't that a little unfair since Vernon is a contestant?" Buck smiled at Vernon, "No offense, ole boy."

"None taken," Vernon said.

"I understand your concern Mr. Boudreaux, but as the nine-time winner, aren't you ready to raise the stakes?" Eugene said.

"Well, yes. I don't plan on giving up my title to anyone, and if Vernon needs a little help to level the playing field, I don't mind a bit."

"Thanks," Vernon said.

"Don't mention it," Buck said.

Coach Ducet was standing by the wall next to Kelvin. "Traditionally folks have respected the Crenshaw's wishes for privacy, so why are we trespassing on their land?"

Eugene turned to Trace for support, who nodded for him to continue. "Actually it's not Crenshaw land anymore."

"What are you talking about? That's absurd," Coach said.

"In an effort to promote economic development, we will develop a nature center and public park for the good of the town. In fact, the developer is here today. Mr. Morgan would you like to add anything?"

"No sir, you're doing just fine," Trace said.

Pastor Foret stood. "Actually if I may interject, just this morning Ms. Crenshaw generously donated her land to the church." He turned to Adele and winked.

Eugene nervously tapped his finger on the side of the lectern. He could feel Trace's gaze burning into his back.

"However, I don't see any reason to stop your plans for the tournament, as long as the church is indemnified against liability, of course," Louis said.

"Mayor, what about the murder?" Blaze said.

The crowd started to talk among themselves in whispers.

"If I could have your attention again folks; that was an accident, not a homicide." Eugene started to sweat from the overhead lights.

"What about Kenny Mouton? My sources tell me that was an attempted murder," Blaze said.

"It's just a rogue bear attack," Andre said.

"Then why was there reptile saliva and venom found in the tissue samples?" Wiley said.

Blaze was surprised he was backing her up for once, and intrigued by the new information.

"That wasn't in my report," Andre said.

"I didn't say the report came from your office," Wiley said.

Blaze tried to smooth over the argument so she could look like a savior. "I don't think the sheriff is trying to scare anybody, but it might be prudent to exercise some caution while in the swamp." She looked directly at Buck. "We wouldn't want anything to happen to our contestants would we?"

"For those not from around here, we have an urban legend that goes way back about a monster that lives in the swamp," Eugene said.

"The Creepler," Beau said.

"Yes, the myth is most popular with our teenagers, as Beau just pointed out. But monsters are not real, I can assure you."

"It's real enough to keep local people away," Beau said.

Kacie elbowed him to be quiet.

Eugene decided to cut it short. "Well, if there are no more questions, please enjoy the refreshments and visit with our contestants."

The crowd clapped and people started to mingle.

"What's wrong with you? Why do you have to embarrass us all the time?" Kacie said.

"Thanks mom. I forgot that my constitutional right to free speech only included saying what you wanted." Beau got up to leave.

"Where are you going now?" Kacie said.

"Someplace where you're not."

Cody stood there, unintentionally listening to the conversation.

"Hey, you want to get out of here?" Beau said.

Cody looked around, unsure if Beau meant him. "Jim and I were going to race."

"Got any room for a passenger?"

"Sure." Cody was amazed that Beau wanted to ride in his car.

As the rest of the crowd mingled, Kelvin and Coach Ducet quietly slipped away to his office and locked the door. Coach retrieved some items from the locked cabinet and handed them to Kelvin.

"I need some help with an upcoming dual match. The boy in this photograph needs an edge over his opponent," Coach said.

"Do you have something personal of his?" Kelvin said.

"Yes, here is his sweatshirt that he wore today."

"Good, how far do you want this to go? Small win or big win?"

"Break some bones if need be," Coach said.

Kelvin laughed, "I always really liked you. Even back in high school you were such a hard-ass."

Beau walked quickly toward the parking lot afraid his mother was going to run after him. He slid into the leather bucket seat of the GTO.

Cody revved the engine and the whole car vibrated.

"Let's go!" Beau said.

"You got it captain." Cody backed the car out and exited the lot with Jim trailing.

"Got any tunes?"

"What do you like?"

"I'm in the mood for Manson or something like that."

"You're in luck. I feel like a *disposable teen* myself sometimes." Cody fumbled with the MP4 player cueing the song.

After driving for a while, the two sports cars approached the entrance to Route 3. The road was clear for miles, just before sunset. Cody pulled along the side of Jim's car. They had their windows rolled down.

"Buckle up," Jim said.

"As our guest, you get to start the count down," Cody said.

"Cool … ready? Three, two, one!" Beau screamed as they took off.

Both drivers mashed the gas pedals as fat rubber tires squealed, leaving black streaks and smoke. They raced down the highway with the music blaring out the windows.

The brisk air invigorated Beau's face. He felt alive and free for the first time.

Each car was neck-and-neck until Cody flipped a special switch releasing nitrous oxide. His car rocketed forward leaving Jim in the dust. Modern engine technology could not compare with the customization of an old classic when it came to beating horses.

Jim slowed, returning to the proper side of the road. He waved them off admitting defeat.

"That was awesome. What a rush!" Beau said.

Cody was all smiles, but his victory was short lived as a thumping sound started growing louder from the car's rear axle.

"Oh no," Cody said.

"What?"

"I think we have a flat." Cody veered off the road into the soft grass. "I've got a spare in the trunk, can you help me?"

As Beau got out of the car, he looked around the woods. Twilight quickly faded to darkness and it became difficult to see. The only sounds were chirping crickets and the approaching rumble of Jim's engine.

Jim pulled up, stopping. "What's wrong?"

"Flat tire," Cody said.

"That's the … pits. Hey, I'm going to … head home," Jim said.

"See you at the party," Cody proceeded to unbolt the rim.

Beau heard a noise in the distance. He scanned the horizon and saw an unrecognizable figure moving between the trees. It looked directly at him with yellow glowing eyes. "Hey, do you see that?" Beau reached down to tug at Cody's shoulder, but by the time he looked up it was gone.

"Where, I don't see anything. What was it?" Cody said.

"I don't know."

People came and went and time rolled on, but there were those tasked with special assignments, the guardians of knowledge too esoteric for the public.

The fire in the basement grew to a roar. Adele poked at the hickory logs causing a stir of embers. She sprinkled a powdery dust on top not made by pixies.

Those who believed in fairies had fervent imaginations. In the old days, snake-oil salesmen and charlatans preyed on these impressionable people. However, Adele's group possessed a divine knowledge that only they were worthy of receiving.

Adele's knowledge was sacred and she knew there was no point to convey it to those whose minds were not capable of understanding. She and three others were the only ones blessed with the ability to comprehend the sacred wisdom.

She acquired the secret knowledge through birthright as a descendent of LeCretia. Adele was the firstborn female, beating her twin sister into the world by two minutes, and there could be only one with the special powers.

LeCretia foretold the day would come when a female heir would rein the cult. Because of this, her descendants faithfully toiled in the ceremonies. The repeated ritual sacrifices and incantations proved successful five generations later. Adele retained both the passed down knowledge and the inherent power to manifest the spirit world.

The Creepler incarnated into physical form solely because Adele imagined it into existence, although the concept was something that LeCretia first envisioned. In the *Book of Shadows*, LeCretia carefully sketched out her plans to bring to life a guardian for the land. After Anton's brutal attack and the assault on her home, she vowed never again to witness violence waged upon her family.

Adele the High Priestess was a witch by contemporary terms, but not a Wiccan or Satanist. There was no special sect to which she associated, secret handshake or cryptic symbols. She could create whatever she intended without the need for a label. Other cults were more rooted in the acquisition of power and money. Her realm focused on genuine practical magic.

Kelvin was a second-generation Haitian warlock; able to help Adele cast magic. His ancestry practiced Vodun and worshipped multiple lesser deities. His male energy balanced her female power.

Kelvin was a patient man, dedicated to their cause. Working as a janitor afforded him a level of anonymity in the town. No one really noticed him in the background, like a potted plant sitting silently in the corner. He went about his daily routine undetected, disguised in plain sight.

Tonight, Adele really needed him.

Kelvin unrolled a clean piece of parchment, tearing it down the center. On one piece, he wrote: *Saylor*. On the other, he wrote: *Beau*. Then he placed them on top of each other with the names facing. He held them between both palms, touching fingers as if in a prayer. The armholes of his evergreen robe hung low, while his forearms protruded.

Adele rested her open palms on top of his elbows to contribute her energy. She faced him in her robe wearing the mask and hood.

"I am the witch, hear my prayer," Adele said.

"I am the warlock, hear my prayer," Kelvin said.

They chanted together. "We balance all that is. We call on you, oh Great Spirit, to bind these two children in perfect union for your holy consecration."

In the center of the room, a leather wrapped chair hovered an inch above the floor. Vernon rested comfortably as it floated. He wore blue jeans, but was shirtless. The lover's talisman hung from his neck. He had a black silk bag over his head.

Wearing an evergreen robe and mask, Andre stood within the pentagram on the floor that circled the chair. Vernon laid down his right arm on the armrest, exposing his palm as Andre laced the thin leather restraints around his wrist. Written on his skin in red marker was: *Kacie*.

Standing on the other side of the chair, Coach Ducet laced the leather restraints around Vernon's left arm, palm down on the armrest. Written on the back of his hand in red marker was: *Vernon*.

Once the restraints were tight, Coach removed the hood from Vernon's head.

Andre held up a pewter chalice filled with wine to Vernon's lips. As he drank, some spilled, running down the corner of his mouth. It magically turned from red wine to human blood.

Coach replaced the hood back over Vernon's head.

"I am the Atheist, hear my prayer," Andre said.

"I am the Christian, hear my prayer," Coach said.

They chanted together. "We balance all that is. We call on you, oh Great Spirit, to bind these two adults in perfect union for your holy consecration."

Vernon felt something scratching his left arm. It tore into his skin cutting deeper and deeper. He felt his warm blood oozing from the trenches. The pain was dreadful.

A voice softly called from somewhere distant in his mind. He could see Kacie coming into view out of the darkness. She was naked. She smiled but did not speak. He felt her supple hand slowly move up the inside of his thigh. It gently stroked regions arousing a beast inside. Paralyzed, he tried to flinch. She slowly moved closer whispering his name, *Vernn … nonnn*. The words came from inside his head, but he heard them. For a moment, he was lost in the lyrical sound of her voice.

She was almost touching that part of him, the one he reserved just for her. His body pulsated and burned with an internal fire. Each moment was pure ecstasy. The anticipation of holding her again was killing him. He longed for her touch, to smell her scent and to taste the sweetness of her lips again.

Just when he expected some relief, she vanished from view replaced by a hideous sight. Something so heinously disgusting, he almost vomited. The blood wine curdled inside his stomach, begging for release.

Hairy tarantulas crawled all over his naked body. One crept across his mouth. He feared screaming would anger it, resulting in a sting. The spider moved closer and closer toward his eye, slowly creeping across his nose. Each hairy leg tickled and pricked. He could see it staring back at him with multiple black eyes. Before it could inject venom into his cornea, they all vanished.

Kacie returned to his consciousness. Her familiar face comforted him. She looked at him with endearing eyes. She opened her arms as if to hug him. He longed for her embrace, to feel her soft flesh again. She moved toward him with lips so close to his, he could feel her warm breath.

Then he felt pressure around his neck and leg. The darkness returned revealing serpents slinking around his vulnerable body. A large albino Boa Constrictor wrapped around his neck. Vernon could not breathe. It was crushing his windpipe. He struggled to scream.

Hoping the cycle of pain and pleasure would end soon, Vernon then felt his arm on fire. He looked out of the corner of his eye to see a soaring blaze. Andre stood there holding a gasoline can. The fire burned his skin. He could feel it destroying layer after layer. The seared meat smelled of acrid soot. The pain was too intense to stand.

The snake's constriction caused him to slip into unconsciousness, while the group continued to chant in the background.

A beam of light radiated, casting illumination on a dark tradition. The elliptical headlights tilted to project demonic shapes dancing through smoke. The figures rejoiced in reverie, free to cavort on the ground surface. All in a row, the parked vehicles focused their lights on the main attraction amid interspersed trucks with open tailgates welcoming the ceremony around the lake.

Courtesy of Coach Ducet, Marvin's truck bed contained an iced keg. He dispensed the elixir into plastic cups. The entire class was there, at least everyone that mattered.

The annual fall festival of teenagers degrading themselves into drunken debauchery was a senior custom. The town braced for a night of degenerates causing random mischief. Like Halloween tricks and juvenile pranks, they received a pass from the adults.

The unpopular students fell victim to the hazing rituals of the commanding seniors, as they attempted to gain access to the social club before graduation. Tonight was also the perfect chance for the misfits to find prom dates, as the beer would work in their favor. Everyone's inhibitions would be gone followed by lowered standards.

Cody's prospects were slim, and his dad's unfortunate accident was not helping matters. He had been assisting at the store afterschool, leaving little time left to socialize with the other seniors. He vowed not to skip the prom, ask a junior classmen or go stag. Only the losers without a car would have those limited options.

He drove up to the party with the destructive bass sounds of grunge metal vibrating the car spoiler. The failing hatch seal and the juxtaposition of the rear speakers made it convulse. Tonight he was determined not to leave empty handed. He parked the car on the outskirts of the popular teenagers, which was still too close for their liking.

Amber stood next to her friend Sally. They were talking when Cody spied them. He rolled down the window, so they would be impressed with the wattage of his speakers. The window crank came off in his hand. It was not the first time. He punched it back into contact with the gear. He tried to turn the shaft smoothly without them noticing his difficulty. The glass became stuck with a few inches still showing, so he left it alone.

He got out of the car and walked in a straight line toward them thinking about what he was going to say. He strutted closer like a shark moving into striking range, when the football hit him. It bounced off his side and fell dead on the ground. Amid the rock music, he could hear sounds of laughter all directed at him. The girls whispered about him, chipping away at his waning confidence.

He briefly stumbled, picked up the ball and blindly threw it back into the crowd. Then he resumed the swagger of a gangster missing a leg. By the time he made it to the girls, they stopped whispering, now content to stare. They already had discussed every flaw about him.

"Evening ladies, can I get you a drink?" Cody said.

The girls looked at each other restraining laughter. Sally stated the obvious while holding a red cup in front of his face. "We have drinks, moron."

The response made Cody self-conscious and he realized he was still wearing sunshades. "Okay, I'll just get one for myself." At that point, the worm in him took over and he retreated to hide from their ridicule.

Sally laughed at his stupidity, but Amber only blushed.

Cody set a new course for the brew truck surrounded by the football team. He became more nervous every step, but was determined to get a red cup in hand.

The muscular boys glared at him, as he continued to walk toward them knowing their intimidation was all for show. He was the best friend of the mayor's son and that gave him a magic shield, or so he thought.

Marvin smiled and handed down a cup to Walter. He held it high in the air over Cody's head. Each time he would reach for it, Walter would move it and the guys would laugh.

"Leave him alone," Marvin said.

Walter offered the cup as if reaching out for a handshake. Cody went to accept it, but Walter spilled some on his hand. Everyone laughed again.

"Stop wasting it," Marvin said.

Cody grabbed the drink and hurried away retreating into the dark shadows.

Devil's Hole was a small freshwater lake fed by a natural spring. It contained sunken logs, algae, trout, brim and bass. The water quality varied between crystal-clear spots and dingy murk. The temperature was usually cool.

A flat dirt area worn clear from vehicle traffic was next to the lake. The elevation sloped down toward the water. There was a forty-foot wooden dock for launching boats. The surrounding area was treeless except for one giant live oak, which had useful limbs for a tire swing.

The lake was a hot spot for summer fishing and swimming, especially skinny-dipping. Every spring Pastor Foret would baptize converts there. It was named for all the sins being washed away, sinking to the bottom. In addition, there were other bad things on the bottom, but Officer Aucoin let them rest.

The music thrashed distorted instruments; electric guitar feedback, booming drums and growling vocals screaming lyrics filled with angst and social alienation set to a slow tempo. It was not the kind of music easily lip-sinked because no one could decipher the words, but every teenager resonated with the abysmal void from which it originated.

Beau sat on the hood of Saylor's roadster on top of a white furry throw. It was a bit feminine for his taste, but she said it reminded her of snow, the weather event southern states rarely experienced.

He relaxed, leaning back on the windshield nursing a fresh bottle of whiskey, the one he stole from the family wet bar. He hoped his dad would reach for the bottle only to be disappointed. Beau knew if that happened he would catch hell for it, but he did not care.

Today on the eve of his eighteenth birthday, he was especially angry with his parents. He could not blame one without the other, for they were a team. When he was little, he would be in his room keeping to himself and they would invade his space to discuss the latest atrocity. They would blame him for something he did not do.

The scenario was always the same. One would ask: *Did you do this?* He would say: *No.* And they would pronounce him guilty anyway. He would argue his case and they would pass a sentence because he was the only one there to blame. At least the only one they could see. They never considered it could be a spirit playing tricks. Or that the spirit could be his deceased twin brother.

Despite Beau's anger at the latest events, he also felt liberated. In a few hours, he would be an adult and capable of legally walking out of the door never to return. Just the thought alone was powerful, like an unlit stick of dynamite waiting for a match.

He planned to go to the college of his choice, find a way to pay for it, and start living his own life. He hoped Saylor would understand, and that they could remain friends if nothing else. Despite her expected response to the news, Beau had to make a move and he was willing to endure the consequences no matter what.

Saylor hopped up on the hood and snuggled under his arm. "What-cha doing birthday boy?"

"Looking at the stars. See Orion and his belt?" Beau pointed the neck of the bottle toward the sky. "He's a great warrior, like me."

"So when are you going to plunder my village, oh great warrior?" Saylor looked especially attractive. Her red hair burned as bright as the bonfire flames and her outlined eyes were smoky grey.

"I thought that you wanted to wait?" Beau slurred his words. He made a considerable dent in the bottle contents, the taste of which he did like.

"I do, we should but…." She leaned to kiss him and felt the magnetism before their lips touched. She gently caressed his in hers. Their noses danced around each other occasionally touching. She held his cheek in the palm of her hand, and could feel the warmth emanating from inside.

Beau's arm splayed across the tiny roadster, with one still clutching the bottle. He laid there focusing on the dark sky as she took control of his body. She kissed him intently for periods of time and occasionally came up for air. In those moments, he could see the stars again.

She tried hard to elicit a passionate response but he was preoccupied. She slowly traced the outline of his mouth with her tongue. Her saliva tasted like sweet cherries, the kind that had a sugary tartness in the meat concealing a rocky pit.

She straddled on top of him, leaning down to kiss his face, his cheeks cupped in both of her palms. She breathed heavier than normal and had her eyes closed. She smelled of lavender. Their tongues entwined in a circle dance of cascading waterfalls. She had an effect on his body. She drew him closer and he could feel a restriction around his neck. The air was getting thin, as the oxygen left his brain.

He touched her velvet back between the shoulders and pulled her close. He held her tight, as they continued to kiss. Then he rested the bottle between the windshield and the hood, and quickly rolled her onto her back. Her skull would have slammed against the glass if he had not shielded it. She could feel his firm weight as he pressed down with manly desire.

"Do you want me?" Saylor said.

Beau paused not sure how to answer the question. His body expressed affirmation, but his conscience knew better than to say *yes* though she was hard to deny.

The crowd had noticed the romance and was chanting in the distance. Riley led them, "Do it … do it … do it!" The alcohol lowered Beau's inhibitions, and his own best friend was cheering him on.

The bonfire raged out of control. Colored plumes scattered with glitter, erupted in solar flares. The wood planks stood upright forming a pyramid. The flames reached ten-feet tall, illuminating the area. The human ashes scattered on top swirled in purple clouds. The brisk air, fire's inferno and the guttural moans of the crowd cast a spell on the lovers.

Saylor wrapped her legs around the backs of his knees pinning him down. She waited for a response.

Beau moved up her side with his hand, reaching under her sweater. The soft angora fur tickled his knuckles as he explored her body. The tips of his fingers encountered her bra. He walked across the lace tracing the patterns with his fingers.

They kissed feverously. It was wet and sensual. The heat from their breath was visible in the cool air.

The palm of his hand cupped her breast. He clawed his fingernails over the top of her push-up bra encountering her soft flesh.

He pressed harder with his pelvis causing her inner thigh tendon to ache. She relegated to shallow breaths as her tiny frame bore the full weight of his body.

His hands slithered around her legs and landed on her perfectly round buttocks. He held them, squeezing the firmness.

The crowd continued to chant. The rhythmic mantra created a power from the unified energy. It took on a life of its own.

He could sense his mind receding, as his body mechanized.

Saylor had her hand down the back of his jeans, wedged between the belt. Her fingers were like icicles biting into his skin. She whispered seductively in his ear, "Take me now."

The words echoed in the recesses of his intoxicated mind: *take me, take me, take me.* Beau paused staring into her beguiling eyes. Then something strange came over him, a clarity. He looked around the lake, realizing everyone was watching them. The sudden awareness lifted the spell. He sat up to gather his composure and gently pushed her aside.

She seemed both embarrassed and mortified by his sudden rejection.

He tried to make light of the situation and formed an excuse. "If you'll excuse me, I have to take a leak really bad." Beau hopped off the car hood and walked toward Riley.

The athletes clapped. Marvin started spraying down everyone around the truck with the keg hose, "Get a room you perverts." Beau ducked to escape the shower.

Someone screamed, "Crank up the music!"

Beau walked over to the large oak tree to relieve himself. He had his back to the crowd.

Saylor ran off to the solace of her friends. The papier-mâché cake was in the cheerleading van. She jumped in the back to change into her one-piece swimsuit. She slipped on her tennis shoes, determined to become a woman tonight, despite what Beau wanted. When she hopped out of the van, Jennifer and Meghan were ready with cans of whipped cream.

"You sure about this?" Meghan said.

"Just do it, I'm freezing," Saylor said.

The girls sprayed her with white foam, while some of the boys drug out the four-tiered cake. They helped Saylor hide inside and replaced on the top piece.

When Beau had finished, he stumbled over to Riley.

"Look at that," Riley pointed to the giant cake sitting in the middle of the parking lot.

Beau started to zigzag toward it, and the crowd formed a parade route around him. Everyone started singing the *Happy Birthday* song.

Beau found walking in a straight line impossible; the whiskey lessened his motor functions.

At the end of the compulsory singing, Saylor burst out of the cake, covered from the neck down in cotton-like clouds of ivory. Several clumps flung from her arms as she reached for the sky, "Tada ... happy birthday Beau!"

Beau tried to move but could not; his feet stuck to the dirt. All he could do was witness the next series of events as a spectator.

Saylor stepped down out of the cake, like a princess descending from a throne. She danced wildly as the loud music echoed in Beau's head with throbbing beats.

The fire responded with serpentine flames twisting into sharp points.

The onlooker's faces disappeared into the blackness, leaving peering eyes. They watched and chanted in an ancient language. Beau could not understand their hypnotic words, but felt compelled to participate in the strange event.

Saylor's movements became more erratic, flailing and jumping about. She made several revolutions around the fire pit before running into Marvin.

He stood there ready to receive her. The son of a High Magus reached out stopping her forward motion. He held her still around the waist. His black fingers contrasted her milky white skin.

She looked up at him as if in a trance. He towered over her. She felt drawn by an unseen force to kiss him. His lips were frosty and sent shivers down her spine. He held her so tightly, his claws cut deep into her flesh.

The crowd continued to chant as Beau watched Marvin lick the whipped cream off her chest. His serpent-like tongue extended out of his mouth touching her breastbone. It explored the valley wandering around before retreating into the black hole of his mouth.

Beau screamed inside *Stop*, but nothing came out.

Saylor's head cocked back, arching her neck. The whites of her eyeballs rolled backward with bulging veins. She moaned possessed by his complete control.

When the crowd reached a feverish pitch, Marvin signaled the others to join. The athletes marched toward Jim. He backed away from them protesting. They grabbed his arms lifting him overhead and moved toward the oak. On his back, he could see every star in the clear night's sky twinkling in varying intensities.

Riley draped a rope over one derelict branch. He fashioned a slipknot on the other end. The boys held Jim up as Riley slid the noose around his right ankle. Riley pulled on the opposite end, hoisting Jim into the air upside down. Jim demanded freedom. The boys raised him higher and tied the rope around the tree.

Jim's left leg bent at the knee with his ankle resting on the right kneecap. The hangman configuration resembled a number-four Tarot card. His arms dangled helplessly below his head.

Beau was powerless to stop them.

The rest of the class danced around the fire. Even the unpopular ones joined in the festival.

Then the athletes fixated on Amber. They held her arms and blindfolded her with a black-satin tie. She stood there silent and motionless. Riley removed her puffy vest, and then her sweatshirt. She was wearing a ribbed tank top underneath. He removed her denim skirt exposing white cotton waist-high panties. Her legs were bare except for black patent leather knee-high boots. They hoisted her overhead on her back and paraded around the fire.

Marvin still had Saylor in his grasp. She kissed him feverishly and he wove his scaly tongue in and out of her mouth, a tangled mass of brumous light and dark, opposite forces straining for control, as razor blades sliced brittle wood leaving behind valleys of scars.

Forming on her face, droplets of bodily fluid grew into a volcanic explosive puss-laced fibrous keratin smelling of rotten eggs. The capsule's veneer stretched out of shape into a flabby sheet billowing in the wind. Pressure built as internal forces demanded release.

Beau saw a sea of blood rising from the ground about to envelope them all. Reptilian monsters swam in the mess as the surface moved. The garnet liquid swirled around them.

Saylor wrapped her arms around Marvin's neck as he lifted her up. She straddled his waist curling her legs around him. He supported her bottom with his hands. She was slippery from the whip cream, but he was not letting go of her.

They continued to kiss. She bit his lip drawing blood. He raised his head to the stars and howled like an animal.

The athletes wove around the crowd offering Amber to the sky. Her pale body was lifeless and brittle.

Over by the tree, Jennifer and Meghan alternated tormenting Jim's head, investigating each orifice with their tongues. Meghan licked inside his ear. He laughed from the sensation, about to pass out from the blood settling in his skull.

Jennifer poured beer into his mouth, some of which entered his nostrils. He choked and spit the rest out. The more he discarded, the more she poured. "Drink it you pig!"

Meghan spun him around in circles winding up the rope. When she let go, he turned like a top spinning out of control. The momentum made him ill. He could feel the prickly stomach acid knocking at his throat. He started to gag. Meghan jabbed her tongue inside his mouth, holding his head still so he could not vomit.

"Choke on it pig," Jennifer said.

Meghan's tongue burned and stung, but he wanted more. Once he let his psyche free to discover the new sensations, he catapulted into a forbidden world of lust and lucidity. He felt each cut and the throbbing pain that followed.

Jennifer pulled Meghan away. Their eyes met and communicated a subliminal message to investigate each other's bodies. Jennifer dominated, and Meghan submitted to her will. They touched deep valleys and soft hills traveling through dales caressing puckered lips ripe like fruit ready for harvesting. Each kiss was more passionate than the last, and Jim felt tortured. "Hey you guys, what about me?"

Jennifer responded by clenching his throat. She pressed so hard he turned blue from loss of oxygen. "Die you pig, die."

Marvin carried Saylor onto the wooden pier. Her eyes were as black as his skin with voids of empty nothingness. He walked to the edge of the boards. She let out a sinister laugh, one that sounded like there were several demons inside her.

Then they jumped cannonball fashion into the water. They broke the still surface casting an arching wave over the dock. The water was frigid. The whip cream floated away. They came up from the murk still clinging to each other.

The athletes threw Amber in the lake. She screamed with delight as they ejected her into the air.

Suddenly, Beau's feet were free from the stranglehold.

Others who had been dancing around the fire also jumped into the water. They laughed and splashed in the polar temperature.

Beau slowly approached the dock. He thought everyone had gone crazy. Though he was drunk, he did not feel the same compulsions, until a strong force booted him from behind. He could feel his body falling in slow motion as if in a nightmare.

As his nose greeted the water's surface, he felt a chill crawl over him and saw hands reaching up from the depths pulling him down. The discolored limbs bore rotten flesh riddled with sores and he could even make out crusted blood under their nails. They sucked him into the darkness, floating farther into the abyss.

Then he felt a hand under his throat pushing him back up. It was Riley raising his intoxicated head above water. "Hey, breathe man. What are you trying to do, kill yourself?"

As Beau became reoriented with reality, he saw people standing on the shore strangely looking at him. Saylor now dressed, was standing next to her friends. The athletes huddled around the keg. Cody and Jim grilled hot dogs on a charcoal pit. Marvin strummed a guitar, while Amber sang a folk song. The rest congregated in small conversational groups around the fire.

Beau was confused, like he had been dreaming the whole time, but it felt so real. His head ached from the confusion.

"Can we get out of the water now? It's shrinking my balls," Riley said.

"Maybe I should head home. What time is it?" Beau said.

Riley looked at his sports watch. "3:05 dude."

"Can you take me home?"

"What about Saylor?" Riley said.

"I can't deal with her right now. Can we go please?" Beau said.

"Sure dude, you're the birthday boy."

CHAPTER 6

Fine grit sandpaper dipped in gooseberry jam was the sensation Beau felt on his face. Sampson licked the crusted drool that formed a staircase down his cheek. Each lash from the dog's tongue made Beau aware of how much his head throbbed.

With one eye partially open, he could see two things; morning had replaced the last time he was conscious and his father towered over him.

Buck bumped the porch swing with his knee. "Rough night, sport?"

Beau shielded the glare from his eyes. "What do you want?"

"Get up, we're going fishing."

"No, leave me alone. I need sleep."

"You can sleep when you're dead." Buck offered black coffee in a travel mug as a sign of sympathy.

Beau slowly sat up, looking around through bloodshot eyes. His body felt miserable from sleeping outdoors in a crumbled heap.

"There's a muffin in the truck from your mother, if you're hungry." Buck tossed a clean flannel shirt down to him. "Damn boy, you smell worse than the dog."

Kacie stuck her head out of the screen door, smiling as it creaked. "You two have a nice time, but don't be late for service."

Buck approached her, kissing her cheek. "I know; I'll get around to fixing that door one day."

Kacie smiled back with her usual patience. "Catch a big one honey."

Beau was dressed, standing canted to one side as if he were going to fall over.

Buck grabbed him by the back of the shirt collar and pushed him down the porch steps.

"Hey, cut it out," Beau said.

Buck wrapped his arm around Beau's neck squeezing him in a man hug. "You complain that we never do anything." He opened the passenger-side door to the truck. "Get in."

Sampson followed in his one speed, lumbering swagger.

The truck was brand new, a fully loaded American-made model with an extended cabin. The two-toned limited edition even had Buck's initials embroidered in the leather headrests.

Sampson jumped in the backseat, ready to go wherever.

Beau crawled in, slipping into a comfortable slouch, pawing for the hot coffee, which was black with no sugar. It tasted bitter. The whiskey left a barren wasteland pitting in his stomach. Milk would have been better to coat the irritated lining.

Buck should have known how Beau felt; he had spent plenty of time drinking too much throughout his adulthood. The vicious cycle of binges and abstinence had damaged all of his relationships. When binging, he found himself sleeping in strange places; behind the steering wheel in Fourchette's parking lot, on the back porch of the house, face down in front of the toilet and occasionally under the kitchen table. And for a brief period, he found himself sleeping in a strange place with someone else.

Kacie knew about the affair. In fact, she could predict when and where it was going to happen without the powers of psychic ability. Her internal compass honed in on a force that pulled Buck into the arms of his ex-girlfriend.

Those days had long been over. As soon as Kacie found out she was pregnant again, Buck walked away from the whiskey. He was so excited about the prospect of having a little girl that nothing else mattered.

The day he found out Kacie was having a boy, was the day he abandoned sobriety. Like a spoiled child that didn't get its way, he slid back into Blaze's clutches. But the truth was, he could never be satisfied. He would still be bouncing between them today, if it had not been for Kacie's accident.

One morning she awoke, realizing that Buck had not come home. She went through her routine cooking breakfast for Beau and lied saying Buck had gone fishing in the early-morning hours. Beau ate unconcerned about his dad's absence and went off to school.

Kacie proceeded with her mundane daily life, filling the agonizing moments with household chores. As she moved through the bedrooms collecting dirty clothes into a basket, she thought about how angry she was. Her pregnancy plan to stop Buck's adultery had backfired. He was drinking again and she was going to be stuck caring for another needy man. Life was very unfair.

Maybe the soul searching caused her foot to slip at the top of the landing. The clothes basket jettisoned over the railing, as Kacie fell in slow motion, tumbling down the straight run of stairs to the foyer floor below.

Buck came home and found her unconscious in a pool of blood.

The doctors tried to save the first-trimester baby, but it was too late. Blunt force caused the amniotic sack to rupture.

Kacie stayed in bed for weeks afterward, too depressed to bathe. She did not eat or speak, hibernating in the master bedroom with the curtains drawn.

Buck found sobriety when his fans rallied around him. Their support helped him regain his focus. He ended the relationship with Blaze for the last time.

When Kacie finally emerged from her exile, they never spoke again of the tragedy. Instead, they stocked away piles of blame and resentment for each other.

Sampson stuck his head out of the truck window. His jowls flapped in the wind. Long streaks of saliva danced on the air. He panted and licked his chops.

The truck pulled up to Ricky's Bait Shack, a tiny establishment operated by Skeeter.

"Stay here, I'll be right back," Buck said.

Beau finished the blueberry muffin trying to catch the crumbs. Then the sensation came over him of a strong need to urinate. He got out of the truck. Approaching the screen door, he heard voices that ceased when he entered.

"Mind if I use your facilities? Beau said.

"Naw, go on," Skeeter said.

Beau walked down an aisle of live minnow wells, listening to the sound of water cascading from the filter into the tank. It made his bladder hurt.

The corner restroom had standing room only. He shut the door and unzipped his jeans. The pressure in his abdomen was so painful, the urine burned upon exit as his body released the toxins.

His ears tuned into a conversation the men were having. The sound amplified through the wall air vent. He delayed flushing, zipped up and leaned closer to the vent.

"This aint easy to come by," Skeeter said.

"Are you sure it will work?" Buck said.

"Sure as a cock crows. Just a dab will do ya."

Beau opened the door a little and video recorded the transaction on his cell phone.

"So this pheromone will attract the big ones?" Buck held up a small vial of liquid.

"Look here, them shiners has been basting in it. I marked 'em with a black dot."

"Give me a couple of those too. I will try them out today. And don't go telling anyone about this."

"Don't ya worry." Skeeter placed the items in a brown paper bag.

Beau could not believe what he witnessed. His dad was a cheater. He thought about the irony as he flushed the toilet. Now all he had to do was pretend that he did not know the truth and save the information for later.

"Everything okay, sport?" Buck said.

"Yes, I resampled mom's muffin, although it wasn't as good the second time."

"I hear that." Buck retrieved the bag. "Skeeter, we'll settle up later."

"Y'all come back now."

The bait shack was just an eighth of a mile from the fishing spot and Devil's Hole was the last place in the world where Beau wanted to return.

The deserted parking lot had no evidence that anything had taken place there last night, except for the remnants of the bonfire. Marvin must have cleaned up all the trash.

The water was placid, not like the demonic eruptions he remembered.

"Looks like we have the whole lake to ourselves," Buck said.

"Fabulous." Beau hopped out of the truck with Sampson in tow and headed for the pier.

Buck spun the truck around and backed the boat down the ramp next to the dock so that the tail end was floating. Then he got out to release the wench hook.

Once the boat was adrift, Beau grabbed the rope pulling it toward the pier.

Buck drove off to park the truck and trailer. He returned wearing a canvas fishing vest with cargo pockets.

Sampson jumped onto the boat deck causing it to rock, then took the helm waiting patiently for something exciting to happen.

Beau looked around the cabin for some sunshades, with no luck.

Buck approached holding a baseball cap with embroidered words: *#1 DAD*. He tossed it to Beau. "Remember this?"

"That was long ago." Beau gave the hat to his dad ten years ago for Father's Day at the insistence of his mother.

Buck wasn't a bad father in the sense that he was physically abusive or irresponsible. He had been there, doing his time, but without an emotional connection. He

166

acted the role of dad without understanding that it was not what he was doing that was wrong, it was what he could not give; unconditional love.

Buck loved his son with a kind of surface emotion, one that looked pretty on Christmas cards. It floated like pond scum, hiding what was just below the surface. In the depths lurked manipulation, demands, invasions of privacy, trampled boundaries and lots of anger.

To the rest of the world, the Boudreauxs were the perfect family, a single lie that tormented Beau. He could no longer stomach the false reality that had become his life.

With this new mindset, his parents were having an arduous time manipulating him because their usual tactics were not working. They pushed buttons knowing his programmed response. Instead, they encountered defiance.

This troubled them because they never treated him like a real person or took the time to get to know him; all that mattered was that he played his role in the family.

However, the role of dotting son had gotten old quickly. Pretending to have feelings contrary to how he really felt manifested in physical illness. He spent many hours with an upset stomach, visiting the restroom. The expulsion cleansed the stuffed emotions as each chunk of food representing negative energy released. He watched the remnants of pain circle in a vortex down the toilet bowl. A temporary relief, but the depletion of electrolytes ruined his health. Each time he was sick, a piece of him floated away never to return.

Father and son stood on the pier waiting for something to happen. Each had expectations that the other could not meet. Each waited for an apology. The growing quiet was uncomfortable.

Buck hopped onto the boat and lowered the motor.

Beau took a deep breath, and pushed the boat away from the pier. He moved to the front seat trying to create some distance between them.

They motored to somewhere in the middle of the lake.

Sampson sat on his hunches panting; the wind gently furrowed his ears. Once the boat stopped moving, he curled up in a ball under the pedestal seat.

Buck handed a can of worms and a rod to Beau. They did not speak.

Beau removed the plastic lid, which had small puncture holes so the worms could breathe. They were slimy and wriggling amid the charcoal dirt clumps. He pinched one between his fingers and it flailed violently in protest. Then he pierced its bulbous mocha skin with a treble hook. The point caused olive puss to ooze. He wrapped the worm's body around the hook a few times and stuck it again. More secretions extruded.

"Make sure you double hook it," Buck said.

Beau rolled his eyes. "Yes Dad." He looked back to where Buck was standing, so he could get a clean cast off without reliving the last incident. Previously, he accidentally hooked Buck in the shoulder with a heavy bronze 4/0 J hook. The barb sank deep, tearing through a half-inch of flesh on the exit.

The only sound on the lake that morning was an occasional frog croak or overhead crow cawing.

Beau released the monofilament, which sung as it soared through the air. The reel clicked when he flipped the bail. Then he drew in a little slack line. The lead weight did its duty resting on the bottom. He cocked the baseball cap down over his eyes and hoped to sleep.

"How's it feel to be a man?" Buck said.

"No different."

"I guess it's time for us to have that talk, you know the one about how romance works."

"Dad please, spare us both. I've got it covered."

Buck let out a chuckle. "That's my boy. I didn't think you were still a virgin, not with that little philly around. Go on; get it out of your system while you can."

"I didn't say that, never mind." Beau reeled in the line and recast. He threw it so hard, the rod almost slipped out of his hand. "Why do you guys dislike her so much?"

"Oh, she's a fine girl for somebody else, just not you."

"Why exactly?" Beau said.

"She's the wrong pedigree."

"Right, because we're dogs with papers."

"Don't get offended, I'm just saying when you get to college, it's going to be a whole new world. Those gals are real women." Buck adjusted his fishing cap decorated with his signature lures. "And it's going to be important for your law career to marry the right one that makes you look good."

"About that—," Beau said.

"When I was in high school, I played the field. I had fun sampling whatever I could get away with. Then at your age, I became a responsible adult and married your mom."

"I thought she dated Vern?" Beau said.

"How do you know about that? Did she say something to you?"

Beau paused for a moment, "I've seen her high school yearbook."

"Oh, they dated for a while. But that's exactly my point; high school is the time when you should be dating without serious intentions. Hell, I even dated Blaze once. So what's the big deal about your mother and Vernon?"

"Nothing I guess, I just thought they were more than that." Beau's words cut like razor-sharp knives, slicing tough meat. The pain lingered in the air, ceasing all further communications. Father and son were still distant, another attempt at bonding resulted in the status quo.

Kacie leaned into the doorway of Andre's office. He sat behind a huge mahogany desk with an embossed leather top divided into three sections. "Thanks for seeing me on such short notice."

"I was here anyway, drowning in paperwork." A pile of charts stacked on top of the desk waited for his review. "So tell me what's going on."

"I'm tired all the time from the anemia, and still bleeding."

"I have your file right here." Andre thumbed through the pages. "Unfortunately, your pap smear results came back abnormal. I recommend a biopsy to see what's going on."

Kacie sat nervously in the chair, "What do you think it is?"

"It's too soon to go labeling anything."

"When do you want to do this?" Kacie said.

"Right now."

"Today's not really good for me. I have the church bake sale, then I'm hosting Beau's birthday lunch."

"How is he?" Andre said.

"Honestly, I think he's a little hung over today."

"You don't say."

"I'm embarrassed but I think he only made it as far as the porch last night."

"Boys will be boys. So what about you and your health? Let's get you set up for that procedure," Andre said.

"I don't think my doctor is available."

"Not a big deal, I'll be happy to do it myself."

"Thanks but, I'm sure you have more important things to do," Kacie said.

"You flatter me. What good is it to be the wife of a celebrity if you can't get any special treatment?"

A crowd gathered around the portable table outside the church. Mabel ran the bake sale, dispensing sugary confections with the same organizational skills she used at the restaurant. The pies stacked by flavor were precut into slices. Frosted cupcakes aligned symmetrically in rows by color. Cookies and brownies sat on the outer fringe, meant to be impulse buys. She made it easy to toss down a quarter and grab one on the way into service.

Kacie sat in the truck feeling the guilt of arriving late, the tray of New Orleans' style bread pudding rested on her lap as a reminder.

Buck opened her door and offered a hand, a true southern gentleman. He was dressed in a tailored dark-platinum suit with a coral tie that matched her chiffon dress. His freshly shaven face smelled of spice.

Beau wore a suit after showering away the sins of the previous evening. His bloodshot eyes were the only remaining evidence of his transgressions. He lagged behind his parents who were already at the bake sale.

"I'm so sorry we are late. The boys had to go fishing," Kacie said.

"Just glad your bread pudding has arrived. I'll take the first piece," Mabel said.

"Can I help you with anything?"

"I've got it covered. You go on inside, you look tired."

The white exterior of the little chapel had all the typical architectural features: horizontal wood clapboard, three steps to the entrance to represent the Trinity, a bell steeple, high cathedral ceilings, tall stained-glass windows and a sanctimonious preacher at the door welcoming the flock.

Inside was a full house with not much room left to spare. The Boudreauxs took their customary reserved seats in the second row. Beau entered first, followed by Kacie. She often sat between father and son to keep the peace.

The choir sang a rendition of *Our God*. Regular members did not need Hymn books, everyone had heard this song since birth.

Beau scanned the audience searching for one of his kind. Then he spied Riley who sat next to his mom and Ms. Guidry. The ladies whispered behind their programs.

"You should have seen her fawning all over Buck at the press conference," Linn said.

"Tart," Betty said.

"Then she had the audacity to question the Mayor in front of all of those people."

"No respect."

"I saw her slink away with Mr. Morgan after," Linn said.

"Gold digger."

"I know, in high school she was voted: *most likely to steal.*"

They laughed.

Blaze sat four rows directly in front of them. She could hear the faint murmurs of sarcastic comments. Although she had just left Trace smiling in the motel room, she fantasized about Buck. Their quality time faded, now that her dream man was in view. Her mind drifted to the past.

The feathered roach clip hung from the rear-view mirror of his Trans Am. It sashayed in the air-conditioning, rocking gently.

His crystal-blue eyes danced in the moonlight. Buck had a freedom about his spirit that was inspiring and breathtaking.

The night he picked her up, Blaze felt invincible. They drove around town without a destination, cruising around. She gazed at the star-filled sky, cool breeze blowing on her skin and she forgot everything lost in the moment.

It was their first date, the one she dreamt of and so far, it was perfection.

The cassette player cranked out a mix tape of classic rock. Blaze especially remembered the loud wattage of classic rock ringing in her head. *All her love* was all she could give, and tonight she would give it all if asked.

Buck thumped her shoulder with the neck of a twist-top wine bottle lifted from a convenience store. She guzzled the sanguine grapes as the sweetness turned to bitter paste. Buck talked about something that lost her fascination. His rubescent lips moved at half speed as she treaded water in a deep pool of gelatin lost in his gaze.

The twinkling stars yelled in her eye sockets with flashing neon. The glitter dust was only visible with a magnifying lens under a red lamp. All the solid shaped objects vibrated, zigzag forms melted into butter.

When he called her name, it echoed in her skull as if it were a hollow warehouse. She could feel his touch but it tasted foreign. Blaze screamed inside, but all he heard was her silence.

He laughed at her, the loud obnoxious kind. His face was distorted, his eyeballs dissolved in their oculars, his flesh dripped from his jaw. She screamed louder and louder to no avail.

"Breathe girl. Here, take a sip of this slowly. I thought you did this before?" Buck said.

"Sure I have." Blaze lied to impress him. Dropping acid was not something she had ever done, and after that night never did again.

Now Blaze sat in church so many years later staring at the back of Kacie's head with her prefect silky sable hair, thinking of all the shattered plans and what could have been if only she did not exist. But she did.

That night in the car parked by the lake, Blaze thought it was the beginning of the rest of her life. Buck leaned in to kiss her and when their lips finally touched, it was magic. Sparks flew in cosmic eruptions of gooey sticky stardust. The way he looked at her, held her head in his palms, the way he was into her, those things were paramount.

He held her close and she felt safe. He noticed her, acknowledged her presence and allowed her to be near him. They moved together as a cohesive unit responding to each trigger, contorting and twisting into a tangled mess of passion, navigating the stick shift as each deep exhale painted the windows with fog.

It did not matter to her that it was their first date. She knew it would not be the last.

It did not matter to him that it was their first date. He did not give seconds.

Their brief interlude was over before the cassette tape reached the white space. He had already forgotten her name on the drive home.

Life rolled on for him, but she was stuck living in the past. She thought about the night repeatedly, analyzing each move to find justification as to why he had dumped her. If only there had been an explanation, a simple reason for the cold way he treated her afterward.

Some would say he was a stand-up guy for driving her to the clinic and handing her enough cash to solve the problem. But in her mind, it never should have been that way. They were seniors and he could have faced his responsibilities like a man. Instead, he acted like she and her situation needed to go away. So she did.

Kacie got up to visit the restroom. She was not paying any attention to Blaze who was fixated on her movements. She learned long ago to ignore the other women who clamored for Buck's affections. They were as he would say: *a dime a dozen and worth ten dollars put together.*

Kacie was Ms. Buck Boudreaux, and no one was going to take that away from her. She had him embroiled in their lives. As long as he stayed sober, everything was marvelous.

The Mouton family sat together in a pew several rows back. Kenny wore a dress shirt with the collar unbuttoned because of his bandaged neck. The tender skin needed time to heal. He was doing well considering he nearly bled to death in the woods. Francine insisted that he take it easy, but he would not listen.

"Dad, can I please borrow some money for prom?" Cody said.

"What about the money you still owe me for the tire repair?"

"Kenny, its prom. Leave the boy alone," Francine said.

"Why can't he eat at the local diner with the other kids?"

"We want some privacy, besides Mesquite Chuck's has ambience."

"You want ambience, Clovis can dim the lights. You want steak, he can grill a burger. No need for you to go clear to the next town for grub."

"Kenny, leave him alone. You should be happy he even has a date."

Kacie stepped outside the sanctuary to check on Mabel. "How are sales going?"

"Great. Your bread pudding is selling out. Wish we had some more."

"The secret is the rum, but don't tell anyone."

"Ms. Guidry's pies aren't moving at all. She's going to be angry," Mabel said.

"It's probably because she had the flu. No one wants to get sick."

Pastor Foret approached them. "Ladies are you ready to step inside?"

"Looks like I'm done here for now. Eighty-six that bread pudding," Mabel said.

"Kacie did you do as I asked?" Louis probed as they walked inside.

"Yes Dad."

"And how'd it go?"

"Well don't take up a collection plate just yet, but you may want to start praying."

Louis hugged his daughter and kissed her on the forehead. "I always pray for you, my dearest."

The choir sang a joyous hymn and jostled to punctuate each note.

The sanctuary was bare of graven images. Each empty white wall gave more emphasis to the bronze cross atop the altar. Two huge floor vases flanked the pulpit full of white gladiolas. The only other decorations were hanging banners.

The pews overflowed with Bible touting virtuous believers who demanded dogma, guidance and salvation. Their hunger for redemption was unquenchable. Each Sunday they primped and preened into the pristine few who would spend an hour in the house to wash away the envy, lust and sloth that pervaded each week. Excuses for bad actions and bargaining for recompense were commonplace.

Still Louis tended to his flock, ever the caring shepherd. "Stand and rejoice with me."

The congregation stood, raising their palms toward the heavens.

The choir resonated inside the hallowed walls shaking the foundation. They praised the same God with reverence and an expectation of deliverance.

Pastor Foret assumed his position at the pulpit standing above those who bankrolled his existence. He did not mind taking the high ground, while being responsible for their emancipation. It was his God-given destiny to guide them along the straight and narrow path to the Promised Land.

He raised his hands up. "Let us bow our heads. Heavenly Father, we come before you today asking for your forgiveness, for we are weak. How many times have we spoken ill of our brother? Let me get an *Amen* if this is you."

Linn spoke, "Amen, Reverend."

"How many times have we looked to our neighbor's possessions and thought, boy I'd like to have that?"

Blaze spoke, "Amen, Reverend."

"And for those of you who have not owned up to the truth, we'll pray for you." The pastor stepped down and stood by the altar.

Mayor Rousseau stepped up. "Today we have a reading from the Book of James, Chapter four, verses eleven through twelve … *Speak not evil of another, brethren. He that speaketh evil of his brother, judge the law, thou art not a doer of the law, but a judge. There is only one lawgiver, who is able to save and destroy.*" Eugene closed the Bible, bowed and kissed the cover. Then he rejoined the congregation.

The Pastor started to pace in front of the altar. "So what is James speaking of when he talks about evil? Can good people do bad things or is evil just a concept relegated to cultists? I am asked this question all the time, and my answer is always the same. How do you define bad? People make mistakes and those mistakes can be bad things: things that end careers, break up homes and damn our souls. So friends I ask you to investigate your definition of bad. If it includes coveting your neighbor's husband, cheating to get ahead or keeping secrets then you are guilty. And the only lawgiver that can judge you is our Almighty Lord … Let us pray as we make our offerings to God."

Ms. Chillingham sang solo in front of the choir accompanied by Lillian on the organ.

Kelvin and Marvin passed the collection baskets. Tin clanked as it shuffled around making a gentle percussion sound in the background.

Beau stared out the stained-glass window. The light rays filtered through a particular piece of red glass. They touched his arm burning like a laser. He could see each beam terminate on his skin. Then he felt her clench his palm. Their fingers interlaced. She squeezed and a glimmer of light radiated from her ring finger. A solitaire diamond sparkled in the sunlight.

Out of his periphery vision, he noticed a pregnant girl close to full term sitting next to him, smiling with a look of familiarity. He expected to greet Saylor, but to his horror saw Amber's face. She was the one sitting between him and his mother.

Beau looked around and everyone was listening to the service. He felt himself drowning in boiling oil. It pricked and stung with slippery cool. He could not make sense of what he was seeing.

Amber smiled at him like a puppy dog ready to lick his face. His mother leaned over with a big grin. She patted his knee. Then his dad leaned over and waved. They all had a transfixed smile with vacant black eyes.

Beau felt the air thinning. He started to sweat. He reached in his jacket pocket to pull out a handkerchief, but pulled out a business card instead. It had black raised ink imprinted on cream-linen cardstock. The words read: *Beau Reginald Boudreaux, Attorney at Law, 12 Main Street, Stray Oaks, Louisiana, 70507. (337) 555-LAW1.*

Beau looked up again searching for a familiar face, but all he saw was a room filled with clones of himself staring back at him, expressionless and silent. They did not blink. Cabernet blood seeped from each orifice. At first it was just a drip, then a flow until finally gushing. He tasted rusted iron on the back of his throat.

A boney skeletal hand jabbed him in the shoulder. It was Kacie with the look of a disgusted parent. "Wake up!" She whispered.

The high-back William and Mary chairs perfectly aligned with twelve place settings. Pink Depression Era glass goblets loomed over the scalloped pewter plates as if waiting for a king to arrive. The centerpiece was a galvanized tub filled with wild brown-eyed Susan flowers.

The décor of the dining room was rustic Medieval and not to Kacie's liking, but that is how Eleanor left her house. Each chair had needlepoint cushions in a floral tapestry pattern. The head chairs had the Boudreaux family crest depicting their French heritage with Napoleon's fleur-de-lys.

After Eleanor's death, Kacie redecorated the entire house except this one room. She left it alone as a remembrance of her, because they seldom used it.

When Buck and Kacie were married at Town Hall, following their high school graduation, they moved in with Eleanor and never left. Five months later the twins were born, although only one boy came home from the hospital.

The room that would have been Jessie's remained untouched with the door locked. No one ever went in there. The unused nursery was perfectly arranged and now a shrine, a monument for remembering the pain.

On the porch Buck, Pastor Foret and Riley discussed his varsity wrestling career. The season had just begun and the Panthers were determined to take the state championship.

Spectators of the sport did not understand that most of wrestling occurred outside the ring. The match preparation was all about self-control through diet and exercise. Riley even practiced Hatha Yoga to stretch his muscles and improve his concentration.

Weigh-in days were extremely stressful for him. It was like standing in front of a judge, sweating the moments before a sentencing. 3,500 calories sounded like a big number, but one pound was not, though it was enough to have him disqualified.

"Riley, sometimes I think you are way too hard on yourself. That was a great dual meet between two seasoned pros," Buck said.

"Plus you were wrestling one class above your weight," Louis said.

"Coach didn't think I needed to worry, but I have to admit I was scared going in. Brad is the Wolverine's team captain and all," Riley said.

"You made it look so easy. The matches went by quickly," Buck said.

"Sometimes six minutes seems like six hours to me," Riley said.

"But you've got to admit the Sudden Victory Tie, then the Tie Breaker resulting in an Ultimate Tie Breaker was an extraordinary two minutes of a match of wills," Louis said.

"Then you got the fall right before the clock ran out, that was amazing showmanship," Buck said.

"Thank God for Half Nelsons," Louis said.

They all laughed.

"Yeah, Coach added it to my highlights reel. I just hope it is good enough to get that scholarship," Riley said.

Upstairs Beau hid in his room, lying on his side in the tiny twin bed he had since Kindergarten. His whole body ached and he wanted to sleep. He had just closed his heavy eye lids when his cell phone vibrated in his slacks. "Beau speaking."

"Hello, this is Ms. Dubois from the Savannah School of Art."

"Good morning Ma'am."

"I'm the Photography School Director and I wanted to welcome you to our freshman class, congratulations," Ms. Dubois said.

"Really, I was accepted?" Beau said.

"You will receive an official letter in the mail. It's just that we haven't seen someone with your raw talent in a long time. And as you know, our students are the crème-de-le-crème."

"I'm honored. This is a dream come true," Beau said.

"In addition since you requested financial aid, we wanted to give you a partial merit scholarship."

"May I ask about housing?"

"The endowment also provides for a dorm room and meal plan. We understand that private education is very costly, but well worth the investment."

"Is there anything else I need to do?"

"Just keep up the good grades and graduate. That should be easy for you. Oh and Happy Birthday!"

"Thank you so much, Ma'am. Good day."

Beau laid there in his quiet confines with a smile on his face, thinking of the future. This was everything he had worked for and wanted. But instead of being happy, he had mixed feelings. There were going to be huge ramifications for his charted course and he needed to prepare for the fallout.

Somehow in the next seven months, he had to convince his parents that it was his life and his decision to make. The only way he could gain control was to win them over, starting with his mother. Swaying her would be easier.

A compromise was in order. The only battleground besides college was his choice in girlfriends. If Beau ditched Saylor and dated someone they deemed respectable, then maybe his mom would cave. Amber was someone whom they loved, but the thought made him shudder.

The brass skeleton key turned the tumbler with a loud clunk. Beau had not heard that sound in a long time. Across the hall, Kacie entered the room that no one ever went in. She left the door wide open.

Beau carefully opened his door enough to peek.

Inside Jessie's room, Kacie approached a diaper-changing table. She glided her hand along the smooth painted wood as if in a trance. A couple of infant sized stuffed animals rested on the top pad. She picked up a teddy bear and cradled it in her arms, while humming a lullaby. The song was one Beau remembered from his childhood.

Inside a drawer, she shuffled items around pulling out a photograph. Beau could not see who was in it from where he stood, but he could see Kacie's expression. She stared at it intently, as a single tear rolled down her cheek.

She unfolded a hand-written letter on loose-leaf paper. The contents proved to be more emotion provoking than the photograph. Whatever it was all about was exceedingly painful to her.

There was also a raised seal document that read: *Death Certificate*. Kacie caressed it with shaking hands as streams of saline carved deep trenches in her façade.

"Darling, we've arrived. Where are you?" Haley's voice echoed up the staircase. She was not alone. Her offspring anxiously searched for signs of Beau.

184

Kacie put the precious things back in their sarcophagus for safekeeping. She wiped her cheeks and hurried out the room locking the door. "Up here. I'm coming."

Beau hid behind his door and waited for her to leave. Then he quietly closed it and crawled back into bed. He was going to wait until he was summoned to join the party.

Kacie resumed her lunch preparations trying not to make eye contact. She did not want her guests to know she had been crying.

"Can we help you with anything?" Haley said.

"Amber could pour the tea," Kacie said.

"Fabulous darling, you know I'm not very domestic."

Kacie sliced lemons on a butcher block, while Amber stirred sugar into the pitcher. "So what are your plans after graduation?"

"I have a full scholarship to state," Amber said.

"Very impressive, I guess it pays to be an honors student." The lemon slices were perfectly arranged in a crystal dish. "What fields are you interested in?"

"I want to be a social worker and maybe spend some time with the Peace Corps."

"You're such a thoughtful young lady; I wish I could get my son to date you."

Beau heard them talking as he entered the room, the perfect segue. "Amber, maybe we could grab some ice cream afterschool?" He was willing to make this concession if it would help his cause.

"Gosh, that would be super!" Amber's face looked like an overstuffed pink balloon right before it exploded. "By the way, happy birthday."

"Thanks." Beau smiled looking down, tugging on his ear.

Riley noticed the guy code distress signal as he came in from the front porch. "Hey Beau, can you show me that thing you were talking about?"

"It's on my computer."

They ran up the stairs.

Shortly thereafter, Saylor arrived. She was dressed in a tight polyester dress with spaghetti straps. She reeked of overpowering department store perfume that lingered in the air. The three ladies greeted her with the friendly demeanor of a badger. She felt a cold chill up her spine, though the fireplace was ablaze.

"Has Buck placed all the sponsor stickers on the boat?" Haley said.

"I believe so, and the vest arrived yesterday with Fishermen World's embroidered logo on the back," Kacie said.

"Lovely, one less thing for me to worry about; there are so many details. I'm about to go mad."

Amber walked to the powder room passing Saylor on the way. She had a weird smile on her face, harboring a secret no one else knew.

Saylor followed her, sensing a threat to her territory. She patiently waited in the hallway outside the door.

When Amber came out, she stopped in her tracks. Saylor stood very close to her and calmly said, "Why are you always hanging around my boyfriend?"

186

"I was invited."

"Only because of your mother."

"Maybe you should ask Beau about that," Amber said.

"Drop the delusion, sweetheart. He doesn't like you. Find a prom date someplace else."

"I already have one. I'm going with Cody," Amber said.

"Good, stick to your own kind, the island of trolls," Saylor said.

Kacie gathered the guests. "Everyone please, let's take our seats." She leaned into the stairwell yelling, "Boys, lunch is ready."

Each person took their seat, making an unconscious choice about whom they wanted to sit by. The outcome resulted in alliances and betrayals. Once seated, the hubbub simmered down to a dull rumble.

"Dad, would you mind?" Kacie said.

"Family and friends, let's bow our heads. Heavenly Father, we come before you to celebrate Beau's eighteenth birthday and we ask you to watch over him on his journey into adulthood. Bless this food to nourish our bodies and protect us from evil. Amen."

"Thanks Louis. I'd like to add a few things before we start this wonderful meal. First, I'd like to thank my wife for arranging such a lovely get together and cooking my duck, even though she hates meat. Second, I'd like to thank you all for sharing this special occasion with us. And to the honoree, boy, I never thought we would make it. When are you leaving?"

"Buck!" Kacie said.

"I'm just kidding. Seriously, you are officially a young man and soon you will be graduating and going off to college. I can't tell you how happy I am; because it's something I never got to do myself."

"And we'll get to the rest of the birthday hoopla after we eat. Please go ahead before it gets cold," Kacie said.

"It looks simply fab darling. Could you pass the sweet potato casserole?" Haley dumped heaping piles on her plate.

"Wouldn't you like something else to go with that?" Kacie said.

"You know me; I never met a potato I didn't like."

"It's the Irish gene," Amber said.

"I thought that was for beer," Saylor said.

The group feasted as the ice tea flowed, breaking off into intimate conversations about various topics.

Kacie sat at the far end of the table closest to the kitchen. She looked around the room and had the strangest feeling, as if this was the last time she would be eating with everyone. She ignored the sensation.

The meal wound down with remnants of a bird carcass scattered about. The guests grew uncomfortable as gastric pressure pushed on their waistlines.

Kacie got up to clear the dishes from the table. Before Saylor could wipe her mouth, Amber jumped up to assist. It was obvious she was brown nosing. Their little talk by the restroom had not worked.

In the kitchen, Ms. Guidry's rolled fondant specialty cake awaited. It was Beau's favorite flavor; carrot cake, but the shape was in a clown's face.

Amber and Kacie slowly carried it into the dining room with eighteen burning candles. Everyone broke out in song, the annoying one reminding Beau he was one day closer to death.

He took it all in with sportsman-like reserve, being genuinely happy when it was over. "So where's my present?"

Buck tossed a petite box wrapped in black foil at him. "Catch!"

Beau shook it, hearing a jingle inside. He ripped open the box to find German car keys with a nifty chevron logo. "No way!"

"It's outside," Buck said.

Beau sprang up and flew out the door. He raced over the porch steps to see a glossy black sedan parked gracefully between the monster truck and hybrid skate. It had a familiar emblem ornamenting the hood, a symbol of wealth.

The crowd followed him outside forming a half circle around him.

Beau opened the car door startled by Mr. Stumpy, who crawled out holding a bunch of multicolored helium balloons. He waddled around in big red clown shoes handing them out. The blue and white striped satin costume squished between his thighs. He blew into a kazoo and made some offensive bodily noises.

Inside the car, it smelled of well-oiled leather. The rosewood dashboard glistened in the sunlight. Beau sat in the driver's seat fondling the steering wheel when Mr. Stumpy approached. He wedged his deformed body in the door opening and proceeded to create a balloon animal.

Beau could feel the hair standing up on the back of his neck. Clowns were the epitome of evil, and he was trapped inside the car with no way out.

"So kid, a preacher and a rabbi walk into a bar—," Mr. Stumpy said.

"Do you know any about attorneys?"

"Sure, let me think." He finished twisting the neck of a blue dog. "What do you call a lawyer with an intelligence quotient of one hundred?"

"I don't know," Beau said.

"Your Honor … What do you call a lawyer with an intelligence quotient of fifty?"

"What?" Beau said.

"Senator, of course."

"Yeah, you're right!"

"Boys, how about some cake?" Kacie said.

The group headed back inside, while Mr. Stumpy made obscene balloon hats.

Beau grabbed his mother's arm holding her in place as everyone walked by. "Mom, you know I'm not ten anymore. Why do you have to embarrass me in front of my friends?"

"What's wrong with a clown?"

"He's a freak!" Beau said.

"Where are your manners? God made him that way," Kacie said.

"Not his size. He's a clown and all clowns are freaks."

In early morning, a thick layer of fog hovered above the placid surface crawling along in waves;

uncoordinated smoky appendages grappled for some place to cling.

The lake embroiled with spectators vied for connection to the celebrities. Some were amateurs, others were dedicated fans of the sport and some just wanted to touch a star.

Monday was the first of a two-day tournament. Eugene grandstanded, it was time to go over rules and garner some free press coverage. He needed everything to go smoothly. There could be no screw-ups, accidents or murders; his reelection was riding on it.

His phone jostled violently against his thigh. A cursory glance at the view screen showed trouble. Without wanting to answer, "Mayor speaking."

"Damn it, you better fix this," Trace said.

"I understand how you feel, but there is nothing I can do; please understand my hands are tied."

"Look here, I'm not going to be outsmarted by an old bag. So help me, if I find out you are pulling a fast one—," Trace said.

"I don't take kindly to threats," Eugene said.

"But you do take kindly to bribes. What's that chick's name down at the station?"

"Oh come now, you know more than her name."

"If that's so, you should be very afraid of what I could expose."

"I think it would be far worse for you. Bribing a government official is a felony, besides you wouldn't want all that negative press to tank your corporate stock would you?" Eugene said.

There was silence on the phone for a minute. Eugene knew the golden rule: *he who speaks last loses*. He kept his mouth shut, though the dead air was killing him. Finally, the caller spoke.

"Bravo Eugene, Bravo. I see you've grown a pair. Too bad your wife's not still around."

"Is there anything else I can do for you Mr. Morgan?"

"Not right now, I'll be in touch." Trace cut the line.

Eugene had a flurry of people around him; just what he needed to stroke his ego.

Lin situated the press; cameras ready in position.

On the other side, the marshals gathered. Kenny approached Eugene and handed a clipboard full of entrance forms.

"Are all the boats inspected?" Eugene said.

"Yes, we're good to go," Kenny said.

Eugene signaled the television film crew. They turned on their camera lights.

"Welcome to the fiftieth anniversary of the Stray Oaks Fishing Tournament, part of the hunt for the Southern Trail. It is my honor as town mayor to officiate a wonderful exhibition of professional angler's and their protégés," Eugene said.

The crowd clapped while Eugene paused. All ten entrants were standing in pods off to the side. They were noticeable by their long sleeved jerseys covered in sponsor logos.

"Louisiana is a bounty of natural wildlife and I am pleased to open the beautiful wetlands of Shallow Basin as our official fishing grounds."

Lin handed him a piece of paper, reminding him to go over some business.

"Now for some quick rules: obey the marshals, check in with them periodically, no live bait or leaving your boat, stay fifty yards away from each other. Don't return any fish from your live well, no more than five in the box at one time and keep them healthy for weigh-in."

Eugene motioned for Wiley to speak.

"This is a wild habitat full of poisonous snakes, alligators, snapping turtles and God knows what else. Be careful, be safe and call on the radio if there is a problem. In addition, gentlemen, mind altering substances are prohibited. Good luck."

The crowd cheered and whistled.

"And with that, let the good times roll," Eugene said.

Blaze jumped up dragging Ed by the shirtsleeve. He had the camera resting on his shoulder.

"Come on, I want to interview Buck before he leaves." Blaze rudely pushed through the crowd. "Buck, can I have a word?"

Buck turned around, "Sure, but make it quick."

Skeeter was standing next to him chewing tobacco. He focused on Blaze's semi unbuttoned satin blouse, shifting his eyes around trying to get a peek.

"What's your strategy for today?"

"Well, I've studied the map and I have some spots picked out. We're going to do some crankbait retrieves to locate fish alternating burn it and stop and go presentations, test the water conditions and try out some of the gear," Buck said.

"Sounds like a winning plan. Good luck on your tenth victory. Catch a lunker guys."

"Thanks Blaze, see you back at base camp."

All of the fishermen loaded their pickup trucks, preparing to trailer to the launch site. Wiley led them behind his official truck with the light bar flashing. They exited the parking area in single fashion, a small convoy on Route 3.

It was a short drive to the site, less than a mile. As the winner from last year, Buck got to launch first. He was anxious to get to work.

"You got everything we need?" Buck said.

"Yep, but don't eat none of them pork rinds," Skeeter said.

"I meant the gear."

"We're good on that too."

Top Dawg as she was named, was the top of the line in professional bass boats. She had an "XL" in the model number, which stood for extra luxury, only the best for someone who really did not need it.

Buck knew how to fish. He had a natural ability to locate them wherever they were hiding. He could think like them, a predator searching for a victim. And that was why he was at the top of his field.

His high-profile sponsors graciously donated most of his expensive gear in exchange for his feedback. Shimano cared about his opinion. They financed and produced his signature lure line, which sold in the millions. They also devised the concept for the instructional video series that demonstrated how to use the lures. Ever the competitor, Buck would never fully give away all of his tricks.

It was midmorning. The fog had burned off in the intense sunlight. The water temperature was fifty-five degrees, which meant the fish would be sluggish. They would need some coaxing to come out from under cover.

Largemouth bass were intelligent creatures. They had the ability to avoid a bait after one encounter. That meant they could reason. The bigger they were, the older and wiser. A lunker would have seven years of experience and know what not to chase.

Buck could not outsmart them and he did not try too. Instead he tempted them, pitching the bait close to cover. No fish could resist an easy ambush striking a short distance. After all, they had to eat.

"Lead the way Hoss," Skeeter said as he adjusted the leather bucket seat.

Buck cranked the 250 horse power outboard engine. It grumbled slightly vibrating the composite construction hull.

"Where we going to first?" Skeeter said.

"I want to scout the shallow areas and see if we can set a hook on anything." Buck steered to a clear open area, trimmed the motor and planed at eighteen miles per hour. After a short jaunt, they were at the first spot. He killed the engine. "I'll bring us closer with the trolling motor." He set up the pedestal seat and turned on the fish finder. The fore deck had forty square feet of room even with the chair in place.

Skeeter checked the live well, which was full of water. A pump aerated it. "I like the rounded walls. This is a mighty fine boat."

Buck was not listening to Skeeter babble about the numerous features of his metallic red and white super sport. He was already in the zone, being quiet and moving methodically.

The boat pointed toward the shoreline, which undulated in little pockets covered by lily pads and floating water lettuce. The shadows provided by the foliage were a perfect place to cast a shad colored scatter-rap bait.

Skeeter dug through the portside rod tray, "Which one do you want?"

"Let me have the seven-foot heavy action graphite," Buck said.

Skeeter looked through the various rods and started to pull one out.

"No, not that one. Here let me." Buck picked the one he wanted, resting it on the carpeted deck. "Why don't you try this one on the aft deck? It is a fiberglass-spinning rod that has some flexibility, but the cork handle will hold your grip. Look around for cruising fish."

"Which lure?"

"I like this watermelon creature bait with a ¼ oz. tungsten weight and a 4/0 straight shank," Buck said.

"I got it."

Buck adjusted his baseball cap and removed the life vest tossing it into the driver's seat. He held the rod assuming his usual stance at the bow. He liked to place his right foot slightly behind his hip to distribute his weight evenly.

The touchscreen fish finder showed the depth, three dimensional bottom terrain and had a color chartplotter. It had a GPS antenna to mark coordinates and a removable secure digital memory card to record hot spots for safekeeping.

Skeeter liked to fish, but he did not get out much since the bait shack was always open. He inherited the place after his uncle died and ran it alone, which was not difficult to do since he was raised there, dropping out of school in the seventh grade.

Buck aimed at his target, held the rod tip slightly above eye level and cast punching through the matted vegetation. He landed the ball bullet sized split sinker right where he wanted. After every forth crank he paused, allowing the lure to fall simulating an injured fish. The three treble hook minnow worked great in the shallows. He got several test strikes but no hookset. The extra wide cup created a tight waffle, which proved irresistible. Buck could feel the pressure from each tug. It was a big resident fish. He reeled in the rest of the twenty-pound fluorocarbon test.

Skeeter was burning water, covering much ground in a short amount of time.

Buck observed a few rookie mistakes. "Go fast but steady; don't vary your cadence so much." Buck marked his location. "Are you getting anything back there?"

"Naw, water is clear though."

"Try a double-bladed buzzbait. Use the black one. Hopefully this breeze will help conceal the noise it makes." Buck went back to pursuit of his hiding fish.

He put a small piece of pork on a rugby shaped jig. It had a super sharp hook that he turned three degrees off the closed eye. A relatively new design, it had a plastic keeper barb and was tied with a Snell knot.

Buck liked to use braided line with teeth to cut through reeds and a short six-inch leader so the fish would not see it. He kept the rod pointed at ten o'clock to control the retrieve speed. He brought the lure close to cover then slowed it down. The crank handle made the rod tip throb with each kick of the bait. Clack, clack, clack then a boom as water exploded in all directions. A big fish clamped down on pheromone laced pork. Buck quickly retrieved, as the rod bent under immense resistance. He was patient, waiting for the fish to tire. When he could feel slack in the line, he cranked a few turns. The rod bent shaped like a horseshoe.

"Ya think it's a cat fish?" Skeeter said.

"No, but it's under the boat moving toward you." Buck walked around the deck perimeter holding the rod, past the cockpit to the rear. "Grab the net."

The bass struggled just below the surface. Its tail flapped violently spraying fans of water. Once the leader was above the surface, Skeeter scooped the net under the fish and they laid it on the deck. Buck used needle-nose pliers to remove the hook. The fish wiggled in protest.

"Don't lose it," Buck said.

"That's a big'en," Skeeter said.

"A keeper of at least six pounds." Buck released it into the live well. It swam around in circles a few times before settling on the bottom. "You just relax in there for a while big boy, I'll get you some company soon."

"I'll send the coordinates back to the Marshals at base camp," Skeeter said.

"Just use the scoring app on my smartphone."

The rest of the afternoon was peppered with small victories and some missed opportunities. But the weather held out and provided a nice first day of fishing. Occasionally they would pass another boat, but for the most part, it was isolated fishing grounds.

Each team packed it in as the sun went down, heading back to base camp. Kenny was there ready to check their live wells. The spectators cheered eager to see the days haul. Clovis had a portable grill full of Angus burgers, T-bone steaks and spare ribs, complimentary to each contestant.

It had been a long day with plenty left to do. Some of the high school football team members volunteered to wash the boats. That freed the fishermen to retie gear for tomorrow. They needed to rise early to take advantage of nocturnal feeding.

After all the preparatory work was completed, the group gathered around the campfire to eat barbecue. Clovis liked to cut his own steaks from a loin, which meant he bought the highest quality meat. But the real ingredient that made them so mouth-watering was the aged whiskey in the homemade sauce. The men gorged themselves, as Clovis passed out a round of free beers.

"You're the master," Buck said.

"Can I get you gentlemen anything else before I head to my real job?" Clovis said.

The men shook their heads in negation as exhaustion set in.

"Very well, I'm off. Good luck tomorrow."

The fire burned steady, crackling and roaring. For a while, there was silence among the group. Vernon's coangler Phil spoke first, "So how'd y'all do?"

"It was sure different out there. Not really what I expected. I've fished other swamps before, just not like this," Buck said.

"Yeah, no oil rigs," Vernon said.

"So Vernon, how did you do today? I bet you've got this one in the bag," Buck said.

"Why do you think that?"

"You grew up there. Didn't Earl take you fishing?"

"Paw and I went out all the time before his accident. I love it out there in the open air, nobody around just peace and seclusion," Vernon said.

"So it must be pretty lousy to lose your inheritance to the church. Any idea why Adele did that? You must have pissed her off good," Buck said.

"The transfer is just on paper, nothing has changed. We're still the caretakers for life. The only real change is I don't have to worry about taxes."

"That's a smart move," Skeeter said.

Phil leaned in offering a toast. "I'll drink too that."

"What about the big ones, you must know where some are?" Morty said.

"There's a granddaddy out there. I've seen it before," Vernon said.

"George Perry grand?" Buck said.

"I doubt no one's seen no twenty-two pound fish around these parts, that'd be a fish tale for sure," Skeeter said.

"It's not quiet that big, maybe eighteen or so," Vernon said.

"How come you've never caught it? If I had a fish that size in my backyard I'd be out morning, noon and night trying to land it," Buck said.

"Oh I've caught it a few times, but I always let it go," Vernon said.

"That's crazy!" Morty said.

"I guess I have too much respect for nature," Vernon said.

"Why, that place doesn't care about you. It will continue on in spite of your intrusions," Buck said.

"So if you don't want to catch it, mind telling us where it is?" Morty said.

"It's getting late. I'm going to turn in. You guys have a nice evening, and just remember the early bird gets the worm," Vernon said.

"Don't run off yet. Why don't you tell us about your twin?" Buck said.

"What's there to tell?" Vernon said.

"Wasn't he a better fisherman than you, until the mysterious car crash?" Buck wiped his hands. "Then to go away to prison for all those years, isn't that why Kacie left you?"

Vernon just stared at Buck not willing to join in the fight he was trying to instigate. If Adele had taught him anything, it was to keep his cool. "I'm just glad you were there for second choice."

The next morning, the moon was almost full except for a missing sliver. It was frigid outside, and breath left steam in the air. The best time to fish was a few days before a full moon. The teams were in pursuit of fish traveling to shallow grounds to fatten up for winter. Bass would look for hard-bottomed rocky areas that would absorb the sun's heat. Each day they would migrate to a new location looking for food.

Vernon used a larger lure to simulate the actual size of the baitfish. He caught them first to match the size, and then released them. It was an extra step but the little things he did made a difference: regularly checking the gear, sharpening the hook after a few hours of usage, removing nicked line, and retying knots.

The boat maneuvered through a tight pass with the headlights off. There were downed trees on either side. Pine branches protruded like arms reaching for help. Spanish moss hung from limbs higher up. It was quiet as Vernon guided Ms. Sunshine right to the spot where he wanted to go. He took his foot off the trolling motor foot pedal and used the end of an ore to push along the bottom feeling his way.

"Don't you want to use the electronics?" Phil said.

"Too much light. Stop worrying, I know where we are. Snap that glow stick if it will make you feel better."

Phil fumbled in the cockpit above the dashboard groping for a small plastic tube. When he bent it in half, a chemical reaction produced an eerie green glow. "That's better."

At the front deck, Vernon went to work taking his time with each deliberate move. He had a system of feeling the fishing, using all senses to evaluate the present conditions and adjusting his presentation accordingly. Not only did he know the layout of the area, but also he understood the inhabitants. This relaxed approach of patiently waiting for the fish to be hungry proved to be a winning strategy. He had three keepers in the live well already.

Warm colors decorated the gymnasium, set up for the annual fall fair. Small game booths in rows dominated the center court. The periphery had the smells of refreshments. The school band sat in the bleachers practicing for the next football game. It was noisy and crowded inside.

Saylor paraded around the floor with Beau on her arm like a charm bracelet. She smiled at everyone as they passed, even the unpopular students. Her goal was to convince them she should be prom queen.

Beau wanted to tell her about his plan to use Amber to win over his mother. He waited for the right opportunity. "I need to tell you something. Can we go somewhere a little quieter and talk?"

"Now is not really a good time. It's important that our peers see us. Would you please smile at everyone?"

"Why, this is stupid?" Beau said.

"Look, do you want to be prom king or not?"

"Now that you bring it up, no, not really."

"Well, you're definitely not helping our cause with that attitude." Saylor saw a gypsy sitting behind a card table. "Let's go get our fortunes told!"

"It's surprising how you can go from hating me too happy in zero point five seconds," Beau said.

"Come on, I want to do this," Saylor said.

Madame Sadira wore a purple-silk wrap embellished with gold-coin fringe. A scarf draped across her nose like a robber's mask. She waved her elderly arm, motioning for them to sit. "May I help you?"

"Yes, we would like a reading," Saylor said as she pulled up a chair.

"Which one of you is the nonbeliever?"

"That would be me," Beau said.

"Then you it is." Sadira shuffled the stack of Tarot cards. "First, I must tell you that this reading is for entertainment purposes only."

"Yeah, yeah. We get it; you're part of the psychic network," Beau said.

"Very well then." Sadira fanned the cards on the table in an arch face down. "Choose."

Beau hovered above the stack finally landing on a left-end card.

Sadira placed the card face down in front of him. "This represents the present." She gathered the rest of the deck and placed one card on each side, aligned in a horizontal row. She pointed to the left card. "This is the past." She pointed to the remaining card. "This is the future." She held the deck tightly sandwiched between her palms. "Now tap the back of the three cards lightly with your hand to infuse your energy, and concentrate."

Beau rolled his eyes at Saylor. "Really?"

"Just play along."

Sadira turned the center card face up; it was the devil.

Saylor laughed, "I could have told you he was evil."

"That's not what it means." Sadira turned up the past card; it was the hangman. She leaned back in her stack chair, staring at the table for a moment. "Listen boy, I want you to really concentrate on the future." Her eyes were as cold as stones.

"All right Esmeralda, I'm focused now."

Sadira turned up the final card; it was death. "Oh, no." She laid the remaining cards down.

"So what's it all mean?" Beau said.

"You will be experiencing life-changing events; that will have long-term consequences. Pay close attention to any life lessons in the near future or you won't be able to progress on your journey," Sadira said.

"Okay, isn't that true for everyone?" Buck said.

"The deep insight I'm about to reveal to you stems from a great collective awareness. It would do you well to respect this power and heed my warning."

Beau looked at Saylor in disbelief. "Here it comes, the load of horse manure."

"Your three card spread is very disturbing to me. You chose all Major Arcana cards."

"Speak-ease Madame Sadira," Saylor said.

"Trump cards of significance. It's unusual and it holds special meaning. I don't think I should say anymore."

"What a rip off," Beau said.

"Beau please!" Saylor had a little more faith in the Occult. "Madame Sadira please tell us what the cards mean."

"Very well child." She politely smiled at Saylor then turned a frightening grimace toward Beau and spoke in a bone chilling tone. "One you know will die, one will wish for death and one will bring death upon us all."

Beau laughed holding his stomach. "Oh my God, and you know this how?"

"The hangman represents sacrifice ... someone you know will die because of their past. The devil could stand for bondage ... someone you know will be held against their will and wish for death. Both things will happen very soon."

"Go on, this is just starting to get interesting," Beau said.

"Death is a transformation, with every end there is a new beginning. Something will bring death upon us all. Its presence will effectively kill the future."

Beau started clapping as he rose from the table. "Awesome, you're good. But next time maybe you should tell your rube that they'd win the lottery. That would be more exciting." He walked away in a huff.

Saylor apologized for his disrespect and chased him. "What's wrong with you?"

"Nothing!" Beau snapped.

"You've been acting really weird lately, ever since you spent time with Mr. Crenshaw. What's your major dysfunction? I'm getting tired of your bad attitude."

"Maybe I'm sick of you nagging me all the time," Beau said.

Saylor felt self-conscious, as the argument started to draw attention. "Fine, have it your way, jerk!"

But Beau had already walked away. He headed outside for some fresh air, when he remembered that he had escape wheels. On his way to the car, he looked back to see if anyone was watching. No one was around.

Rows of endless clothes hung silently on plastic hangers. Divided by type, each section of the walk-in closet had evening gowns, cocktail dresses, skirts, blouses and pants. There were numerous drawers full of undergarments filled with mismatched socks. The maple shelves piled high with sweaters, T-shirts and shorts overflowed. Behind a tiny door were seasonal crates in a cedar-lined room. Racks of shoes, ten pair of each color imaginable, and some never taken out of their boxes stacked high on the floor.

Why Kacie needed all this stuff was beyond her. She tended to wear the same clothes each day, relying on comfort versus fashion. All these garments required purging. The church mission would have better use for the donations.

She attempted to clean out the closet, while no one was around. It was a big job, enough work to keep her busy all day and keep her mind off the worrying. Waiting for test results was the worst part of being sick. And deep down she knew she was sick; mere patience would not fix what was wrong.

A lab test could not reveal the answer to the mystery. No doctor could predict the future or garner magical powers to heal her. The outcome was already determined. All she could do now was wait for the call.

In the wake of the news, there would be a flood of condolences. She would be angry in general, then angry with God, finally settling on acceptance of the situation. People would talk about the inadequacies of medical science. But the only person she would blame was herself.

Each time she canceled an annual checkup because of a publicity event for Buck or for something she had to do at Beau's school or a last minute need of the church was a time when she sacrificed her health for others. She promised the nurse to reschedule when she had a chance to look at her day planner, but that day never came. Then after too much time went by, she was embarrassed about breaking a promise so she let it go until the next year.

She thought she was a healthy person who took care of herself but really she took care of others, living to fulfill their needs at the expense of her own. This long-standing pattern of self-sacrifice caught up to her, though she continued to ignore the signs. The bitter truth was visible; still she chose to bury herself in rearranging cotton, wool and polyester garments.

The house phone rang. The high-pitched chirp of the digital set echoed in each room. It made her skin crawl. She scampered over a pile of clothes, knocking over a stack of shoeboxes when she tripped on a belt loop that lassoed her ankle. She grasped the receiver before the call went to voice mail.

"Boudreaux residence," Kacie said.

"I have your pathology results from the biopsy," Andre said.

"And?"

"It's not good and there is no way to say it with sugar. You have stage four ovarian cancer. I'm sorry."

Kacie focused her attention outside the bedroom window. There was a crow perched on the rim of a birdbath. It stared back at her with one dark eye, an eye that seemed an endless void where light squelched nothingness.

"Are you still there?" Andre said.

"Yes, is there a treatment?"

"Maybe if we caught it sooner. Your file says you missed your annuals a few years in a row."

"Yes, that's my fault," Kacie said.

"That's not what I meant. At this stage, it's too late to do anything."

"So there will be no chemotherapy or radiation?"

"It would be pointless," Andre said.

"How much time do I have left?"

"Hard to say, maybe six months or so."

"Good, I want to see my son graduate," Kacie said.

"Is there anything I can do for you?"

"No, it's already done." Kacie returned the phone to its cradle without saying goodbye, noticing when the display panel turned to black. That was how she felt, extinguished.

She sat on the edge of the king-sized mattress with her hands in her lap. The mess she made with the clothes was indicative of her life.

She thought about how everyone else would react to the news. There would be media attention, and it would affect Buck's performance. Then there was Beau, so close to becoming a man. He needed to leave the nest without looking back. Her illness would bring them all down.

So she chose not to tell anyone. They would find out soon enough once the symptoms were apparent. At least her last days would be as normal as possible; she could continue to suffer in silence and die a martyr.

Kacie heard a knock at the back door and ran downstairs.

Blaze stood on the other side of the screen. "I'm sorry to bother you, but I was wondering if I could get a sound byte for my midday tournament report?"

"Of course, come in. Make yourself at home." Kacie filled a kettle with water. "Would you like some tea?"

"Sure, if it's not too much trouble." Blaze looked around the room, not as someone who admired the décor but rather as an investigator searching for clues.

The kitchen was very welcoming. It felt like the heart of the house. Blaze envisioned herself standing before the vintage gas stove wearing a ruffled apron frying a hen's egg in a cast-iron skillet; over easy lathered in butter with no browning.

Buck would be seated at the table sipping on freshly squeezed orange juice that came from the tree out back. The only sound he would make would be the occasional noise of newspaper pages turning. He would be engrossed in Blaze's front-page story.

She would be a top-notch reporter writing facts in literary prose, carefully choosing words to convey meaning. Each sentence would be poetic, adding color to an entertaining story. Each period would punctuate like a torch in the sand. She was in love with the thought of him being in love with her.

Kacie withdrew the chair to take a seat. She seemed distant. "I'm sorry, what was it you needed?"

"Have you heard from Buck? He's going to win again I'm sure, but a little edge before the weigh-in would be much appreciated."

"All I know is he's after a big one," Kacie said.

The kettle started to whistle in the background, reaching a crescendo. Kacie just sat there with a blank look on her face.

"Shall I get that for you?" Blaze said.

"Oh, I'm sorry, my manners." Kacie removed the boiling water like she had done a thousand times and set the empty pot on a cold burner. "I hope you drink Earl Grey; I'm out of the other."

"Anything will be fine." Blaze looked around. "This is a nice place."

"It's old. It was Eleanor's house. I never wanted to live here." There was bitterness in Kacie's tone that aroused Blaze's curiosity.

"Then why did you? Certainly Buck loves you enough to follow you anywhere."

"I don't know, I never really thought about it. We moved in and never left."

Blaze sipped on the tea. "You know, he and I dated once in high school?"

"He told me," Kacie said.

"Did he tell you everything?"

Kacie remained as stone cold as a statue. "All that I need to know."

"It's just that I would have given anything to be in your shoes now. I always hoped to be married with children."

"Look at it from his point of view; why buy what you can get for free?"

Blaze was taken aback by Kacie's uncharacteristic meanness. Usually she was polite. Something must be dreadfully wrong. "Do you mind if I use the restroom?"

"There's one in the hall, help yourself." Kacie remained seated, stirring her china cup. The spoon circled, scraping the bottom.

Inside the small room were family mementos: a wicker shelf above the toilet had a tropical themed framed photograph, a cruise ship coffee mug and a plastic snow globe from an amusement park. Blaze fondled the small photograph taken at the beach. Family fun day included Kacie standing next to Buck wearing plastic Hawaiian leis and Beau holding a coconut shell drink.

It was a great picture of Buck standing in the sand next to a dune. He had a shirtless tan and a smile a mile wide. The others subjects were like sandpipers lurking in the background, waiting for free food to drop from the sky.

Blaze did the unthinkable; she removed the picture and slid it into her skirt pocket.

On the back of the door, a robe hook held a man's extra-large flannel long-sleeve shirt. She grabbed the cuff and sniffed, breathing in his scent. It was exactly as she remembered, woody spice. When she inhaled, memories flooded back into her consciousness. If there had been a way she could have stolen the shirt and walked out of there, she would have. But as it was, she had spent too much time lingering alone.

Buck and Skeeter left base camp late. Buck spent the early morning mapping a plan to find the fish of legends so he could win big. Not only would his face adorn the town's commemorative plate, but also he would have the satisfaction of beating Vernon again.

"I think I figured out where that bucket-mouth lives," Buck said as he steered the boat.

"How'd you do that?"

"I was studying the map focused on a spot and got a strange feeling about it. Besides, Vernon will avoid the area where it lives."

"So we go where he aint?"

"Precisely." Buck stopped the motor when they reached the destination. "It's got to be right around here somewhere." He hopped out of the driver's seat. The wake gently rocked the boat as it rolled by.

Buck knelt digging in the bait tray. It stored five plastic snap-lid containers upright in specially designed slots. Each box was sorted by type, and marked for easy identification. "Get that pork ready."

Skeeter raised the forward step to reveal an icebox that contained sodas, bottled water, a couple of tuna sandwiches and the pork cutlets soaked in his secret concoction of bait scents, cyanine pepper and fish pheromones individually wrapped in foil and refrigerated to preserve the smell.

The boat floated in an open area, free to drift with the wind.

Buck fished a top spot hard while scanning the surface. "Look for boiling water. That will be a school of baitfish being chased." Buck cast overhand, lifting on the backstroke. Once the lure hit the water, he transferred the rod from his casting hand to his left hand so he could reel with his right.

"There's something over yonder." Skeeter pointed to air bubbles on the surface.

Buck quickly retrieved the rest of the line, and sidearm cast in that direction. He felt a tug, naturally dropping the rod tip in response. He waited a few seconds for the fish to take the lure into its mouth. The rod pointed toward the fish. Buck reeled in the slack line dropping the rod tip, then lifted straight up to set the hook.

Now the game was on. Catching a fish was easy. Fighting a fish was harder. Landing the same fish was the most difficult. The goal was to tire the fish as soon as possible since lactic acid would build up in its muscles.

Buck pulled up and reeled down in a rhythm, moving around the boat deck following the fish darting from side to side. Sometimes the fish would take more line out as it got a glimpse of the boat. Buck counteracted each maneuver gaining inches that would eventually close the gap.

Occasionally, the line would rise as the fish cleared the water desperate to throw the hook. The body was dark grey with an emerald lateral stripe. The two-sectioned dorsal fin had hard spines that protruded like sharp quills. They stood up under distress. Many an inexperienced angler had tried to pick up a fish like this while landing it, only to learn that a moist net was better to protect the mucous-coated fish skin. Buck received such a warning as a boy, requiring stitches and a course of antibiotics. Still, it was beautiful to watch the desperate fish struggle for its life.

"Is it the big one?" Skeeter said.

"I can't tell, but whatever it is, it's a tough bugger."

"You're making me tired just watching." Skeeter ripped back a pop tab, while seated on the rear deck with his feet dangling over the passenger's chair. "Want some of my sandwich?"

Buck ignored him focusing on the behemoth, running away with his line. It sang as it flew off the spool. The fish darted in odd directions trying to break free. There was little chance it could bust the braided line fighting in the open, but it might weaken a knot.

The sun beat down reflecting white light on the surface. The glare made it difficult to see without polarized sunglasses. Buck had the kind that wrapped around his head so they would not slip off. He leaned back trying to compensate for the fish's forward momentum. His legs were tired of standing, and his arms felt like jelly.

Skeeter chewed the sandwich the same way he worked tobacco around his cud. His jaw swirled in a circular pattern. "Are you going to land that big boy anytime soon?"

Buck reeled down when he could; resting in the seconds between. The fish covered a lot of ground, finally losing steam. "It's looking for a place to hide, but there's nowhere to run baby."

The leader was within view. Buck reeled in a straight line. The fish thrashed violently from side to side, jumping up once. It was huge. A giant gapping mouth with a fuzzy lure hooked behind the upper lip appeared. "Get the net ready."

Skeeter tripped on his untied shoelace walking through the cockpit. He knelt holding onto the deck edge, reached under the fish and scooped. It was heavy. He grabbed the hoop of the net for extra support. "Hot damn, what a looker."

Buck laid the rod down on the deck and reached in his back pocket for the pliers. "Hold him still."

"I got him, don't you worry."

Buck jimmied the wedged hook for a while and blood sprayed across his tan loafers. The bass wiggled on its side, but could do nothing out of water. As oxygen quickly faded from its vessels, it became docile. Finally, the hook barb worked free. Buck had a good grasp of the fish's lower lip between his thumb and fore fingers. "We need to get it into water fast."

Skeeter lifted the live well cover. "Are you sure it will fit? There are four in here already."

"I'll make it fit." Buck cradled the fish in his arms. It was the size of an infant.

"How long is it?"

"I'd say two feet easy." Buck carefully lowered the fish into the live well, tail first. The other fish swam in circles at the bottom trying to get away. The water overflowed from the fish's displacement, spilling onto the deck. Buck held the lip, dipping its head so it could oxygenate. Its eyes looked around independently and the side fins started to flutter. Buck let go. "Call in the coordinates and stow the gear. Tell them we're coming in."

Less than a mile away, Morty and his nephew Doug pursued the shoreline, hoping a big fish would hide in the shade of bankside trees.

Morty saw dragonflies hovering over lily pads. Easy bugs to mimic, he pitched a plug on top of a lily pad, rested for a few moments, twitched it and a ferocious jaw clamped down as water sprayed in all directions.

The large mouth took the plug below the surface and felt the prick of a sharp point against its soft pad. It screamed without making a sound. The jaw that extended past its eyes showed signs of pain. The fish jumped out of the water, and dove back down causing the line to wrap around a cypress knot.

Morty brought the boat in to shore as close as possible. He kept tension on the line, so the fish could not move. It was wedged in a hole.

Doug tried to get the net under it while leaning over the bow edge. The fish hid in roots under a thin layer of slime.

"Don't step off the boat, or we'll be disqualified," Morty said.

"I can't get the net in there. Do we have anything smaller?" Doug said.

"You'll have to look, I can't let go of the rod."

Doug searched through various storage compartments finding a discarded sixteen-ounce plastic drinking cup from a convenience store. "What about this?"

"Try it and hurry. My arms are getting tired," Morty said.

Doug was 6'-2" and thin as a string bean. He had long limbs and the flexibility of youth. He stretched his lean body over the edge, held onto an upright root and scooped violently in the water. The cup fit better in the hole than the net. The fish squirmed around tethered to the stump.

In the woods, a lens zoomed on a centipede as it traversed the burl knot of an oak. The shutter clicked. The multi-legged insect responded to the intrusion by smiling with one russet eye, antenna flailing like radar. The camera clicked again.

Beau loved photography. He lost himself in the observation of his surroundings, momentarily forgetting he had problems. The world he observed was suddenly visible through his photographs. Nature was beautiful, but could be destructive. It was pristine and pure, but could be easily spoiled.

This special place by the creek was his spot for solitude. Gentle ripples of falling water calmed him. Moss grew on rocks; trees added another ring and time rolled on.

He walked along the edge of the water in the direction of the current, curious of where the flow discharged. Granite rocks with jagged edges lined the bank. Some were enormous. Centuries of abrasion smoothed others under the water.

His own hiking boots left a footprint in the moist sand. Beau became interested in the impression, a contrast between man and nature. Fascinated, he set off on a journey surveying for animal tracks.

Fallen leaves covered most of the ground. Now and then, there was a clear patch of dirt, leaving room for an animal to forage. Beau searched for a mark, and found one.

It resembled small deer hooves, pointed toward the water. Beau snapped pictures from several angles.

A chill hit his body. The afternoon temperature dropped especially in the shade. He forgot about time, and had nowhere important to be for a while. The new car afforded him some freedom.

The animal tracks ended at the creek. He stepped over the tops of large boulders making his way downstream. The rapids became louder when he arrived at a change in elevation. A minor cliff extended, producing a miniature waterfall. It stretched across seven feet and created a pool below, where water pushed out trickling down an incline toward the mouth opening.

Beau took several photographs. There was a rainbow effect arching in a beam of sunlight. The crystal water roared by in a blurred transparency forming surface pockets of taupe foam.

A burgundy maple leaf curled upward floated by like a sailing ship. It fell in the treacherous current with no way to steer its course, but survived. Beau thought about his situation. He too had become like the leaf, a victim of fate. He desperately wanted to control his destiny.

Beau hurried to keep up with the leaf as it washed farther downstream. It wedged between two rocks, suspended in animation.

That is when he saw the outline of something bizarre on the ground. It resembled a distorted man's footprint. The oval heel depression was normal, but the rest was different. The sickle-shaped ball was a triangular pad, and a few inches farther were four clawed toes. The total length was more than twelve inches.

Beau quickly imagined what it could not be: a bear, deer, cougar, boar or alligator. It definitely was not a rabbit or raccoon. Maybe it was a Sasquatch, zombie, space alien or werewolf.

Excited about the prospect, he took pictures from all angles, even one with his own foot next to it for scale. He marked the GPS coordinates on his phone, so he could lead authorities back there. This was a rare find indeed.

In the distance a twig snapped. Beau looked up from the viewfinder to see a dark figure move through the trees. He flipped the dial to shutter burst, trying to capture the moving image in succession.

Within a few seconds, it was gone. He reviewed the shots and increased the image size. All he could see was a blurry shape contrasting the tree trunks, but nothing definite. He could edit the photograph with software to enhance the image, but it was not a great picture to work with.

A traditionalist, he preferred a clean original image with little afterward manipulation. Anyone could doctor a photograph, crop and recolor, but he framed the composition correctly from the start and used the proper F-stop and lens filter.

He looked at his watch. The mysterious creature would have to wait another day. It was late and he promised Amber ice cream afterschool. Beau draped the camera over his shoulder and hiked out of the woods.

Morty grew impatient with Doug's inability to capture the ornery fish. "Just grab the dang thing. Pull on the line, it's attached at the other end."

"I'm trying; I can't reach it without falling off the boat."

"Be a little quicker!"

The bushes rattled on the bank nearby, something moved through them. It rapidly approached. A long scaly arm sliced through the air. Razor-like claws ripped across Doug's back leaving crimson streaks, as they cut his shirt. He could not see what hit him bent upside down in the hole. The force knocked him off the deck. He tumbled onto the protruding cypress knees. The water splashed.

The creature pulled Doug away, while he screamed. He grasped for any handhold, clawing deep gouges into the moist dirt. The monster had him by the ankles face down. His mouth collected leaves and debris. "Uncle Mort ... Help me, please!"

Morty could do nothing. He froze stiff holding the rod. When Doug disappeared into the shadows, he dropped it.

He raced to the cockpit and throttled the engine in reverse. It shot water diagonally into the air. The partially submerged propeller was trimmed up for the shallow depth. Morty flipped a switch to lower it, but he went too far.

His eyes could not move, fixated on the horrifying sight. Instinct told him to run, even though his nephew was still out there.

The propeller made a squeal as it bound on a tree stump. One fin blade nicked and another bent, but it still spun on the shaft.

Morty raised the motor a few inches and shoved the console mount control forward. Water spit out of the propeller blades but *Second Mistress* floated out of the shoal.

The motor sputtered while the boat turned bringing it into the open water. Morty cut the curve so abruptly, the radio resting on the passenger dashboard fell overboard.

"Hell's bells!" Morty groped in his pockets for the cell phone but he remembered Doug had it last. There was no way to call for help and no one was around. Several other boats had already returned to base camp with their limit, passing by hours ago.

The motor made a strange noise as if the gears locked, then completely shut down. He repeatedly tried to crank it. The only sound was the click of the ignition key. The damaged propeller was the problem. Now Morty was dead in the water with that thing still out there.

The sun was setting. Soon it would be dark. That thing could come back for him anytime. The only protection he had was a flare gun. He debated whether to use it to signal for help.

Morty looked around helplessly. He sat down on the rear deck and wept.

The eyes of a mature alligator surfaced near the boat. It sat motionless staring. There were no birds overhead or sounds of frogs, just bitter silence.

What would he say to his sister when he returned home without her son? He pondered this for a while. He had to go after Doug.

Morty dove into the opaque water without his life vest. He was a poor swimmer. He misjudged the distance to the shore. Two days of fishing out in the sun with few hours of sleep and minimal food had drained his energy reserves.

The water was much colder than he anticipated. It went inside his inner ear as his head bobbed to stay afloat. His swollen eyes, red from crying could barely see.

Morty splashed and kicked trying to reach the elusive shore that only seemed to mover farther away. The more he exerted himself, the weaker he became.

He drank the pea soup and choked. His head sank below the surface. A water ring rippled out in all directions.

The vacant boat drifted by, as the alligator descended with its meal.

While Clovis worked the outdoor grill at the lake for the tournament spectators, Mabel managed the restaurant. She seated guests, waited tables, bussed dirty dishes, operated the cash register, answered the phone and refilled drinks. Business was slower than usual, but she was busy preparing the dining room and bar for the dinner crowd.

Surprised to see Beau with Amber, she seated them in a booth toward the back. Mabel did not have time to gossip or believe in its merits, but did often overhear people talking. It was not difficult to connect all the dots, especially after hearing the stories that Clovis absorbed at the bar. In a way, she lived vicariously through others.

She could have gone to college, become a trapeze artist or moved to Bangladesh, but she chose to remain living and working with her father. He needed her more than her own need for adventure. That is why she stayed secluded inside the confines of the family namesake.

Mabel would have ventured outside, but Lorelei was somewhere in the world. The thought of possibly crossing paths by accident terrified her. Ample pent-up emotion, frustration and rage simmered under a polite façade waiting to explode. One wrong look, word or gesture to hug her would set off a storm of violence so heinous, even Officer Aucoin would throw away the key.

The callousness did not come from her abandonment; it was from what Lorelei did to Clovis. He was the perfect husband; providing a good home, faithful and patient. Still, she trampled on his fragile heart as if it was gutter trash left out in the rain.

Mabel needed clinical therapy and a professional psychologist to discuss what happened. Instead, she neatly folded the injuries into a combination-lock briefcase, chained to her arm by a handcuff.

The baggage left no room in her heart for anyone else, and much less room for a man. Coupled with her fear to venture outside, she would probably never marry or start a family of her own. She had an aversion to commitment for different reasons than her mother, but the outcome was the same. In that way, she was just like her mother.

Beau requested the booth in the back so no one would see them. Amber thought he was trying to be romantic in the darkness. They were off track with each other, but still he played along entertaining her fantasy.

"What will it be kids?" Mabel said.

"How's about two hot fudge Sundaes with extra peanuts?" Beau said.

"Coming right up."

"And two glasses of milk please," Amber said.

Mabel rushed off to fill the order leaving uncomfortable dead air.

Amber was aggressive for a shy girl. Like her mother, she was good at seizing opportunities. She spoke first. "Do you think your dad will win again tonight?"

"That's why I asked you for ice cream instead of dinner. I have to go to the weigh-in ceremony after this."

"Would you mind if I tagged along? My mom will be there anyway. Then you won't have to drive me home," Amber said.

Beau's intestines were already nervous about their meeting, and the possible repercussions with Saylor were moving toward flat-out distress. He thought about how Amber's presence at the ceremony might work to his advantage. "Sure, I'll be taking pictures. You can hang around my mom. I'm sure she'd like that."

"So how much money is the first-place prize?"

"Twenty-five thousand."

"Wow! That is a lot of cash. What's your dad going to do with it all?"

"Probably add it to the pile in the mattress."

Mabel delivered the beverages and deserts.

Beau took out a white packet of pills. "Excuse me while I take this medicine. I'm allergic to dairy."

"Oh gosh, I couldn't live without cheese." Amber attacked the molten fudge, drowning the cherry in dark goo. Then she scooped up the peanuts crumbs, while talking too much.

Beau mostly swirled his spoon around allowing the French vanilla to melt into a milky soup, listening to her incessant dribble.

"Where are you going for college? I hope you picked state. That's where I'm going."

"That's a loaded question. Actually, I want to go anywhere but there."

"Why? That's where everyone from high school is going," Amber said.

"Exactly my point."

"Just think of all the friends you'll already have."

"Wouldn't you rather meet new people?" Beau said.

"Why waste all the connections you've spent twelve years making. No, I'd rather keep my friends and build from there. Sally's big sister is already at State and she says it's awesome."

"I may go to a private school. I haven't decided." Beau looked at his watch. "I hate to rush you but it's getting late. We should be going."

Amber laughed. "I can't believe Beau Boudreaux is taking me to the lake. Isn't that where kids make out? Oh my God!"

Overhead, the lake seemed completely surrounded. Recreational vehicles lined one area of the parking lot in rows, their contents spilled outside forming makeshift yards. Most of them had out-of-state license plates.

The visitors' interest in the winner, sparked from a rivalry between two contestants, was all that mattered. Media attention, partly drummed up by Blaze's command of drama, created a world where competing Gladiators fought for their lives.

This was a possible tenth straight victory for the favored warrior, a feat propelling him into hall of fame territory. He was the one everyone bet on to win.

Buck's career was solid. His record for attending the most prestigious competitions and subsequent wins earned him celebrity status and a hefty purse. He always came out on top, no matter how difficult the challenge.

His natural-born confidence morphed into his present day arrogance. He took his abilities for granted. He used nature as a tool to feed his ego. He sucked up the attention like an emotional vampire, enslaved by his own fame.

Obsessed fans wanted to touch him, as if he had powers of a messiah to heal the sick. Women wanted him to father their next child. Little boys dreamed one day of being just like him. Just not his own son.

Beau liked Buck the public figure. He respected his father's career accomplishments and was happy for his success, but he did not appreciate Buck the father.

He met the responsibilities of providing for necessities like checking off a list for emergency preparedness. Food and shelter were stellar.

Buck excelled at gift giving, often spending more than was appropriate as a form of servitude. He intended for each neatly wrapped present with hooked chains to ensnare the intended recipient. The hooks had curved shafts with several barbs to prevent escape. Once the hook embedded deep into the subcutaneous tissue, the chain of debt would drag on the floor making noise. The sound of metal scraping reminded the recipient of the gratitude owned to the gift barer.

The exchange of gifts transferred guilt, their guilt from failed parenting. What they refused to give was replaced by store-bought items they could afford.

Beau had a simple list of things he craved: honesty, an emotional connection, respect to make his own decisions and unconditional love. He did not understand why it was so difficult for them to give any of those items. His parents guarded them, as if they were the last drop of drinking water in a desert.

Beau's parents loved him in a modified version: when he did exactly what they expected, or when he met their goals for achievements that they deemed worthy and also when he reflected well on them in public. For eighteen years, Beau had done those things.

It was easy to applaud Buck's career achievements, because parenting was not his best work. Beau thought of this forgetting that he was not alone in the lookout tower.

Amber gazed down on the people below walking around the campgrounds. "They look like ants from way up here. How'd you know about this place?"

"It's a forestry lookout tower, a summer lifeguard stand and the boy scouts use it for training. Just be glad I didn't make you climb the rope to get up here," Beau said.

"The ladder was difficult enough. This place is pretty nifty, although the plywood walls could use some paint. I'd go with pink and maybe put a throw rug."

"It's supposed to be rustic and blend with the natural surroundings."

"Seems like a sweet make-out spot. Bet you come here a lot with Saylor. Not that I'm trying to pry."

"This is my secret alone place; besides we had a fight."

"I was wondering why she's not here tonight. I hope it's not because of me. Gosh, I would hate to cause problems."

The comment puzzled Beau. "We should get down there and find my mom. She'll be looking for me."

A crowd of fans gathered around Buck, some people were interested in his experiences landing the lunker and others were interested in him.

Kacie pushed through politely excusing herself along the way. "Pardon me ... Hello, how are you ... May I get through please?"

Buck returned an autograph to a little girl. His eyes lit up when he saw his wife. "Baby!"

She was dressed in soft pink adorned with long strands of pearls. He craved her feminine touch. She embraced him as if it were the last time they would be together. Today she received the worst news of her life, and she also needed a hug.

"You smell good, and you look beautiful too. I missed you so much," Buck said.

"You smell nice too honey," Kacie said.

"I took a shower and changed after I called you. Let's go to the press tent. Haley should be there by now."

"Have you seen Beau?" Buck said.

"No, isn't he with you?" Kacie said.

"I'm right here." Beau and Amber walked up behind them.

Kacie looked surprised to see them together. She smiled. "I wouldn't have expected to see the two of you together." She squeezed his cheeks. "What a nice surprise."

"Mom, stop it. You're embarrassing me."

"Can't a mother love her only son?"

Buck led them to the scoreboard area in the tent. His name was the first on the list, with a star behind it for winning last year. There were ten columns for individual fish weights, and the eleventh reserved for the total. Numbers filled most columns, large for typical bass weights. The total column was empty to add to the suspense. In Buck's ninth column, a red question mark signified that he had boated a limit.

The mystery fish sat in the bottom corner of a 300-gallon aquarium. Its partially opened mouth, breathed through its gills. The tiny pectoral fins stroked in reverse to hold it stationary.

Young children jumped up and down to harass the fish, a spectacle of enormous proportions. They tapped on the glass to aggravate it, though the sign read: *Do Not Touch.*

Buck led his family there, proud of his accomplishments.

"Oh my, what a big one. Honey, that's larger than I thought a bass could grow," Kacie said.

"Must be all that toxic waste in the basin," Beau said.

"Beau please, can't you be a little more supportive of your father? Especially in front of your guest."

"You're right. Great job Dad, for killing the oldest fish known to man."

"It's going back to where it came from, that's why we give the GPS coordinates," Buck said.

"Wow Mr. Boudreaux, that's so noble," Amber said.

Vernon stood at the back of the tent, talking to some people from Bakersfield. He noticed Kacie immediately as she walked in.

She was stunning. The older they became, the more attractive she seemed. Time had been good to her appearance with hardly any wrinkles on her face, and only a few laugh lines when she smiled.

Distracted by her presence, Vernon was unable to focus on the interviewer. His lack of interest in discussing the details of his hookset dismayed the reporter enough to go elsewhere.

Kacie felt his staring gaze. She peered around the tent using peripheral vision to see him standing alone watching her. There was a slack smile on his jaw, but his eyes beamed rays of love. Once she made eye contact, Vernon approached her unable to resist her attraction.

"Vernon ole boy. Just the guy I wanted to see. So tell me, is this the one you were talking about?" Buck said.

"I don't know. Only if it has a scar above the eye." Vernon moved closer to the tank to get a better look.

The other fish frantically swam around in circles. The big one just sat on the bottom. It turned to look at him with sad eyes. "Hey, big fella." Vernon pressed his palm to the glass.

Kacie could see the pain in his eyes, and empathized. She was accustomed to Buck's disrespect toward him, especially when she was present. Usually it was a territorial display. This was different. She could see Buck's arousal from Vernon's suffering. It was as if he had run over his dog.

"Don't worry old friend, he's going back to the swamp once I'm crowned the winner. Of course, I'll have a fiberglass replica hanging in our living room to remind me of the experience. Kacie and I will enjoy looking at it when we snuggle on the couch," Buck said.

Vernon did not respond to the taunt. He stared at Kacie, whose eyes were on the verge of watering.

"Vern, how'd you do?" Beau tried to lighten the mood.

"Okay I guess. It was a nice couple of days, good weather for November and solid fishing."

Eugene huddled with the marshals in a deep discussion about some urgent matter, as the crowd gathered under the tent. It was almost weigh-in time.

"He didn't check in. Last time I heard from him was around lunch," Kenny said.

"Do we have his location?" Eugene said.

"The signal is gone."

"How do we lose a GPS? I thought you said these transmitters worked no matter what."

"Usually they do, unless…," Kenny said.

"Unless what? Spit it out Kenny. People are waiting."

"Something bad could have happened."

"Such as?"

"I don't know Mayor, maybe the boat sunk."

Officer Aucoin walked up. "What's the problem?"

"We have a missing boat, number eight," Eugene said.

"It's probably nothing. I'll drive over there, and check it out."

"All right, we'll hold off here for a few minutes. Hurry up though."

As Wiley exited the tent, Blaze stepped in front of him. "Something wrong Officer?"

"Nothing to report yet ma'am. If you'll excuse me?" Wiley pushed her aside.

Inside the tent, people held conversations, some ate barbecue, and others drank beer. The press milled around taking photographs and doing interviews. Everyone waited for the big event to start.

Eugene walked up to the lectern and flipped on the microphone, which squealed as he adjusted it. "Excuse me, folks, if I can have your attention. We will be starting soon. Sorry for the delay. We have one boat still out. Please enjoy some fine refreshments provided by Fourchette's Bar & Grill, one of our local sponsors. Thank you for your patience."

Lin handed him bottled water. "Need something stronger?"

"Not yet, ask me in ten minutes. Have you seen my boy?"

"Behind the tent with the other kids, likely smoking," Lin said.

"Great, just what I need. Go get him please."

"You don't pay me enough to be his mother too."

"Fine, you've been promoted. Expect a check in the mail," Eugene said.

"Ha, ha, Mayor, very funny."

Wiley turned off Route 3 into a clearing in the woods. He saw Morty's truck and trailer still sitting where they had been since morning. He parked the truck in the middle of the clearing with the engine running and headlights on high beam. He grabbed the flashlight and unsnapped his holster as a safety precaution.

"Hello, Morty, Doug. Anybody out there?"

The only sounds that greeted him were evening crickets, frogs and an interested barn owl who watched his every move. He walked around shining the flashlight through the trees. The landing area was vacant, no signs of life or foul play.

Behind the tent, Jim, Cody and a couple of Goth teenagers from Bakersfield High School passed around a cigarette. One freakishly large teenager looked too mature to be a student. Held back a few years, he offered a bottle in a crumpled brown bag. Store bought twist-top wine made from subpar grapes was just what Cody needed to appease his frustration.

He saw Amber and Beau climbing down from the lookout tower, and assumed that she was two-timing him. He easily jumped to conclusions with low self-esteem. She was not one of the popular girls, but she still was a girl, which automatically made her out of his league.

Cody grew up in the family grocery store stocking shelves, mopping the floor and gathering shopping carts. It was menial work, but it afforded him a weekly allowance.

His parents worked hard, and he learned a strong work ethic. But because they were always at the store, he did not have much of a home life. They even ate dinner in the stockroom. Cody did homework in the office while Francine managed the accounting books. Though they were always together, they rarely did anything but work tasks.

The store, which had its financial woes through the years, would be his inheritance if it survived the unstable economy. That would be a blessing and a curse. Cody had a way to earn a living, but he did not have what he really wanted, a home life.

The key to fulfilling his life dream was a *Ms. Mouton*. His endgame was to go home at the end of each day to a wife and family. The children would be useful for free labor. Cody intended to work them, but *she* was as elusive as winning the lottery.

Going through the process to find a wife terrified him. All girls were frightening. It was not the fear of asking them out or of the certain rejection that followed, but rather that his heart would be in mortal jeopardy.

Cody believed men were the superior gender, when women were not around. As soon as they entered the picture, everything changed. They embodied the one thing a man could never get on his own, compassion.

Women were soft, tender and comforting. Like air, necessary to exist. But the feature that drew him in could easily be reversed into an equal emotion of brutality.

He witnessed this behavior firsthand in his mother, who was mentally bi-polar. Francine exhibited symptoms that confused him about women and what to expect. He feared they were all unpredictable like her, his gold standard.

To survive, Cody tried to control her mood swings. When she was depressed, he thought he was the cause. He absorbed her manic energy when she worked herself into a tizzy. He cycled through the multitude of her emotions, which did not correlate to the environment.

Talking himself into asking Amber to prom was extremely difficult, a simple question made of seven small words harder than climbing Mount Kilimanjaro.

Her positive response was unexpected. It caught him off guard. He had not thought beyond the question. He feared the power she now possessed over him.

He felt very small. At any moment, Amber could crush him like a bug. Her options were limitless: she could change her mind and stay home, go with a better offer to prom or cancel and go alone. Fear of the unknown paralyzed him.

When Cody saw them together, it was proof that his nightmare was about to come true. Amber had her foot firmly placed above his exoskeleton ready to pounce with all of her might. He withered at the mere thought.

Wiley looked concerned when he returned from the boat launch. He stood in the back of the tent far away from the others, motioning for Eugene to join him in a private conversation.

The press set up in the front of the tent near the lectern. Most of the spectators sat in rows of foldout chairs, occupying every seat. The rest stood around the tent perimeter, like a church revival.

The Boudreauxs sat in the first row of the reserved section, surrounded by the other anglers and their families. Beau excused himself to find a portable toilet. He passed Wiley and Eugene who looked serious.

"What did you find?" Eugene said.

"Nothing, the truck is right where they left it," Wiley said.

"Then I'll have to disqualifying them. I'll say they went out of bounds."

"Aren't you concerned?"

"That's your job. Send a search party out tomorrow. I'm sure it's just engine trouble," Eugene said.

"What if it's something else?" Wiley said.

"Like what, another bear attack?" Eugene said.

Beau heard what they were discussing. His eyes suddenly turned jet black. He interrupted them and spoke in a deep sinister voice as if possessed, "Something is eating the competition."

"Excuse me son?" Eugene said.

Then Beau's body released from the momentary occupation. His voice and face returned to normal. "I was out there in the woods today taking pictures. Please don't tell my parents that I cut class. Anyway, I saw a strange shadowy figure walking around. I've seen it before there.

Here, look at these photographs." Beau played back the camera memory card.

"Oh my, that's odd. Maybe Blaze is right. Can you email these to me?" Wiley said.

Eugene rolled his eyes and approached the lectern. "I'd like to get started. Folks, quiet please."

The crowd stilled, as camera lights created a spotlight on him.

"Welcome to the awards ceremony of the fiftieth Annual Stray Oaks Fishing Tournament. First, I'd like to thank the volunteers and sponsors who organized the event. Second, I'd like to thank our contestants for assisting with the catch and release program. We will return all these lovely specimens in the aquarium to their homes without harm. Third, I'd like to thank Calvary Chapel for graciously allowing usage of their property." Eugene clapped and the audience followed. "Unfortunately, one of the contestants went out of bounds. Marshal, please remove number eight from the score board."

Kenny drew a red line through Morty's name. The crowd murmured in disbelief.

Buck turned around to Vernon seated behind him. "Looks like your odds of winning just improved."

"Yours too," Vernon said.

"Marshal please tally all the final scores," Eugene said.

Kenny filled in the totals for all the anglers except Buck. Vernon's score was the highest, at seventy-pounds-three-ounces. Buck's score without his last fish was sixty-pounds-two-ounces. He needed a minimum of ten-pounds-four-ounces to win.

The crowd became restless as they realized that the lunker was much more than ten pounds. Cameras flashed at the scoreboard.

"Come on Mayor, we're dying to know, how much does the trophy fish weigh?" Blaze said.

Eugene hesitated and leaned into the microphone. "It's a new record for this competition. The final fish weighs twenty-pounds-five-ounces bringing Mr. Boudreaux's total score to eighty-pounds-seven-ounces."

Buck jumped up, "Yes!" He turned around to Vernon and reached to shake his hand. "Sorry mate, better luck next time."

The crowd cheered, and chanted his name. Camera lights flashed sporadically creating a strobe light effect.

"That would make Mr. Boudreaux our tenth straight winner. Buck, could you come up here please?" Eugene said.

"Certainly Mayor." Buck leaned down and sensuously kissed Kacie, cupping her cheeks between his palms. He lingered for a while caressing her lips with his. As he pulled away to step into the aisle, he grabbed her hand clenching firmly. He kissed her fingers repeatedly before letting go.

Kacie blew him a kiss and smiled as he looked back at her. Buck approached the lectern.

Eugene held the crystal obelisk trophy in the air. People clapped and cheered.

"Buck Boudreaux, as mayor of Stray Oaks, may I present to you this trophy in recognition of winning our fiftieth annual fishing tournament."

Buck accepted the trophy glancing down at the etched words and studied them, as a tear formed in the corner of his eye. He wiped the tear, seeming humbled by the experience and reached out to shake Eugene's hand.

They paused smiling at the cameras as bulbs flashed.

"Thank you Mayor and the good people of Stray Oaks. I would like to thank my sponsors for their continued support. Without them, this would not be possible. And please do not forget that my signature lure line and instructional DVDs make great Christmas gifts available at Fishermen's World. In addition, I would like to thank my family for everything they do. And special thanks to my coangler for helping me land this baby, Skeeter please take a bow." Buck clapped.

Skeeter stood. "No problem Hoss, anytime."

"Buck, tell us how you landed that fish," Blaze said.

"Well, we looked for running bait schools and followed them. Then we worked the top water, hard. I knew it would be won out in the open. It just took a little expertise and a whole lot of patience."

Beau coughed and thought about the hypocrisy. He had nothing to gain by exposing his father as a fraud. He remained silent to keep the peace. Graduation would come soon enough.

"What will you do next?" Blaze said.

"This win gives me enough points to secure a spot in the Southern Trail Championship, so I will be busy preparing for that. Also I have an autobiography coming out in a few weeks."

"Sounds exciting!" Blaze said.

Eugene stepped up to the lectern to interrupt Blaze's monopolizing of the spotlight. "I'm sure our anglers are hungry. Everyone please enjoy some barbecue from our sponsor, Fourchette's Bar & Grill. Oh, and please vote for me as mayor. I promise to continue to provide quality family events just like this. Thanks again for coming out."

CHAPTER 7

Five months later, piles of shipping boxes sat next to the reception counter unopened. A thin layer of dust coated the tops. The boxes were in the way of customers trying to access the checkout counter. One patron even stubbed her toe on the corner, resulting in a verbal tirade unusual for inside the quiet library.

Kacie normally was a taskmaster and a neatness freak. Those boxes would have been broken down and the books shelved, but ever since the bad news, nothing remained the same. This was not a typical workday; it was the very short rest of her life.

The cancer changed everything. No longer could Kacie live day after day tending to the needs of others at the expense of herself. Nor could she fight an invisible foe coursing through her veins. Her own cells rebelled against her body. The symptoms of the illness were apparent and soon everyone else would know the bitter truth.

Bad news like this would spread fast across the small town as Blaze exclaimed it from the highest mountain top.

Buck's career would suffer, as his corporate sponsors questioned the stability of his sobriety and feared the worst.

Kacie would not be there to mediate between father and son. What would become of Beau's bright future?

No one would be there to manage the minute details that Kacie labored over daily. She wondered if anyone would even notice she was gone. Those things haunted her now that time had turned against her.

The boxes waited for attention, but they would have to wait even longer still.

A cool breeze washed through her body in a wave. It prickled parts of her extremities. A sensation of calm came over her like the effects of medication. Something soothed her ailing body, quietly slipping past.

A sparrow caught her attention perched on the back of the porch swing. It stared at her curiously through the imperfect glass of the historic window. It chirped a few times and then broke out in spring song. The brief melody of happy sounds made her feel content. The internal fear subsided. She let go of the binding chains; the obligations, the regrets and freed herself. Her remaining time on Earth would not be spent drowning in abject misery.

The phone distracted her. "Chaisson Library," Kacie said.

"Hey hun, I talked with Wilbur last night. He came by after his shift to see the kid and drop off some money," Lillian said.

"Did you patch things up yet?"

"He admitted what I already knew, that he started an affair with some guy six months ago. He said it was an accident, and that he had never done that before."

"Are they in love?"

"Why does that matter?" Lillian said.

"Well, a fling is one thing but an intimate connection is something entirely different."

"That's what Remy says. Oops; I wasn't going to tell you."

"So you are dating Coach?"

"We have talked about my situation and he has been so understanding and supportive," Lillian said.

"I know that it's nice to have someone pay attention to you, but you shouldn't be discussing your marriage with another man."

"He really cares about me," Lillian said.

"Then I guess you aren't planning on staying married for long."

"Maybe Wilbur and I just need a mutual break for a while."

"Marriage is supposed to be a full-time union of two people in love who want to be together. Not an arrangement for cheating."

"Kacie what's wrong? You usually don't preach."

"I don't mean to be rude to you. I'm sure you will work it out in time."

The front doorbell jiggled and Adele entered with a smile.

"Can I call you back later?" Kacie hung up without waiting for an answer.

Adele seamlessly glided into the reception area. Her long skirt did not flutter as she moved. She held coffee in to-go cups. "Have a mocha latte dear. It will make you feel better."

"Thanks. What brings you in today?" Kacie said.

"Come sit with me on the sofa and chat for a while," Adele said.

Kacie plopped onto the worn-out cushions. Her body, which was five pounds lighter than a week ago sunk into the antique springs.

"So how is Buck doing after his tenth win? You must be proud," Adele said.

"I would have been just as happy for Vernon to win the tournament, but you know that. How is he?"

"I didn't know you still cared. He's fine dear, but thanks for asking."

"Has this sofa always been so uncomfortable? I swear, I feel like my bones are breaking in half," Kacie said.

"I'm worried about you. Have you lost weight? Your complexion looks a bit yellow. That's why I brought you more of my homemade soup."

Kacie paused, sipped her coffee and politely blurted, "I'm dying." It was the first time she spoke those words aloud. The three syllables hung heavy in the air, but she suddenly felt unburdened by the admission.

"I know dear, and I'm sorry for that."

"But how can you know?" Kacie said.

Adele laughed. "I'm a witch, remember? I just wish there was something I could do to change the circumstances."

"Please, you can't tell anyone. No one knows yet. Not even Buck."

"Don't worry yourself. I'm good at keeping secrets." Adele leaned back and adjusted her skirt. "May I ask you a question? I'm just curious; if it wasn't for the accident would you have married Vernon back then?"

Kacie focused on the plastic lid of the polystyrene container. She knew the answer to the question, she thought about it numerous times. Still, she was silent. Her eyes started to water.

"It's okay, dear. I already know the answer. I can see it on your face."

"I don't understand why you are asking me this now. Why does it matter?"

Adele sighed and took Kacie's hands, holding them gently in her palms. "Forgive me for being blunt, but if you have limited time left, don't you want to be happy? You should be happy, no matter what."

Between a pair of griffin bookends stood picture books of the great masters. Beau loved to read the personal story of the artists behind their work. The journey to creating art was often more interesting to him than the results produced. He understood the energy expended in birthing a piece and the emotion contained in the critic's review; in today's world, professional success hinged on public opinion fueled by social media.

Beau cared about what others thought of him, but he did not try to control their perceptions. Observers deserved the freedom to draw their own conclusions about his talents. He respected all points of view, even the ones contrary to his own opinion, but rather than waste time on what he could not control, he focused on producing good solid work.

Each photograph hanging on the wall in his room was a moment captured on film visible through his eyes. The viewfinder framed a composition that he deemed worthy, immortalizing time.

To become a budding artist meant exposing himself to possible ridicule. That part was easy for him, because he endured parental judgments throughout his childhood. He developed skin thick as armor to shield the negative comments oddly veiled as constructive criticism.

His parents did not understand the intangible, and could not assign value to art. They believed art was what people who could not master mathematics or science did with their spare time as a hobby. Small-town environments bred their closed minds.

Farmers had little use for art. Their livelihoods depended on producing top-grade crops measured by the pound. But like a farmer, planting a seed and nurturing it to fruition required faith in something intangible. The eventual crop born out of nothingness formed from the power of the imagination, as an idea became something tangible.

Each photograph told a story of his energy poured into a subject resulting in his vision and later judged by people's emotional response. The subjective part of art scared him, but he did not take photographs to please others or to receive their praise. He endeavored to capture the perfect composition and record a moment in time just for himself.

Beau reclined on his bed with his laptop. He searched the Internet for information about Savannah, Georgia. He had never visited there before.

In advertisements, it seemed like a cozy southern town with rich history and charm. Forsyth Park had live oak trees draped in Spanish moss and a three-tiered water fountain as a centerpiece posed for capture. Horse-drawn carriages, shotgun row houses and the beach lighthouse beckoned him to frame each subject with accurate lighting.

While he was surfing, an instant message from Riley popped up in the lower corner of the computer screen: *Did you talk yet?*

Beau typed a simple reply: *No.*

Riley continued: *Dude, call her. It's prom night. I'll pick you up in one hour.*

Beau leaned back on his pillow with his arms folded above his head, staring at the ceiling. He exhaled a deep breath knowing that Riley was right. He knew he had to call Saylor eventually.

Communication ceased since their last argument. The airwaves were dead for months. It would remain that way until Beau apologized or explained his out-of-character behavior.

He knew what to expect from Saylor, the arctic chill of her conditional love. He got the same response from his parents when he did not do as they wished. The silent undertone of disapproval was common in his house. Beau had almost built-up a tolerance to the rapid temperature changes.

However, Beau understood why she was upset. She normally got her way. To please her he went along with whatever she wanted until now.

Beau wanted to tell Saylor the truth. He needed to be honest with her. She deserved that much. There would not be a fairy tale ending after graduation. Five states would separate them in distance, although more than miles would keep them apart.

Saylor had done nothing wrong. The fight was his fault, and for that his heart ached.

He saw that life was pulling them in separate directions. She wanted a career with marriage and children. He wanted freedom.

She deserved more than what he could give. One day a knight would ride up to her door, it just would not be him. The ironic sound of his father telling him so that day on the boat rang in his ears.

Tonight was the senior prom, a rite of passage and the final social gathering before graduation. Saylor required a handsome gentleman escort, so she could shine as the ultimate prom queen.

While together, Beau could pretend that nothing happened, smile and try desperately to make it up to her. That would only delay the pending demise of their relationship. He owed her the truth. With his mind settled on expressing his true feelings, he dialed the number.

Saylor answered her private phone line on the second ring without speaking.

"I'm sorry about our fight. I know you're pissed, you should be, but I'd like to talk about it tonight at prom," Beau said.

"Oh, you still want to go with me? I wasn't sure. Usually real couples talk at least once a day and are upset when they don't. Gauging by your silence for months, I would think we had broken up already."

"Of course, I want to escort you to prom. We've been together for a long time, and you know what I'm dealing with at home. They're making me crazy. It's not about you and I'm sorry if you feel hurt by my distance of late."

"Fine, what time can I expect you? You are picking me up aren't you?" Saylor said.

"Riley's on his way to get me now. We'll see you in a bit after we pick up Meghan."

Saylor hung up the phone without an acknowledgment, though the force of the receiver slamming into the cradle said it all.

In a rush, Beau hopped in the shower lathering in a quick once over. He got out, quickly dried his body and dumped the tuxedo-bag contents on the bed. He hated formal attire; there were too many parts for his liking.

Kacie walked by his door with a basket of folded laundry. She placed towels on a shelf in the hall linen closet. Carrying the plastic basket, she curiously stuck her head in the doorway. "Can I help you with that?"

Beau stood in front of a dresser mirror fumbling with the bow tie tails. "I hate these things. Why can't I wear a clip-on? No one will know the difference."

"I'll fix it for you, have some patience." Kacie untied the jumbled mess, correctly tying the tails. "There, that's better." She smiled.

"Mom, what am I supposed to do when you're not around any longer to take care of me?" Beau said.

Kacie paused gazing at the black satin fabric. Her fingers froze in place, as she realized the irony of his words. "I'll always be around, when you need me. That's what good mothers do." She evaluated her work, tugging once more on a corner. Her eyes started to water. "You look very handsome son."

Beau kissed her on the cheek, "Thanks, mom. You're the best."

A horn sounded repeatedly in the yard. Beau ran to the window and saw Riley sitting in his car waving. "Riley's here, I've got to motor. See you later. Don't wait up."

"Can't you all come in for some photos? I never get to see you dressed up and prom is only once," Kacie said.

"It's late and we still have to pick up the girls. Besides they'll have a photographer at the gym." Beau ran down the stairs.

"Don't stay out too late. Do you need any money? I've got an extra twenty." The quiet of an empty house answered Kacie's pleas for attention.

Beau was already outside, getting into Riley's car.

When he did not respond, Kacie sat on the bed looking down at the floorboards.

After picking up the girls, Riley pulled into the school parking lot and parked in the back. He wore a rented black tuxedo with a ruffled shirt, a red and white striped cummerbund around his waist and a red tie. His date Meghan wore a black-and-white chiffon dress with a red satin sash tied in a bow.

"I can't believe you two are wearing school colors even to prom, how festive," Beau said from the backseat of the sports coupe. "Not that you don't look beautiful tonight, Riley."

"Thanks a lot Beau, I thought for a minute you were going to compliment me on my stunning beauty," Meghan said.

"You do look marvelous too, Meghan, but you know that Riley is the real queen," Beau said.

"Why thank you kind sir," Riley said glancing in the rearview mirror at Saylor, staring silently out the side window. He gave a bottle of cheap wine in a brown bag to Beau. "Here, maybe this will help melt the ice princess."

Beau offered the bottle to Saylor. "Would you like some before Riley contaminates it with his cooties?"

Saylor ignored him, continuing to stare in a fixed gaze not even blinking.

"All right suit yourself, but I'm going to partake in this fine vintage from just last year," Beau said.

Meghan powdered her nose. "Are you guys ready to crash this party?"

"Sure, let's book. I can't wait to enjoy another school function," Beau said.

It was nighttime, but students were still arriving late from dinner. Flashing colored lights were visible through the upper-level windows of the gymnasium. Muffled music blared from inside the walls.

Saylor trailed behind the group, wearing a pink sequined dress with a side slit. She looked amazing even though the style of the dress was too mature for her age.

Beau tried to hold her hand. "Hey, are you going to speak to me at all?"

She stared at him silently with the cold eyes of death.

"By the way, you look smashing," Beau tried to warm her with compliments.

"Thanks, you look handsome too," Saylor said.

"Please forgive me, please, please?" Beau begged for a reprieve hoping to make her laugh.

"Fine, forget it." She walked off ahead of him.

Riley and Meghan waited patiently holding hands by the door.

"Have you lovebirds made up yet?" Riley held the door open for them.

"Riley, go get bent!" Saylor walked in first.

The room decorations were magical. Blue and green paper streamers hung from a metal grid canopy over the basketball court. Twinkling white holiday lights draped across the frame. Helium balloon sprays lined the perimeter walls. The underwater theme that was Saylor's idea turned out spectacular.

Jennifer collected prom tickets and greeted them at the reception table. "Hey guys, I was wondering where you were. Put on name tags please, so people can vote for you."

Riley drew a smiley face on his sticky label. "To hell with them if they don't know who I am by now."

"You're such a renegade," Beau said.

"Don't forget to cast your vote for king and queen before eight o'clock," Jennifer said.

"Stupid question, can we vote for ourselves?" Beau said.

"Very funny, but you shouldn't have too Beau," Jennifer said.

Marvin stood behind a folding table playing compact discs. He volunteered to disk jockey not interested in escorting a date, since so many girls wanted his attention. However, he noticed Saylor as soon as she entered and winked at her with a warm smile.

She blew him a kiss in return, trying to make Beau jealous.

On the side of the court arranged in clusters were small bistro tables and stack chairs. The girls sat down immediately to gossip about the dresses the other girls were wearing.

"I'll get some refreshments for everybody," Riley said.

"Hey wait up, I'll join you," Beau said.

At the refreshment table, Ms. Chillingham dispensed fruit punch and sugar cookies.

"Can I have a dirty martini with an olive, and whatever my friend wants?" Riley said.

"Very funny Riley. How's about some fruit punch instead?" Ms. Chillingham said.

"Is it spiked? If not, I can fix that," Riley said.

"Riley, don't you dare! I'm watching you and I'm not the only chaperone here. I'll tell Coach to keep an eye on you."

"Geez, Ms. C ... I'm just messing around," Riley said.

Riley and Beau walked back to the table carrying the drinks. Before they made it all the way back, Beau stopped him.

"I've decided to go to Savannah," Beau said.

"That's awesome! Does Saylor know?" Riley said.

"I'm going to tell her the truth tonight, whenever I can find the right moment."

"Sucks to be you dude. Let me know before you do, so I can take cover."

When they got back to the table, Walter and Jennifer had joined the group. They wore all-white formal wear. Walter wore a white tuxedo with crème trim on the lapels and Jennifer modeled a floor length white-lace dress with a scandalous open back.

"Saylor are you excited about the big night? We dressed in honor of your engagement," Jennifer said.

"What specifically should I be excited about?" Saylor said.

Meghan sat behind Saylor, motioning for Jennifer to shut up.

"You know what we talked about, the big proposal from Beau," Jennifer said.

"Why don't you ask him all about it yourself?" Saylor said.

Beau looked confused, unaware of what they were discussing. "I'm sorry, did I miss something?"

Marvin played a mix of popular tunes fading from one song to the next as students danced.

"Oh, I love this song. Riley, can we dance?" Meghan dragged Riley to the crowded dance floor on center court. They pushed in between other couples.

The paper streamers hung low enough to touch. Some students kicked around stray balloons on the floor like balls. Others tried to stomp them out.

"Would you like to dance?" Beau said.

Saylor nodded and got up from the chair carrying a bad attitude.

They pushed through the crowd to find a free spot on the floor.

"We need to talk. There is something I really want to say." Beau screamed over the music.

"About what exactly?" Saylor was curious if he was finally going to pop the question.

"There is no easy way to say this, so here goes. I got accepted to art school and decided to go."

While still dancing, Saylor seemed emotionless. This was not the news she wanted to hear. "So what's the big deal?"

"It's in Georgia," Beau said.

Saylor stopped dancing and looked at him perturbed. "What are you saying Beau? Spit it out."

Beau stopped dancing too. "The school is in Savannah, so I won't be moving with you to New York."

Saylor looked sad and then angry. She ran off the dance floor holding back tears.

Beau ran after her, grabbing her arm. "Wait, and there is something else that I've been trying to tell you."

"What now?" Saylor said.

"I took Amber for ice cream before the tournament ceremony, and a few times afterward."

Saylor's eyes turned red, and she squinted at him. "You did what?"

"Hear me out. It was just to shut up my mom. Don't worry, I truly can't stand the girl."

"How could you humiliate me like that?"

"It's not that big of a deal? No one saw us together from school," Beau said.

Saylor broke free from his grip and ran to the girl's restroom crying.

"Saylor wait!" Beau yelled at her, but did not give chase.

Meghan watched the conversation and ran after her.

In the girl's restroom, Saylor stood by the makeup counter crying.

Meghan handed her some tissue. "What's wrong?"

"He's not going to New York with me."

"Why not?"

Amber walked in to use the facilities at the wrong time. She noticed Saylor, but pretended to ignore her.

"It's because of her." Saylor pointed at Amber.

Amber approached them. "What did I do?"

Saylor grabbed the cup of fruit punch from Meghan's hand and hurled it all over Amber's lavender dress. "Now that's better, what an improvement. Too bad I don't have any pig's blood."

"Oh my God, look at my dress! What have I ever done to you?" Amber wiped off the fabric with paper towels.

"Saylor, that's a bit harsh, you ruined her dress," Meghan said.

"Why does everyone care about this loser? Besides, she ruined my life!" She ran out the restroom in a huff.

When the other girls came out of the restroom, Beau was waiting by the door.

Marvin played their song at Beau's request. He had also picked the wrong time.

"Would you like to dance with me? They're playing our song." Beau grabbed her forearm and pulled Saylor out on the dance floor. It was a slow song, so he hugged her and whispered. "Please let it go, people are watching. And it's not what you think. You are blowing this way out of proportion."

After the song finished, Saylor quietly returned to the table. While everyone else enjoyed the rest of the night, she sat there in silence looking sad.

Amber came out of the restroom, though her dress looked the same. Her face was red from crying. She ran to her friend's table and calmly explained what had happened in the restroom to Cody, Jim and Sally. Embarrassed, she wanted to go home. They complied with her request and left without making a scene.

The school photographer worked through the long line of students and Jennifer and Meghan dragged Saylor and the boys to immortalize the event. The backdrop had a shark with a giant gaping mouth surrounded by seaweed. The boys took a group photo standing backwards and then individuals with their respective girlfriends. Saylor and Beau went last, although she did not smile.

When the group finished with pictures, Coach Ducet gave the voting results to Marvin to announce the winners. He stopped the music and spoke into a microphone. "Can I have your attention please?"

The students quit dancing. Everyone stopped talking and formed a circle around the dance floor.

"I'd like to announce our winners. If I call your name, please come up. By an overwhelming margin and no surprise, prom king is ... Beau Boudreaux and prom queen is of course, Saylor Landry."

Everyone clapped and cheered.

"Oh gosh, that is us." Beau held out his hand to Saylor and walked her into the middle of the crowd. Marvin placed paper crowns on their heads and played a slow song.

They danced together, standing close, but had never been so far apart.

"So I guess this means you won't be proposing to me?" Saylor said.

Beau paused before responding, carefully choosing his words. "I'm sorry, but not at this time."

Saylor stopped dancing even though the song continued. Shock overcame her entire being as the truth settled. She lashed back at him unable to process rejection. "I can't believe I wasted all these years on you, the best years of my life. I knew you weren't good enough for me. I could have had any guy."

"That's a little melodramatic, but then again you are the original drama queen."

"You jerk. I hate you Beau Boudreaux!" Saylor ran off toward the double doors, past Kelvin who was picking up empty cups.

Everyone stared quietly at Beau making him uncomfortable. He threw the crown on the floor. "Next time pick someone more deserving than me. I hate this place anyway."

Saylor slammed her fists into the exterior doors with all her might, knocking flower petals off her wrist corsage.

Outside the night sky stormed a violent rage of wind and water. She ran into the parking lot kicking off her rhinestone pumps. Tears washed makeup down her cheeks and rain ruined her hairdo. The wet dress became heavy, clinging to her fragile frame. She screamed and cried all alone barefoot in the rain.

The next afternoon Saylor arrived at Riley's house demanding that he drive her some place. He complied, being too tired from the late night out to argue. Things went beyond bad after they left the prom. Saylor refused to talk to Beau and spent the night at Meghan's house. In between crying her eyes out, asking *why me* and drinking too much alcohol, she concocted a plan of revenge. All that drama, lack of sleep and anger was influencing her every command. Riley drove down Route 3 as she steered his car from the passenger seat.

"Where are we going anyway?" Riley said.

"Just drive!" Saylor said.

"Are you going to at least tell me what is in the garbage bag?"

Saylor giggled, untying the drawstring. Inside were individual rolls of toilet paper. She took one out and held it before Riley's face. "Turn down Creek Lane."

"Why? That's the Crenshaw's property."

"Brilliant Gump!" Saylor lowered the visor flap to check her hair in the mirror, which was a mess.

"Oh man, I have a really bad feeling about this."

"Riley, you say that about everything."

"What if they are at home?"

"They won't be. On a morning like this, Mr. Crenshaw should be out fishing. See, the boat is gone. And Ms. Crenshaw will be doing witchy things, whatever that is."

Riley slowed the car down to a crawl. "Yeah, like turning us into toads."

"I swear you've got to get out more. Pull over there behind the fence so no one can see your car from the road."

"Yes, Captain." Riley parked the red coupe on the edge of the property behind an overgrown chain-link fence. The Kudzu twisted around the galvanized metal forming a wall of evergreen vines. "Why are we doing this to them?"

"Ever since Beau started hanging around that ex-con, he's been acting real weird."

"Well now that you mention it, he doesn't hang out with me afterschool at the lake any longer, but I don't take it personally. And I don't see what that has to do with the Crenshaws."

They got out of the car continuing the conversation in a soft whisper.

Riley did not want to be there afraid of capture, but he equally feared Saylor's wrath. Her pent-up anger needed a victim and he did not want to volunteer.

Last night was the worst night of Saylor's life, one to remember for all the wrong reasons. The alcohol she consumed afterward did not soothe the pain, leaving instead a massive headache. Coupled with the emotional drama, crying and vomiting, her body still twitched from the devastating experience.

Without giving it much thought, Saylor dressed in shorts, high-top shoes, a T-shirt and a baseball cap that spelled in rhinestones: *SEXY*.

Riley wore a sweatshirt over jeans. The white block letters on the front of the shirt spelled: *SOHS*.

"You may want to flip that shirt inside out, unless you want someone to see where you go to high school."

"Good idea." Riley quickly reversed the shirt. "I'd rather not go to jail."

The Crenshaw house stood on a cleared area of the vast property. However, the tall fence and front yard trees blocked it from view of the highway. The ground cover, a mixture of grass and weeds, had pine needles scattered about mostly congregated at the tree bases. It looked as though no one ever raked the yard, allowing the leaves to fall where they may.

"Wish I had a firecracker right now to blow up their stupid mailbox," Saylor said.

"Gosh girl, you're hell on wheels."

"No, I'm hell in heels, and don't you forget it." Saylor flipped the passenger seat forward to retrieve the black bag. She looked up at the slender trees surrounding the decrepit house. "These trees are perfect, but I don't know if I can throw that high. Good thing you're here."

"I just thought you wanted me as a cell mate."

Saylor dragged the bag on the ground. It overflowed with rolls. She commandeered them from her mother's extreme coupon shopping excursions, stored in the basement. The stuffed bag hardly put a dent in the remaining supply.

Riley got nervous the closer they walked toward the house. "Seriously, what if someone is home?"

"Do you see any vehicles around? Besides, that's half the fun of doing this potentially getting caught."

"I'll remember that when old lady Crenshaw has the barrel of a shotgun stuck in your pretty face."

Saylor handed him a roll. "Just shut up and throw long."

Without thinking about it, Riley pitched high into the air as commanded. The sun was out, but the air was dry. The spool reached the top of a limb as Riley held on to the end of the paper. The tail billowed gently as the projectile succumbed to an invisible force. Its velocity halted by gravity. The roll tumbled down, falling faster until plummeting on the ground.

"Happy? Can we go now?"

"I'm just getting started. Finish off the bag." Saylor ran around the thick trunk of an oak, wrapping paper like a candy cane stripe. The tissue spiraled across the bark diagonally terminating at the roots.

Riley continued to lob the spindles as fast as he could so they could get out of there. Like an ironic homecoming, he filled the branches with sanitary paper made from pulverized trees.

Saylor giggled as she danced around, tripping once on a projected root knot. Still semi-intoxicated from last night, she raged out of control. She needed more excitement, a spoiled child with a voracious appetite for adrenalin. Part of her need for attention was because her parents were never home. They worked as traveling craft show artists going from town to town, leaving her in charge of her little brother.

Riley did his best to placate her unstable emotions.

A small garden surrounded by railroad ties waited for invasion close to the porch. In the center of the untrimmed plants, a wire metal stand displayed a mirrored gazing ball. A malformed shape appeared in the glass. Intrigued by her own reflection, Saylor laughed wickedly. She kicked the ball as hard as she could. It shot in the air and crashed against the porch railing. Tiny fragments of blue-mirrored glass descended on the grass. Shattered remnants of something once beautiful lay in ruin with no hope of patching.

"Woe dude, knock it off. A high school prank is one thing, but I draw the line at vandalism," Riley said.

"Go get bent! I'm just having a little fun." Saylor pounced on the pieces breaking them into tiny glitter.

"Let's go Miss Crazy. I think you've had enough fun for one day." Riley tried to usher her back to the car, but she darted off toward the backyard. She skipped and laughed a sinister sound that gave Riley an uneasy feeling. He chased after her unamused.

Saylor stopped dead in her tracks when she saw the cemetery by the woods. "Oh my God, they even have dead people in the yard, how creepy." She ran down the worn path toward the headstones.

"Wait a minute don't go in there, that's really sacrilegious. I don't think it's a good idea to go messing with corpses, especially from this family."

Saylor entered the fenced area perusing the markers. The largest one belonged to Earl. Noticeable from a distance, its prominence sat high among the others. She sat on top of the manicured mound. "Oh zombie Earl, come ravage me. Wrap your skeletal arms around me and damn my soul."

Riley stood by the broken iron-gate, unsure if he wanted to enter. "This is really disrespectful. Sorry, I'm out of here. If you want a ride home, you better come now." He walked away in a huff, fed up with her antics.

"Wait for me, I'm coming you buzzkill!" Saylor walked toward Riley offering her hand as if to shake. Once in contact distance, she sprinted off toward the woods. "Ha, ha, ha … psych!"

"Look, I'm not going to chase you all day. I want to go home and go to sleep."

Saylor darted through a clearing in the trees. The meandering path continued into the forest. Once inside, it hosted a new world to explore.

Riley hesitated to go after her, but he could not leave without her. He mustered the courage deep within to ignore the red flags swarming in his mind, memories of his mother chiding him about the Creepler. Instead, he focused on doing whatever was necessary to get them out of the woods.

Riley strode in several feet to murky darkness. He looked back at the clearing, but it disappeared. Entombed in a labyrinthine puzzle, all he saw was an endless mass of green vegetation.

A foreboding feeling came over him. In the still air nothing moved. In the distance, lyrical sounds of Saylor traipsing through the thicket caught his attention. She frolicked about deeper into the forest unaware that they were not alone.

Saylor came upon a fawn lapping a spumescent substance at the creek. She hid behind a tangled grove and watched. Its butterscotch coat intermixed with ivory spots seemed to pulsate and change position. Each runty hair fiber protruded on its back, as a cottony tail fluttered nervously.

The baby deer had an angelic face. Saylor was close enough to see long black eyelashes sweeping over glassy eyes. The onyx sockets reflected infinitesimal objects.

The fawn became motionless, wary of danger. Its expressionless gaze shifted to agitated panic. It galloped across the creek, splashing water trying to flee.

"Don't run away little one. I'm not going to hurt you," Saylor said.

Laden with the rank odor of rotten flesh decomposing in the sun, the air quality changed. The impudent stench choked her. She heard the sound of male Cicadas. The sky went dark as a heavy rock smashed the back the back of her skull, knocking off the baseball cap. The booming thud rang in her ears, before succumbing to unconsciousness. Her lineal frame responded to the affront by collapsing.

Riley cowered behind a tree. His body convulsed in fright, incredulous of the grotesque creature before him. He gasped, covering his mouth to conceal his location.

The Creepler dragged Saylor away by one arm. Her pliant body trailed through the muck, soiling her clothing.

The back of the monster had a pronged main fin extending from its cranium and terminating at the tail end. The spikes connected by a scalloped webbed membrane stood erect. Scabrous skin changed color with the environment, shifting in texture and tone.

Riley saw a bipedal animal with pairs of limbs, but it was not human. The anamorphous figure resembled nothing he had ever encountered. Whatever it was, carried Saylor from the creek back to its lair.

Precious minutes slipped away as the weight of Riley's dilemma confounded his exhausted brain. Powerless to overcome such a formidable foe, he did not want to lose sight of Saylor. Without any weapon to defend himself and unable to comprehend his opponent's capabilities, he decided to go for help.

Disoriented by the circling trees, Riley traced his steps back to the beginning. The Crenshaw house had to be in the opposite direction of the creek. He cleared his mind of all thought, closed his eyes and envisioned a path to freedom. With calm deep breaths, he modulated his heart rate lowering his blood pressure. The meditation techniques he used in Yoga helped him regain his composure. He imagined Coach's voice telling him: *there is nothing to fear, you can do this.*

With new resolution to survive, Riley's body animated. He ran as fast as possible, darting past trees, pushing through thickets, jumping over boulders, occasionally glancing over his shoulder. Ahead, he saw sunlight emblazing the path to safety.

Clean air wet his tongue, a thirst longed for quenching. A few steps from the clearing, his spirit lifted. Then his ankle cracked, forced askew by festooning vines amassed in a clump. The ball of his tennis shoe wedged under a contrary knot. As his foot remained stationary, the rest of his body tumbled down hard, smacking the ground. His mouth tasted moist dirt.

Positioned on its side, Riley's head rested. Warm red moisture expelled from his forehead. Rays of sunlight extinguished as the elusive escape retreated, like a drawn window shade blocking the promise of hope.

Later that day through slits in her eyes, Saylor saw crimson liquid encrusted on her eyelashes. A gouge in the back of her head left her hair matted from dried blood, which cascaded in all directions.

Semiconscious without the ability to move much, her head had just enough freedom to glance down at her body tied to a tree by vines. They crisscrossed and circled the trunk, binding her limbs in a standing position.

Alone in an arbor made from palmetto leaves, the makeshift shelter confined. It would deflect rain, but not shield temperature fluctuations. Evening approached bringing with it night terrors. She felt sleepy, her head splintered from a concussion. Intense pain caused her to black out again.

Her mind drifted to graduation day and a high school gymnasium full of seniors dressed in gowns. Instead of the typical ceremonial garments, these were evergreen robes with hoods. Everyone sat in circular rows of metal stack chairs facing the central lectern. The empty bleachers held dark shadows.

Saylor looked around, but could not see any faces. The hoods contained only darkness. One of her classmates stepped up to the lectern. Revealed under the spotlight, she recognized Amber's face who recited a Valedictorian speech.

Her shrill voice grated Saylor's nerves. Instead of talking about their bright futures ahead, Amber spoke in an aggrieved tone about damnation. She stared directly at Saylor, as if they were having an intimate conversation, though she could not understand her words. The context of her undiscernible speech sliced like knives. Each syllable inflicted pain, cutting tender flesh.

The other students remained motionless and silent.

Saylor looked down to realize she was naked. Exposed for all to see, her pristine body had a huge belly; a demilune sack widened from her pale torso under the rib cage. Something inside gyrated. She felt it moving around. The weight of the creature pressed on her bladder, causing tepid yellow liquid to flow uncontrollably from below.

Amber continued to speak, but now the words were audible. "You are worthless thrash, who doesn't deserve to live. No one ever liked you, least of all Beau."

The words echoed in Saylor's head, repeatedly.

The malevolent creature clawed her insides. It burned and stung. She tried to scream. Her vocal cords clenched, sputtering under duress.

Amber spoke again looking directly at Saylor. "How long can you hide the past?"

Saylor's mind drifted back to the time when her parents adopted a Romanian toddler who needed a good home. Before she could voice her objections, Trenton arrived.

Five years her junior, Trenton quickly learned English although he mispronounced her name. Late at night when a thunderstorm scared him, he whispered: *Shay, can I get in bed with you?*

Saylor had sinus problems and customarily slept on her side. Trenton frequently climbed in the tiny twin-size bed, snuggling close to her backside. He liked to drape his arm across her waist, hugging her.

Now a teenager, this behavior still continued although Saylor thought it was inappropriate. One night she told him: *he was too old to sleep in her bed*. The dose of reality proved too much for his fragile self-esteem. He cried, claiming she did not love him like a real brother.

That night after the storm ceased, Saylor awoke to find Trenton's hand on her chest. He was asleep. Alarmed by the situation, she laid there in silence and kept their secret.

Suddenly, Saylor's mind returned to the imagined graduation.

Beau stood behind the lectern next to Amber holding her hand. Their faces were visible, though they did not speak. All at once, the entire class turned toward Saylor. Their shrouded faceless figures stared at her pregnant naked body covered in blood.

At the Crenshaw house, Vernon turned off Route 3 trailering the bass boat. As he entered the gate moving slowly down the bumpy driveway, he saw the toilet paper draped over the trees. "Great, Maw is going to be real angry when she gets home. I better clean it up before she sees it."

He parked the truck around back and went inside the house to get a garbage bag. When he came out the front door, he noticed the car parked off to the side by the fence. Upon closer inspection, he did not recognize the coupe but assumed it belonged to a high school student from the various window stickers. "Damn kids!"

Vernon walked around picking up all the paper he could on the ground and unwrapped the tree trunks. He used a garden hose to shoot water high in the air to blast the paper he could not reach. The fragments caked on limbs stuck in between pine needles.

Adele made an impromptu weekend visit to Annie's house in Bakersfield. Vernon questioned why she needed to go out-of-town so suddenly. Adele said: *they had important things to discuss.*

Vernon hated being alone, although the voices in his head never left him alone. He frantically tried to hide the evidence of teenage mischief. Vernon thought about the possibility of Officer Aucoin paying a visit checking on his parole. The voices said: *what about the car? He will blame you.* Vernon silenced the nuisance, gaining control of his thoughts.

He noticed the broken gazing ball. "Awe shucks, now Maw is really going to be mad, Annie gave her that for her birthday." Vernon retrieved a broom and dustpan to clean the porch. The rest of the blue fragments stuck out easily against the green lawn.

Midnight hopped on the porch railing, carefully balancing on the handrail. Hunger overtook its disdain for Vernon. It *meowed* incessantly for food.

When Vernon finished cleaning the yard as best he could, he dumped some vittles into a stainless bowl for the cat. It sat on its haunches gingerly chewing the morsels.

The abandoned car meant that someone was still on the property. Vernon locked the house doors before he left to go fishing, and the interior remained untouched. The only other place that someone could be was in the woods. Vernon lit an oil lantern and quickly headed down the path. The sun was almost gone.

The narrow walkway meandered down the hill. He stopped at the gate of the cemetery to check there first. The markers were untouched. When he entered the woods, he almost passed by Riley's body slumped on the ground. Vernon knelt and shook him. "Hey kid, are you all right?"

Riley slowly raised his head off the ground, which had dirt and leaves stuck to the side of his face. "What happened?" He tried to sit up, but something had a hold of his leg. As he twisted his spine, he felt sharp pain. "Ouch, my ankle hurts!"

"Wait, let me help you. Just stay still." Vernon cut the constricting vines with a pocketknife. "Can you walk?"

"I don't know. What time is it?"

"Around seven in the evening."

"Is it still Saturday?" Riley said.

"Yes." Vernon offered a hand to help Riley to his feet. "Lean on me and take it slow."

Unsteady, Riley hopped on one foot afraid to put pressure on the injured leg. "I'm dizzy."

"What were you doing out here?"

Riley's sense of time and space slowly returned. "Mr. Crenshaw, I'm so sorry about your house. It wasn't my idea. I tried to stop Saylor, but she was out of control."

"Where is she?" Vernon said.

Riley stopped walking and turned to him with a desperate expression. "Oh God, I saw a monster dragging her away into the woods. I did not know what to do, so I ran for help. I tripped and everything went dark."

Vernon motioned for them to continue walking toward the house. "Monsters aren't real boy. I'm sure you just imagined it."

"No really, I saw this horrible thing. It smelled awful and made a weird noise."

"Let's get to the house. You need medical attention."

"I can't leave her here. Beau is going to kill me."

"Beau, oh yeah, isn't she his girlfriend?" Vernon said.

"Well after prom, that would depend on whom you ask."

Vernon carried Riley up the hill toward the house. All the while, the voices said: *Kill him, while no one is around to see.*

"Oh man, that really hurts. God, please don't let it be permanent."

"What's your name?" Vernon said.

"Riley sir, Riley Payne. My mom is the mayor's secretary."

The voices screamed: *We told you to kill him. The cop works for the mayor. Now you're in deep trouble.*

Once they reached the back porch, Riley sat on the steps clenching his ankle.

"I'll go inside and get you some water. Stay here."

"Don't worry, I'm not going anywhere."

Midnight approached Riley, rubbing against his side. It purred and arched its back, as Riley stroked it.

Vernon returned with a glass of ice water. "Drink it slowly."

Riley was so thirsty, he spilled most of it down his shirt, causing Midnight to scamper away.

"Can you call Beau?" Vernon said.

"What do you want me to say?"

"Just have him come here. Don't say anything else about the situation."

"My phone is in my car."

Vernon handed Riley his cell phone. "Use mine."

Riley nervously dialed the Boudreaux residence, trying to remember the number.

Kacie answered the phone after one ring, recognizing the number on caller ID.

"Ms. Boudreaux, this is Riley ma'am. May I speak with Beau please?" Riley covered the phone. "She's getting him."

"Give it to me." Vernon retrieved the phone and waited for Beau to answer.

"Look before you yell at me about prom—," Beau said.

"Beau this is Vern. Your friend Riley is at my house. I think he sprained his ankle."

"What's he doing there?"

"He and your girlfriend came to TP my house and now she's missing. Can you come over and help me search for her?"

"I'll be right there," Beau said.

"Let's keep this between us," Vernon said as he ended the call, returning the phone to his pocket. "Riley, can you drive?"

"I think so, my other leg is fine," Riley said.

Vernon went inside the kitchen to fill a freezer bag with ice. He placed it over the swollen ankle and secured it with tape. He handed Riley a damp towel to wipe off his face. "Let me help you to your car."

They hobbled along, taking short pauses. Vernon opened the unlocked car door, as Riley slid into the bucket seat. They carefully hoisted Riley's injured leg inside.

"Buckle up kid, and go straight to the hospital. Don't stop for anything."

"All right, and thanks Mr. Crenshaw. Tell Beau I'll call him later, and I'm sorry."

Riley took off in the car and noticed two cell phones in the passenger's seat with blinking lights. Riley picked up the yellow-and-black sport model and redialed the last caller.

An angry Lin answered the phone.

"Mom let me explain; I was horsing around with Beau at the lake and tripped on a rock. I think I sprained my ankle. I'm heading for the hospital now. Can you meet me there?

Lin screamed Vietnamese in his ear for several minutes before hanging up.

Riley dialed the next number on the list of recent calls and got whom he wanted. "Beau, oh dude, I'm so sorry. She's out of control man. I couldn't stop her."

"Calm down Riley and tell me what happened," Beau said.

"We did something really stupid, boy is she pissed at you."

"I'm sure, but what's new?'

"We rolled old lady Crenshaw's house, then Saylor trashed a lawn ornament."

"Sounds pretty juvenile," Beau said.

"She made fun of their cemetery. Then she ran into the woods. I followed her. The opening to the trees closed up and I couldn't find a way out," Riley said.

"Riley, you're not making any sense, what happened to Saylor?"

"It took her off into the woods. The Creepler has Saylor!"

On the back of the porch, Vernon lit another oil lantern. Thoughts raced in his mind about whether to radio Adele. If he told her what happened, she would be angry. If he did not tell her, the truth would come out and she'd be angry anyway.

If he could not find Saylor, her parents would call the sheriff. Wiley would show up with a team of search dogs to scour the property. *What if they found the Creepler?* The voices returned causing him to panic. Anxiety escalated to a critical point. He paced nervously.

Beau drove up, jerking the car to an abrupt stop. The headlights cast light beams down the path. He opened the rear door and Sampson gallivanted out. "I brought us some help." Beau held a birthday card in front of the dog's nose. It was from Saylor and smelled of her perfume. The dog only needed a few whiffs and charged off toward the woods.

"Have a lantern, it's getting dark," Vernon said.

"Sorry about all this Vern, I just hope we can find her."

Vernon patted him on the shoulder. "I know these parts well, don't worry."

They marched after Sampson holding up the light. Vernon had Adele's shotgun draped diagonally across his back. They called out Saylor's name as they walked.

The dog led them in a zigzag pattern around to the creek, then paused sniffing the ground near the bank after finding her baseball cap. It sat and looked up at Beau.

"What's this? Beau picked up the hat.

Sampson cocked his head to the side confused.

"Go on boy, follow the scent."

Sampson ran off into the darkness, meandering around trees, sometimes walking in circles. He stopped and sat down near the entrance to a cave.

"What in the world is this?" Beau said.

"Oh it's nothing, an ancient Indian burial tomb. We leave it alone out of respect."

"Have you ever been inside?"

"Once when Chester and me were kids, then my Paw scolded us and said to stay out, so we did. There is nothing inside but some skeletons."

"Sounds creepy, but how do you know she's not in there?"

"The dog would go in after her, wouldn't he?" Vernon said.

"That's true." Beau sat on a large boulder. "I've got to rest a minute. I'm still hung over from prom."

"What was that like? I didn't get to go to mine."

"Oh it was definitely a night to remember; alcohol, screaming, crying, name calling, embarrassment and then she slapped me in the face before running off into the rain."

"Sounds like fun," Vernon said.

"It's my fault, though. We wouldn't be here if I hadn't broken up with her. She's really angry with me, and taking it out on the wrong people."

"Let's keep searching, we'll find her."

The night dragged on, minutes slipped away one after the other. The forest hosted bizarre sounds of nocturnal animals foraging. They were not alone in the dark.

Sampson scurried about occasionally finding an interesting scent and then quickly lost it. Beau retrieved the birthday card from his back pocket, trying to spark his nose. The fragrance was not in the area. The trail turned cold.

They walked around in circles, exhausted. There was no sign of her anywhere, not another piece of clothing, blood or body part.

"Let's rest for the night, and start again at daybreak," Vernon said.

"Good idea, I'm beat." Beau leaned against the base of a tree. Sampson curled up at his feet, panting. For a while, they all slept.

The next morning, sunlight penetrated an opening between the leaves. The focused rays burned her fragile skin. Saylor tried to move out of the light. Her shoulder pressed against the tree bark, while tight vines constricted her limbs.

Hunger and thirst set in. A foreign object had grated the inside of her throat raw until it bled. An olive-shaded substance around her parched lips formed a crust. The torn corners of her mouth and jaw ached, as if held open for a long time by force.

A gentle tickling on her exposed skin was from an invader crawling around. She looked down to see a large hairy spider with yellow rings sitting on her bare distended abdomen. She tried to scream at the repulsive arachnoid, but the only sound to escape was a raspy whisper.

Nearby a heap of camel fur, tiny bones and meat piled by her feet caused a flurry of swarming horseflies. The mangled animal covered in blood was still warm. The body heat felt comforting, though flies kept landing on her face.

Saylor tried to move her arm. It was free from the elbow down. She brushed the spider off and stretched her fingers into the paltry mush. Her nails clawed at the meat, rearranging enough to reveal a black eyeball with long lashes. It was the slaughtered baby fawn.

Repulsed, she retracted her fingers now covered in decaying animal flesh. She started to sob. She wanted to go home.

The T-shirt bunched under her chest exposed the basketball-sized lump in her belly. She tried to cover it.

Unable to comprehend the malformed thing in her body, she tried to remember what happened; fragmented memories of Riley, something hard against her skull then darkness. *Where was she? What time was it, what day?*

A hand reached across her stomach covered in scales and long claws. The mottled colored arm smelled vile. The digits were cold and wet.

Saylor screamed. This time the sound resonated so loud, it frightened the crows to flight.

Sampson barked, aroused from his slumber. He sprang to his four feet and took off running toward the noise.

Beau and Vernon jumped up disoriented. Vernon had a crick in his back from a tree knot. Beau rubbed his sore butt and ran after Sampson.

"Wait up boy, you don't know what's out there," Vernon said.

The bloodhound led them to an alcove close by.

Vernon retrieved the shotgun and fired one round into the air. It echoed in the quiet morning.

Sampson licked Saylor's fingers clean of the deer meat fragments.

Beau pushed through the dense bushes surrounding the alcove. His eyes came upon a horrific sight. "Oh God!" He ran to her, making a grimace at the mangled deer stench. "Gross, what in the world is that?"

Saylor had a blank stare, looking straight ahead. She was silent but calm. Her face and hair were a mess, far from the perfectly primped girl he knew.

Vernon looked around the campsite, focusing on the surrounding bushes.

"Vern, what are you looking for?" Beau said.

"Nothing, is she all right?" Vernon took out his pocketknife to cut the vines.

Saylor's lifeless body slumped forward.

"There's a bad cut on the back of her head, but it doesn't seem to be bleeding any longer." Beau draped her arm over his shoulder to carry her.

Sampson was more interested in the animal carcass.

"Get away from that!" Beau shooed him away.

Vernon followed as they walked out of the den, ever alert of the surroundings. They slowly made their way back to his house.

A half mile down the road, Wiley and a team investigated the spot where the tournament contestants launched their boats.

A pilot doing recreational flying in his plane saw the tail of a small boat sticking out from under thick cover in the swamp. He radioed authorities, who relayed the message to the Sheriff's Office.

Immediately after the fishing tournament, a team searched the woods with dogs, but could not find Morty or Phil. Several aerial missions canvased the waterways, but could not find the boat. The only thing investigators had was the truck and trailer, which did not yield any clues as to their whereabouts.

The mayor announced the men's status to the media as missing, but secretly hoped the story would lose its fascination after a few months. The sherrif left the case open at the insistence of the Bakersfield Constable.

The case grew cold for months and this latest discovery was fortuitous.

"Did you hear that? Sounds like a gunshot," Kenny said.

"Yeah, I heard it. Can you load Morty's boat onto the trailer, while I go check it out?" Wiley said.

"We've got it under control, go do what you need to," Andre said.

Wiley walked toward his truck, irritated that he had to work on a Sunday.

Kenny secured the bass boat, trying not to look at the corpse sitting in the driver's seat. The sight and smell overpowered him.

Together, they winched it onto the trailer. Andre drove the truck forward enough to get the trailer out of the swamp. Water drained from the motor covered in seaweed. Kenny could see the damaged propeller. "Well, that will ruin a good day of fishing."

"That explains why the engine wouldn't start," Andre said.

"What about the body, is it Morty?"

"I don't think so, though it's hard to tell from the decomposition." Andre zipped the body bag containing the mangled remains. The half-eaten corpse sat for a long time. Other parts were missing, bitten, clawed and infested with maggots.

Wiley drove down Route 3 to Creek Lane. The Crenshaws had the only house in the area, so he went there first. He was cautious, parking by the gate. He looked around and did not see anyone, but noticed the clumps of paper in the trees. Vernon's truck still attached to the trailer sat in the backyard.

With his gun drawn, Wiley walked down the driveway to the back of the house and was startled by Midnight standing on the back porch. "Dang, I hate cats, especially black ones." He stepped over the feline to peer into the windows. The lights were off and the interior uninhabited. Knocking on the door brought no answer.

Quietly, Wiley crept downhill toward the woods passing the family cemetery. The many grave markers reminded him how long the Crenshaws had populated the town. He thought about Blaze's preposterous conspiracy theories, which further incensed him.

Blaze was annoying like a mosquito. Her buzzing was audible when she got close enough to the ear, but swatting the air indignantly never shooed her away. Later she would return to aggravate and leave again. Like any bloodsucker, she drained him of his energy. Wiley tolerated her larks because of his new fondness for Odillia.

As Wiley refocused his thoughts on the investigation, the bushes near the clearing shook. He knelt on one knee, pointing the pistol ready to fire.

A black-and-tan hound dog lumbered out, trotting up the path straight for him. Its enormous paws grappled the earth flinging clumps of clay in all directions. Sampson's momentum almost knocked Wiley over. With drool cascading from his slobbering mouth, he licked his chops and panted from running.

"Easy big fella, where'd you come from?" Wiley said.

Voices emerged from the trees. "Just a few more steps, we're almost there. You can do it," Beau said.

The sight of Beau and Vernon carrying Saylor out of the woods shocked Wiley.

"Call an ambulance, she needs medical attention," Vernon said.

"What happened to her?" Wiley said.

"I don't know. We found her like this."

They made their way slowly up the hill to the house.

Wiley called an ambulance, though he was suspicious of Vernon.

Vernon ran inside to get some water and a quilted blanket.

Saylor sat quietly on the back-porch steps, almost catatonic. She shivered.

"Can you talk?" Beau wrapped the blanket around her.

Saylor continued to stare forward, not even blinking.

Beau tried to get her to sip some water, but it rolled down the cracks of her injured mouth.

In the hospital, Wilbur raced the gurney down the hall into the Emergency Room with Beau gripping onto the side rail.

Flat on her back, Saylor stared at the overhead lights as they made a strobe effect. A combination of dried blood, dirt and leaves mottled her pretty face. Her eyes protruded from recessed eyelids with a frozen expression, as each slightly parted lip collapsed unvoiced.

Beau held her palm and noticed that several faux fingernails were missing. Caked dirt and dried blood wedged in the crevices suggested she tried to claw her way out. "Saylor, can you hear me? You're safe now. The doctors are going to take care of everything." As the words rolled off Beau's tongue, he realized how untrue that statement seemed. The doctors could not fix their dying relationship, nor could they fix whatever was wrong with her.

Wilbur placed an electric thermal blanket over her legs. He pooled it around her feet after removing the high-top shoes.

Dr. Comeau arrived, drawing the privacy curtain behind. "What have we here?" She approached the gurney and waved a tiny flashlight in Saylor's eyes. "Well, that's not good."

"You always say that Doc," Wilbur said.

"If it were good, I wouldn't have a job." She placed an oxygen mask over Saylor's dirty face. "What's going on in this region?" She pointed to the large belly.

"I was hoping you could tell me," Beau said.

Dr. Comeau listened with a stethoscope. "Yep, we've got a live one in there."

"We found her in Creekwoods," Beau said.

"That's a strange place for a young girl to be."

"I hear strange things happen there all the time," Beau said.

"Tell me about it. Dr. Chaisson just brought in another dead body from the swamp. I overheard it might be one of the missing fishermen." Dr. Comeau placed heart monitor contacts on Saylor's body in various places. "I need to go get something, I'll be right back."

Beau could not contain his guilt. He started to cry and whispered as if she could hear. "I'm so sorry, this is my fault. If we wouldn't have argued, you would have never been out there." He clasped her hand.

Saylor slowly turned her head toward the bed rail, catching her reflection in the metal panel. Her bloodshot eyes did not blink. A tear formed in one corner, rolling down her cheek.

She opened her mouth under the mask. The clear plastic fogged as she screamed as loud as she could. Then she started to choke.

"It's okay, just relax. You're safe now."

Dr. Comeau returned with an intravenous feeding bag. "She's probably delirious from dehydration." She swabbed a dirty patch on her arm clean, and inserted a twenty gauge multiport needle. Holding it still, she crisscrossed surgical tape to secure the needle in place. Once the port was steady, she attached a tube hanging from the IV bag. "Fluids should do her some good." Drawn from her labcoat pocket, she administered a syringe full of golden liquid, without writing it down on the medical chart.

"What is that?" Beau said.

"Just a little cocktail of mine to take the edge off. She'll sleep like a baby."

Saylor closed her eyes and her tense muscles relaxed.

"I'll be back later to check in. Cheer up kid, she's still alive. That's half the battle." Dr. Comeau departed leaving the curtain closed.

Beau sat on a guest chair thinking about damage control. Since Saylor's parents were out of town, he did not need to worry about them just yet. His own parents would be wondering where he had been all night. He needed an alibi. Riley was the ticket, and the one he called.

"Dude, what happened, I've been trying to call you," Riley said.

"I know, and I'll fill you in, but first I need you to cover for me. Call my mother and say I stayed at your house last night."

"Sure, anything else?" Riley said.

"Talk to her only, and say I got drunk because we broke up. She'll at least be happy about that. And that I'm still passed out, in case she wants to talk with me. Then call me back later. I've got to get some coffee; it was a rough night in the woods."

Wiley had a lot on his mind. For the first time, stress from too much to do ate at his nerves. He needed to sort the facts and develop a logical chain of events. He had a deserted boat, a corpse, one missing body and a teenage assault. The only common denominator was Vernon Crenshaw the ex-convict.

Wiley knocked on Odillia's office door. "May I come in?"

She stood by an island of low cabinets, reviewing photographs from her confidential file on the Cryptomorph. A warm smile graced her beautiful face. Her demeanor perked from the pleasant interruption. "Officer Aucoin, I was just thinking about you."

Wiley deflected his eyes to the floor as his cheeks filled with blood. His blushing smile revealed dimples. "Sorry but I've brought more bad news."

"The young man from the tournament? I know Dr. Chaisson is performing an autopsy. Wonder what animal attack it will be this time?"

"About that, I need hard evidence before I can accuse him of falsifying documents. All I have is a kid that saw something blurry and a strange footprint that may be a hoax."

"I think the Boudreaux boy just turned eighteen. Plus he comes from a prominent family, making his testimony at least credible."

"True." Wiley leaned his elbow on the counter, listening to the soft way she spoke.

"And you have my reports about the tissue for medical testimony."

"I don't want you involved in this, it's too dangerous. There has to be another way."

"Wait a few hours and see what happens with the girl. I heard she was fine a few nights ago at the prom and now she's full term."

"How is that possible?" Wiley said.

"Medically, it is not." Odillia put the documents back into the file. "I'm going to get some tissue from the autopsy."

"Please be careful."

"Stop worrying. I'll be fine. I did contact my friend, Edna Dixon."

"Isn't she the District Attorney Julian Dixon's wife?"

"You know him?"

"Not personally, just that he is close to the mayor."

"Edna works for the Centers for Disease Control. I asked her to check the government database. She couldn't match the samples to anything in any part of the world."

"Then maybe it's not real, like an elaborate scheme set up by a serial killer to throw us off the trail."

"That is possible, but how do you explain the girl's condition?"

In the lobby, Beau shook the vending machine trying to get the cookies to drop. His cell phone rang. "How did it go?"

"Your mom fell for it. She wants me to have you call her when you wake," Rilcy said.

"How's your leg?"

"I'm out for the rest of the season with a leg cast and stupid crutches."

"I hope it doesn't affect your scholarship," Beau said.

"Doc said I should be fine after graduation, leaving the whole summer for lake activity."

The conversation tone shifted to somber. "Who did this to her?"

"More like what. Dude, I saw something horrible drag her off. It was green with scales, sharp teeth and claws. I almost messed my pants," Riley said.

"How hung over are you? Monsters aren't real."

"I'm telling you, I saw it with my own bloodshot eyes. The legend is real."

"That's impossible … later." Beau hung up the phone, placing it back in his pocket.

Vernon arrived at the hospital and saw Beau standing in the vending area. "How is she?"

"Sedated but stable. Thanks for your help. I really appreciate it."

"I'm just sorry it happened," Vernon said.

Wiley approached and interrupted. "I need a statement from both of you, one at a time. Start from the beginning."

"Riley and Saylor went to roll the Crenshaw's house with toilet paper. Something dragged Saylor into the woods. Riley ran and tripped going for help," Beau said.

"Then I came home and found Riley unconscious. I helped him to his car, and he came here," Vernon said.

"I arrived after they called me. Together we looked for Saylor all night. The next morning we heard a scream and my dog led us to her."

"Did you see anyone else?" Wiley said.

"No," Vernon said.

"I heard a gunshot," Wiley said.

"That was me firing a round in the air, in case a bear was nearby," Vernon said.

"You know you're not supposed to have firearms on parole, but I'll let it slide this once," Wiley said.

"It won't happen again, Officer."

Andre exited the morgue after completing Doug's autopsy. He approached Dr. Comeau who was leaving the physician's lounge with a large cup of black coffee. "How is the girl?"

"I've never seen anything like it. I'm going to check on her now."

"Can I come with you?" Beau said.

Once they both left, Andre turned his attention to Vernon. "Does Adele know?"

"She's still at Annie's, but I can radio her," Vernon said.

Andre said in a curt tone, "Tell her I'll handle it, like I always do."

"Why are you mad at me?"

"It always seems like we are cleaning up your mess."

Dr. Comeau and Beau entered the Emergency Room and heard screaming coming from Saylor's cubicle. She had removed the IV feeding tube and was cutting her arms with the needle in an attempt to slit her wrists.

"Hold her down," Dr. Comeau said.

Beau raced to the side of the bed, grabbed her wrist and shook it violently until she released the blood-covered needle.

Dr. Comeau grabbed the other arm, injecting a sedative.

Saylor still thrashed in the bed screaming. Her protruded eyes expressed terror. The shrill sound of her voice rattled the IV stand.

In a side drawer, Dr. Comeau retrieved thick leather restraints. She fastened the buckles around Saylor's wrists tied to the bed rails. "That should hold her." She dressed the wounds, reinserted the needle and replaced the oxygen mask.

Wiley had a few words with Andre before leaving. He called the mayor while walking out to the parking lot. "Sorry to disturb you sir, but we recovered Morty's boat and found Doug's body. Coroner says it's a gator attack and likely that Morty suffered the same fate."

"That's manageable," Eugene said.

"There's more, a high school girl has been assaulted by something."

"Something?"

"You heard right, and she's carrying something inside her."

"Look, I don't need any hiccups before election day. Do what I pay you to do, contain the situation," Eugene said.

"My job is to report the facts, you spin it however you want." Wiley hung up on the mayor just as Blaze approached him.

"Working on a Sunday, must be big?" Blaze said.

"I'm kind of busy right now."

"My sources say you found a body in the woods?"

"The coroner just finished the autopsy," Wiley said.

"And?" Blaze said.

"It's a gator attack."

"What about the other fisherman?"

"I'm on my way to resume the search." Wiley got in the truck and slammed the door in her face.

Tiny fragments of clumped tissue paper stuck to the ground. Vernon kept busy, waiting for Adele to come home. When he radioed, she was not happy having to cut her visit short, and even less thrilled about the situation at the hospital.

The voices in Vernon's head blamed him: *She's going to punish you. Kill her, do it now.* He dragged the rake gouging the lawn.

290

A warm touch tickled his shoulder. Vernon turned around assuming the spirits that haunted the property were playing tricks on him. He was pleasantly surprised to see Kacie's smiling face. "I didn't hear you drive up."

"It doesn't sound like a normal car ... the motor rarely comes on as slow as I drive." Kacie looked around the yard. "What happened here, teenage antics?"

"A harmless prank." Vernon went back to raking. "Maw is at Annie's."

"I came to see you."

"Listen, whatever he told you, I didn't have anything to do with that girl."

"What are you talking about?"

Vernon realized that Kacie did not know. Maybe Beau lied to her. "Never mind, so you came all the way out here to see me?"

"Can we talk?"

"Sure, let's go inside. Would you like some coffee?"

"That would be nice."

Vernon held the door open for her.

Kacie had not visited the house in a long time. Memories flooded back in her mind from deep recesses, but everything looked the same.

"You seem troubled, Sunshine."

"Unfortunately, I am."

Vernon offered her a seat at the kitchen table. It was Adele's chair. He poured steaming coffee into two mugs. "Would you like sugar?"

"Of course." Kacie stirred the coffee repeatedly looking down at the table. "Please stop encouraging my son. He already has a strained relationship with his father and I don't want him confused."

"About what?"

Kacie met his eyes, the ones that pierced her soul. She could not believe that after all these years; he still had not figured it out.

He recognized her desperation and reached across the table to hold her hand. The embrace of her radiant skin sent electric sparks down his spine. His rough hands engulfed her supple palm sandwiching it in warmth. For a moment, they lingered in close contact.

"I really need a friend right now."

"I'm always here for you," Vernon said.

Kacie sat back in the chair and stirred the coffee, troubled by the weight of her secret. "I don't know where to begin. So much has changed."

Vernon sensed something was terribly wrong. The tears forming in the corners of her beautiful eyes made him instantly saddened. "I don't like to see you hurting like this. Whatever it is that's troubling you, you can lean on me."

He stood to offer a hug and she met his advance. He held her fingers in his hand and kissed them. The bristles of his full mustache tickled her, while his gentle lips lingered on her skin.

"I need to tell you something that may come as a shock." Kacie met his gaze conflicted by longing and denial.

Vernon placed his palms on the side of her head. His fingers touched her neck, tilting her head enough so he could meet her in a simple kiss. Her eyes instinctively closed, as her lips parted, an invitation or surrender. Warm breath and satin skin, she tasted of honey and vanilla.

He held his face close to hers with their noses barely touching. Lingering quietly in her presence intoxicated him. The sensation of her arms wrapped around his back made him squeeze her tightly.

They continued to hug and kiss innocently as if young lovers. He placed her delicate lips between his, and then lightly bit her. She met his playful advance with the tip of her tongue, dancing around the outside of his mouth.

He passionately kissed her cheek repeatedly moving toward her ear. His warm breath made her knees weak. His nose twirled around under her earlobe, as he smelled her scent. "I thought you wanted to talk?"

"Not anymore," Kacie said.

Vernon reached down behind her knees, swooping her in his arms. He carried her up the stairs, while she held his shoulders. Their eyes locked in focus.

So much time had passed since their youthful courtship, without a kind word or a word of any kind. They did not speak, but communicated volumes of sonnets. He in nouns and she in adjectives coloring thoughts. The words produced a perfect harmony of tempo and inflection on syllables translating a language of love.

In her mind, Vernon was the only one for Kacie. She bent every rule her strict father placed, willing to risk his respect for a night of nirvana. Thinking they were soul mates destined for marriage, she rationalized her actions. That is why in the middle of senior year, she sacrificed her purity.

She remembered the blue moon, a rare occasion noteworthy because she had never wanted him so much.

Their perfect union was more than a release of unbridled passion; they conceived twin sons on that night.

They would have married after graduation, raised the boys and loved each other until the end, but life was seldom a fairy tale. One tragic event changed their destiny. In a flash, authorities locked Vernon away, leaving Kacie to deal with the problem growing inside her. The weight of guilt caused Kacie to cover her transgressions with a lie.

One day standing by her locker, Buck approached his, one section over. She smiled at him innocently, but he saw something different. She was alone and vulnerable with Vernon in prison. He seized the opportunity based on his own selfish needs.

Buck routinely collected trinkets to make himself seem more important. The narcissist needed a loyal beautiful wife, who would make him look good. Someone to worship him at home. She was the perfect trophy.

Charming her fragile sensibilities was easy. Buck manipulated her, took advantage of the situation but also kept her secret safe. He knew she was pregnant when she accepted his proposal. He raised the boy so his number one rival could not.

None of those things mattered any longer. Vernon threw Kacie onto his bed. He sat on the side of the mattress staring at her. "I've missed you so much."

"Quiet." Kacie touched his lips with her fingers.

"The way you crinkle your nose when you giggle."

"Don't talk."

"I love —," Vernon said.

"Kiss me," Kacie said.

Vernon's face turned a pale shade of parchment.

"That night under the stars in the woods, I never felt so alive. Being close to you, in that moment I knew I wanted to spend the rest of my life with you."

"I remember it too. I think of you every day, every moment and in the spaces in between. But late at night when I'm alone in my room and the house is quiet, in the silence I can hear my heart break."

Kacie caressed Vernon's beard running her graceful fingers over course hair. His weathered skin bore marks of outdoor living, but his rugged exterior housed a fragile being who understood the intricateness of her connections.

"I waited for you that day by the lake, but you never came. Then I saw the emergency vehicles racing down Route 3 toward your house," Kacie said.

Vernon reached over her to dig in a nightstand drawer, searching for a tiny black box. "I had this for you, but I mistakenly told Chester about it after school. He wanted to celebrate. We drove around town drinking. He was so happy for us. On my way to drop him off at home, we had an accident. A deer bolted out of the woods. He jerked the wheel and I couldn't recover control. We smashed into the tree."

Vernon offered her the box. "I want you to have this so you'll always know how I really feel about you."

Kacie opened the box with trepidation. Her unsteady hands revealed a sparkling diamond solitaire.

"I was going to propose that afternoon as the sun set. It would have been perfect if you said *yes*. Would you have?"

"Oh course, I loved you then."

"And now?" Vernon looked despondent. "The accident ruined everything. I killed my twin. I deserved to rot."

"It was an accident. Vernon don't be so hard on yourself; we were just kids." Kacie rubbed his shoulder. "Why didn't you tell me?"

"Would it have mattered? You deserved more than to be with a convict."

"I'm so sorry that you carried this burden for so long." Kacie held the ring box. "It's beautiful. I would have been blessed to be your wife."

"I left you alone, but I don't blame you for turning to him."

Kacie looked puzzled. "You really don't know do you?"

"Know what?"

"Why I married him."

"What's there to know?"

"Right around the time you started your sentence, I discovered I was pregnant. I was so afraid of my father and didn't know what to do."

Vernon was shocked. "Why didn't you tell me? We would have figured it out."

"What could you have done? Would the news have helped the situation?"

"Did he know?" Vernon said.

"Of course and in some sadistic way I think he got off on it."

Vernon thought about the past and everything he had misunderstood. "I had no idea."

"Why do you think I tried so hard to keep you separated from Beau? I thought for sure, you'd see your own reflection in him. He is so much like you." Kacie rested on his pillow. "Please understand I have grown to love Buck in some way. He's a decent man but he is not you. I will never feel this way about him."

Vernon propped up his head by an elbow. "So what's changed? Why are you telling me this now?"

"Make me feel that way again, like the night in the woods," Kacie said.

In her eyes, he saw conviction. She wanted something only he could give. He kissed the warmth of her quivering lips. The intense attraction allowed them the freedom to act without hesitation. His focus never faded from her direct stare, as he witnessed every quake and moan, peering into her soul.

The two rhythmically merged and receded, like rolling waves of an ocean, torrent water converging with calm. Their minds devoid of thought, present in the moment. Nothing else mattered but their perfect union.

Afterward, Vernon held Kacie in his gentle arms. He rested his head on her chest, falling asleep to the sound of her heartbeat.

She continued to hold him, tracing the outline of his ear with her finger. Feeling at peace, she rested too for a while.

Vernon's snoring woke her up. She carefully untangled herself. Kacie sat on the edge of the bed staring at the nightstand. There was an old photograph of them at the state fair. Vernon gripped a giant teddy bear that he won at the ring toss booth. Their arms conjoined with monumental smiles of innocence. She raised the frame to kiss the glass leaving an imprint of her lipstick.

The dream was over. Bottles of his prescriptions beckoned her to reality. No one deserved to suffer, while she wasted away from cancer. Vernon had experienced enough heartache in one lifetime.

Without reading the labels, she consumed the pills in handfuls guzzling water. She started to gag, covering her mouth so as not to wake him.

The water made her thirstier. She slid open the drawer to find a flask of whiskey. It burned her throat going down and tasted nasty.

The drug mixture quickly made her feel funny. She tiptoed across the wooden planks. Before leaving, she glanced at Vernon's peaceful face one last time. She whispered, "Bye my love. We'll be together again."

Kacie walked out the house wearing Vernon's ring. She had double vision and stumbled down the porch steps. Her loose body slipped into the car seat. She felt giddy for a dying woman mashing the accelerator.

She lowered the windows and opened the sunroof letting in fresh air on her face. Kacie sang along with *their song* playing through the speakers. The digital speedometer flipped higher. Wind blew hair across her face. She laughed wildly, hallucinating fairies chased the car.

Both hands gripped the steering wheel. She suddenly jerked the car to the left. She aimed for the remembrance marker nailed to the tree where Vernon's twin brother died. Her last words were: "God help me."

The tremendous strength of oak crumpled steel under force. Plastic fragments ejected into the air. The deafening sound resonated for a mile, waking Vernon.

Returning home, Adele witnessed the wreck and pulled over to assist. The deployed airbags steamed. Adele ran to the bloodied victim recognizing Kacie, her lifeless body slumped over the hood without a seatbelt.

CHAPTER 8

The television mounted on the wall produced a fuzzy picture from a loose cable connection. On the screen, a commercial touted the virtues of a wondrous product with miracle capabilities. Someone hard-of-hearing turned up the volume too high.

Beau leaned back in the upholstered chair with his head resting on the wall. Exhausted from the events of the last few days, he closed his eyes.

The hospital waiting room had one other person. On the coffee table amid piles of crinkled magazines sat a can of diet cola. The soda carbonation grated at his stomach lining. Cookies from the vending machine produced a raging sugar headache.

Beau wondered how his life has turned sideways so quickly and how he had lost control of the situation. He reevaluated his decision to break up with Saylor.

A commotion came from the entry doors as soon as they slid open. Wilbur rushed a gurney down the hall into the Emergency Room. A female with long dark hair, whose bloody face Beau recognized caused him to run after them.

Dr. Comeau entered the Emergency Room, drawing the privacy curtain. She glanced at Beau puzzled. "We keep running into each other? Another girlfriend?"

Beau ignored her quip, focusing on the patient. "Mom, can you hear me?"

Kacie turned her bruised face toward him; fresh blood trickled down from her forehead. "Dra … wer." Her eyes rolled back into her head, and she slumped on the pillow unconscious.

Dr. Comeau looked in her eyes with a light stick. "Her pupils are really dilated. Is she on any medication?"

"No, not that I know of," Beau said.

"I smell liquor." She drew Kacie's blood and handed the tubes to Wilbur. "Let's get a toxicology panel, stat." Dr. Comeau wiped Kacie's face with a damp towel to clean some of the blood careful of the embedded small pieces of glass. She placed an oxygen mask over her mouth and tended to the many lacerations.

Beau held Kacie's hand. "What happened to her?"

"I heard she had a fight with a tree and the tree won." Dr. Comeau inserted an Intravenous feeding bag needle and placed a pulse monitor on her finger. The number on the display panel was low. She banged on the machine with her fist. The number did not change. "Hum, that's not good."

Kacie's heartbeat crawled along slowly and then stopped. A loud continuous screech came from the monitor.

Dr. Comeau screamed toward the curtain. "We've got a coder!"

Wilbur rushed back in with an automated external defibrillator.

"Get him out of here," she said to Wilbur, who ushered Beau out of the cubicle.

Beau stood alone in the Emergency Room staring at the multicolored privacy curtain as the team frantically worked to revive Kacie. He heard the sound of an electronic charge.

"Stand back, charging 200 ... clear!" Dr. Comeau said.

The monitor still sounded an alarm for a flat line.

"Again, charging 250 … clear!"

This time a faint pulse blipped the machine.

"Excellent, good job Wilbur."

Adele and Vernon walked into the Emergency Room and saw Beau standing there. Vernon had a waxen expression. Beau was equally pale.

"How are you dear? I would have been here sooner, but I had to give a statement to Officer Aucoin at the accident scene," Adele said.

"Were you there? What happened to her?" Beau said.

"I don't know. On my way home, I saw her veer off the road into the oak where my son was killed."

"How is she?" Vernon said.

Dr. Comeau drew back the curtain so Wilbur could wheel Kacie upstairs. She approached Adele. "Are you the gram?"

"That depends on whom you ask. How is she?" Adele said.

"Stable now, heading to intensive care. We pumped her stomach, although I don't know what good it will do. Where would she get schizophrenia medications from?"

Adele turned to Vernon and glared as Dr. Comeau walked away.

"I need to call my grandpa, if you'll excuse me," Beau said. He dialed the pastor's number. "Mom has been in a terrible accident. Can you come to the hospital?"

Outside the hospital, overcast weather changed to a torrential downpour. Heard from inside, lightening boomed in the sky, as violent electrical streaks caused the interior lights to flicker. Everything went dark for a few seconds, before the generators powered on emergency lighting. The fixtures had an amber glow of dim light as if candles burned.

Saylor still asleep, started to twitch tied to the bed. The sedation from heavy narcotics amplified the anxiety from vivid remembrances of violence and terror.

Images of a slimy creature touching her body returned to her subconscious. It smelled of rotten flesh decomposing in the summer heat after rain. The odor was so offensive; it lingered in her nose hairs making it difficult to breathe.

The monster had slanted yellow eyes of a snake and menacing jagged teeth. It licked her skin with a slender tongue the texture of wire bristles coated in an oily puss.

Tied to the tree, she could not move. The ligaments tightly bound her, as she strained to break free. The twisted vines moved on their own, self-aware they adjusted to her movements.

Rough tree bark dug into her back, causing it to bleed.

The creature moved closer. With every step, Saylor screamed louder.

The vines moved slowly up the tree toward the canopy taking Saylor's wrists with them. They stopped once her arms were above her head.

The monster moved so close its stench caused Saylor to choke. Directly in front of her face, it glared at her exposing teeth. Thick foamy saliva drained from its mouth, exhaling putrid breath. Her arms blocked her head from looking away.

The Creepler placed its webbed hands on either side of her waist. It slowly slid them under her shirt and up her sides. She felt sharp claws scraping her back. The terror of not knowing its intentions were far worse than the assault.

It reached the inside of her armpits and held its position clamping down with suction. Precious seconds seemed like hours of torture. The scaly skin turned warm as a probe pierced her flesh, pumping a burning liquid. The reptilian scales changed color from green to rust. The creature vibrated producing a chirping sound, which grew louder.

Saylor lost sense of reality. The world dimmed. All faded to black in her mind.

Louis and Buck arrived in the Emergency Room.

"Where's your mother?" Buck said.

"They moved her upstairs," Beau said.

"Then why are you standing here?" Louis said.

Saylor screamed from behind the curtain.

Dr. Comeau ran past them with Andre and Wilbur. "Her vital signs are dangerously low."

"Get her to the labor and delivery room," Andre said to Wilbur. "I have to get the baby out or she won't survive for much longer," Andre said to Dr. Comeau.

As Wilbur wheeled the gurney away with Saylor screaming and thrashing, Beau did not know what to do. His feet froze like the night at the bonfire.

Buck and Louis walked toward the elevator bank.

"Are you coming with us?" Buck said to Beau.

"Geez Dad, thanks for the understanding. My girlfriend was just rushed to the delivery room."

Wiley hurried into the hospital, brushing past the Boudreauxs by the elevator with nothing more than a nod. The commotion of late had severely upset his regiment of drinking, making him extra cranky.

On her way out from the physician's lounge, Odillia saw Wiley in the hall. They huddled quietly as people passed.

"You wanted to see me?" Wiley said.

"It's the same result. Doug's tissue matches the others."

Wiley leaned against the wall. "Okay, but we still don't know what this is."

Blaze walked into the lobby with her camera operator. "Ed, can you get us some coffee? I'll catch up to you."

Ed nodded and walked away.

"Hey girl, what do you think about the situation?" Dr. Comeau said to Blaze.

"Let's recap: we have a dead hunter, two dead fishermen, two assaults, one sexual and a coroner and mayor covering it up. What do you think Officer?" Blaze said.

"For once I agree with you," Wiley said.

"Oh gosh, where is my camera operator when I need him," Blaze said.

"But, we still don't know what it is. I can't get on television and say we have a monster running around without proof," Wiley said.

"Edna at the Centers for Disease Control reached out to her sources and found no match," Odillia said.

"With government black ops, if they can't explain it, no one can." Blaze turned her attention toward Wiley.

"So that just leaves one question Officer. What are you going to do?"

There was a somber tone upstairs in the intensive care unit. Buck sat by his wife's side clenching her hand and gently sobbing.

Beau sat in the corner unable to keep his eyes open any longer. Fatigue from a lack of sleep and food caused his body to crash hard.

Louis stood at the foot of the bed praying in silence, towering over her frail body.

A ventilator compressed air into Kacie's lungs. Beeping machines kept her bandaged body riddled with tubes alive.

Dr. Comeau walked in with a stern face. "I have the CAT scan results. The combination of blunt-force trauma, pills and alcohol has damaged her brain function."

"What are you saying?" Buck said.

"I'm afraid she will never emerge from this coma," Dr. Comeau said.

Buck turned to Kacie trying to wake her. "No, no baby, please wake up."

"Mr. Boudreaux, if it is any consolation terminal patients often take their lives trying to spare their families from suffering."

"What are you talking about?" Buck said.

"Were you aware that your wife had stage four ovarian cancer?"

"That's not possible." Buck looked at Louis, "Did you know about this?"

"I knew she was having a problem, but not this," Louis said.

"Doc, you said you found pills and alcohol. My mother didn't drink or do drugs," Beau said.

"I'm sure she used the whiskey to wash the pills down, which were not hers."

In the labor and delivery room, white glossy ceramic tiles covered the walls. Sheets of white vinyl flooring grounded the sterile medical equipment. The ceiling plane receded into blackness as multi-head spotlights illuminated the procedure. With arms strapped to the table and feet in stirrups, Saylor's youthful body laid on the slab with her stomach in the air. Blue linens draped over her body, exposing her abdomen.

The nurse stood by her side manually oxygenating her lungs. While unconscious from heavy sedation, something moved around inside her.

"Is the container ready?" Andre said.

The nurse nodded while squeezing the bag.

"Okay, here we go." Andre swabbed Betadine on Saylor's lower region. He focused the lamplight on his headgear and stroked across her abdomen with a scalpel. Blood and fluids spilled onto the linens.

Saylor's eyes opened. She looked at the nurse. She thrashed her head trying to break free from the mask.

"Quiet her!" Andre said.

The nurse tried to cover Saylor's screams with her palm.

Saylor bit her like an animal.

The nurse stuffed a towel down her throat, leaving the nostrils clear.

Saylor's face turned beet red, as she screamed muffled sounds.

Andre used his hands to tear open her skin, pushing muscles out of the way.

The baby jerked around, clawing her insides.

Andre stuck his hand inside grabbing at the baby's tail. Once he had a grip, he used the other hand to pull it out of her. "I've got it, I think."

Saylor's bloodshot eyes were wide open and filled with terror.

Blood spattered across the pristine tiles. A slimy gelatin dripped onto the table.

Andre placed the dark colored creature in a stainless-steel box, locking the lid. The box had air holes in the top and a carrying handle. He injected a needle into Saylor's arm and she slept once again.

When Saylor's eyes had closed, the nurse removed the rag from her mouth.

"I'll close her up. Then move her to the psych ward, with restricted visitation."

Upstairs, Buck slept by Kacie's side holding her hand, while Louis in a meditative state bargained with his God.

Beau left to use the restroom down the hall. He splashed warm water on his face. In the mirror, he saw bloodshot eyes, dark bags and razor stubble.

On the countertop, someone left a newspaper. The headline read: *Tragedy Befalls Local Hero*. Beau picked up the paper and read the front-page story: *Prominent angler's wife comatose from hitting oak. Drugs involved. Authorities investigating possible suicide attempt. A confidential source confirmed terminal illness. Buck Boudreaux unavailable for comment. Fans erect a candlelit shrine outside hospital.*

Beau threw the paper down disgusted, "Trash rag!" He took the elevator down to check on Saylor. He looked around the Emergency Room, but she was not there. He stopped a nurse, "Excuse me, is the girl out of the delivery room yet?"

The nurse just shrugged her shoulders and walked away.

Beau went back into the hall ambling toward the vending area. Nothing in the machines enticed him. His stomach churned for real food. He wandered around and caught the smell of grilled hamburgers. The deli served lunch. He stood in line to order.

In the hall, Wiley was speaking with Adele when Odillia interrupted. "Officer, can I have a word with you in private?"

Adele squinted her wrinkled face at Odillia, which made her very uncomfortable.

"Sure, I'll meet you in your office. I'm just about finished here," Wiley said.

Odillia left them alone, although Adele continued to stare at her.

"I mean no disrespect, but we both know where the medications came from," Wiley said.

"Yes Officer, it's no secret my son is afflicted. But I can assure you, he did not give Kacie those drugs," Adele said.

"Was she at your house?"

"You'll have to ask him. If you'll excuse me, I need to have a word with the administrator." Adele pulled Andre to the side. "Where is it?"

"Safe, don't worry."

"Vernon knows about the boy and Kacie is as good as dead."

"What now?" Andre said.

"We move our focus to the bond between father and son."

"What about Buck?"

"I'll take care of him," Adele said.

"And the baby?"

"You handle that. Oh, and keep an eye on that biologist. She could be trouble."

Wiley had a steaming cup of specialty coffee for Odillia as a gift. Her office door was open. "Brought you a little pick-me-up."

"You're so sweet." Odillia closed the door. "They took something out of her alive."

"What kind of something?"

"No one is talking, but I bribed an orderly who said the delivery room was covered in blood and slime."

"Slime?" Wiley said.

"Whatever it was is still here in the hospital. Can you get a warrant?"

"For what, Administrator hides monster baby? The judge will laugh me out of his chamber," Wiley said.

"You better think of something, the whole town could be in danger now."

"I still can't reach the girl's parents, but maybe I can talk with her," Wiley said.

"She's locked in the mental ward with restricted access."

In the deli, Beau finished the last bite of burger when Andre walked by. "Excuse me sir." He chased him. "I'm trying to find my girlfriend, they moved her."

Andre looked at him puzzled. "Oh, you mean that girl."

"Is she all right?" Beau said.

"Sleeping like a baby," Andre said.

"Can I see her?"

"Because of the trauma inflicted on this poor girl, she is under psychiatric evaluation. I'll have a nurse contact you when she can have visitors." Andre rushed off.

Standing alone, Beau shifted his attention back to his mother. He felt the distress of needing to be in two places at the same time.

In the elevator, he thought of the last time they spoke. It was right before he left to go looking for Saylor. Kacie sat at the kitchen table drinking freshly squeezed orange juice. She wanted to talk, but Beau did not have time. Instead, he kissed her on the cheek and ran out the door.

The prospect of never knowing what she wanted haunted him.

As Beau turned the corner to the intensive care unit, he noticed the deafening quiet. He heard Buck wailing but no beeping machines. Louis also cried. They held Kacie's lifeless hands. The familiar numerals on the display monitor were gone. The equipment keeping his mother alive was off. The tubes were gone. Kacie laid stoically in the bed with eyes closed not breathing.

Cold air washed through his body like a wave. "What have you done?"

Buck raised his red eyes. "We thought it would be better if you weren't around. Your mother had a living will."

"You killed her?" Beau said.

"It was her will son, we only followed her wishes," Louis said.

Beau started crying. "No, no!" He grabbed his mother's feet. He shook her, but she did not respond. "Mom don't leave me." When he realized she was gone forever, he turned to his father and screamed, "I hate you!"

Spring brought with it the promise of hope. New life emerged from a frosty slumber. Plants and flowers reached for the sky eager to bask in sunlight's glory. Outside the chapel, beauty sprung to immortal essence.

All were somber surrounding a void in the earth. The dark-colored clothing, a blackwash across the landscape, contrasted nature's intentions.

Filed in rows, mourners grieved. Some did so moved by emotion, others out of a sense of duty. Beau stood in the front row between Vernon and Adele, frowning at the casket.

The silver metal sarcophagus glistened in the morning. It sparkled against the purity of flesh colored rose buds, slightly opened revealing a crème center. Each casket corner decorated in golden cherub faces reflected the sunlight. Beau could not take his eyes off the grandeur of his mother's eternal resting place. Even with the lid closed, she radiated beauty.

Adele put her arm around Beau and squeezed. Rarely moved by human emotion, she ached inside. Kacie was like a daughter to her. She felt the loss just like everyone else.

Across the chasm, Buck stood in a tailored suit surrounded by his fans. He wobbled, reeking of whiskey. Blaze lingered nearby behind him. The rest of the people were faceless concrete statues taking up precious space.

Pastor Foret dressed in a minister's uniform, clutched a worn Bible. The tough leather binding showed cracks. He tried to perform the service his only daughter deserved, but could not speak without sobbing.

Many times in the past, he performed funerals knowing the words by heart, but this time was different. Always removed from the sadness, he now felt it full force.

Eventually Louis said the words, though Beau heard nothing. His mind drifted to a time long ago when life was simple.

As a child, Kacie tucked him in bed at night. She read to him swaddled in his astronaut sheets. She spoke the words of *Ferdinand*. The sweet sound of her lyrical voice conveyed every emotion of the bull. Beau listened to the fictitious story about a loner who was different from everyone else. Kacie conveyed each word, as her approval to dare to be unique.

Other times he took for granted, were more examples of her nurturing; leaving the nightlight on with the hall door slightly opened, homemade chocolate chip cookies in his lunch box and the last time they did speak, Kacie promised to be there for him always.

"Where are you now?" Beau said realizing he spoke aloud.

Pastor Foret could not find the right words. He looked at his grandson, now his inspiration. "So many people ask me that question, where do we go when we die? I don't really know, but I'd like to believe my daughter is in a better place. One filled with beauty and eternal joy."

A solitary tear streamed down his cheek, as he nodded for Kenny to lower the casket. "I now invite you all to say your final good-byes."

One by one people approached the pit casting flowers and handfuls of earth atop the coffin.

Buck stepped up to the carpeted edge, fumbled in his pocket and threw down her wedding ring, the one he gave her eighteen years ago. The coroner found the simple gold band in her pocket. Buck did not speak, cry or throw anything else. Intoxicated, he almost fell into the hole. His entourage propped him up. He walked away sipping a flask.

Pastor Foret pulled a handkerchief from his pocket, blowing his nose. "I'm so sorry my dear Kacie, I've failed you." He walked away in tears.

The others said their peace and left Beau alone in the cemetery. He looked around at the grave markers, human flesh replaced by cold stone.

The crowd gathered in the parking lot, talking in faint murmurs.

"Please join us at the Boudreaux residence for refreshments," Adele said.

Lillian helped Adele arrange the food on the dining table in Beau's home. It was a large feast for such a woeful occasion.

"I think we made too much to eat," Adele said.

Lillian sampled a cocktail shrimp. "Um, who knew funeral food could taste so good."

"Thanks for helping with this dear."

"Where did Vernon go? I haven't seen him since the service," Lillian said.

"He's not feeling well. I told him to go home," Adele said.

"He must be torn up inside. I feel so bad for him."

"I guess it's no secret that he still had feelings for Kacie."

"That's understandable. She was a great girl, my best friend and Lord knows; I'm going to miss her too."

In the drawing room, Buck raised his voice enough for people to stare. "I have it, I tell you, so just back off Louis!"

"I have one too, right here. What's the date on yours?" Louis said.

"We drew these wills up when we married." Buck shoved the document in Louis's face.

"Mine is from one week ago."

Buck wavered back and forth astonished. "Why would she draw up a new will without telling me?"

Louis felt disappointment that his once respectable son-in-law digressed into a drunken jerk. "Seems like there is a lot she never told you."

"What are you implying old man?"

Louis handed Buck the document. "Read it for yourself, then drink some coffee for a change. You're a disgrace to my daughter's memory."

Buck stepped close to Louis, reeking of alcohol. "I'm the disgraced one. Why was your little angel wearing another man's ring? Why was she near the Crenshaw place? Where did she get the pills?"

"I don't know."

Buck stumbled backward. "You're precious daughter may not have been the saint you think she is. That's all I'm saying."

The noise from the room caught Beau's attention. People could hear what should have remained private. Beau interrupted them, "Can you keep it down? What's the problem?"

Buck proceeded to read aloud and slur the words. "I leave two-thirds of my estate to my husband and one-third to my son. Well, there you go."

Beau looked confused, "So how much is that?"

"A quarter of a million. Congratulations, you've won what's behind door number two," Buck said.

"I'd rather have my mother back."

Blaze wove her way through the entourage, carrying caffeine. "Buck honey, have some coffee."

"Why thank you. Glad somebody cares about me, unlike my own family."

Beau rolled his eyes. "I can't talk to you when you're like this." He pushed through the crowd to get to the staircase. As he pounded the wooden steps, he thought of his mother's last word. Suddenly, the two mumbled syllables made sense. She said: *drawer* and he knew just the one.

In her bedroom that smelled of lavender, under a rosewood jewelry box a hidden skeleton key opened Jessie's room.

While everyone mingled downstairs, Beau opened the door to the shrine. The room was dark and cold. A thin layer of dust congregated on planer surfaces. Beau raised the window shade enough to shed light on her dark secret.

The drawer Kacie often referenced would be a window into her soul. It housed photographs of better times when she was somebody else, times when life was simple and carefree.

The official document memorializing Jessie's short life had fingerprints on the edges from Kacie's repeated touch. Signed by Dr. Andre Chaisson, the Death Certificate read: *smaller male twin stillborn*. Beau thought about the irony, if Jessie was dead before he came out of the womb then how was he ever really born. If Jessie was never born, then his mother's pain and suffering over the loss of a child was a figment of her imagination. Why did she cling to the sorrow?

As Beau set the document down, he noticed the name under *paternal father: Vernon Earl Crenshaw*. While Beau made sense of what the words meant, downstairs in the hall a Ming vase fell crashing to the floor. Buck bumped into it on his way to the restroom. The shattered porcelain cast the stench of stagnant floral water asunder. The stench wafted up the staircase.

Embarrassed by his Dad's behavior, Beau returned the contents to the drawer. He closed the drawer and a light pink parchment envelope corner protruded. He opened the drawer again to push it in and noticed the prison address. The letter also lacked any postage.

He opened the unsealed envelope to retrieve a handwritten letter. It was his mother's penmanship; fluid strokes of a ballpoint pen and bubble dots on *i's*.

Beau thought about returning the artifact to its museum, but something internal pushed him to read it. His hands shook as he strained to focus on the words: *My love, you will never know how my heart breaks to see you locked away. I waited for you that day, but you never came. I heard about the car crash, Chester's death and then you were gone. Today I write to speak the truth; we will have twin sons from our night in the woods. They grow inside me like my eternal love for you.*

Beau's eyes welled up overcome with emotion. He had longed all his life for this honesty. Now he knew why his relationship with Buck strained and the ease of Vernon's company relaxed him. In Creekwoods he felt normal and at peace amid the wildlife, because he was truly home.

Beau returned the contents to the drawer. He thought about the gift that his mother had given him. All the puzzle pieces finally fell into place.

He walked over to the window. In the yard, the sun shined brightly on Riley balancing on crutches talking with Coach. Beau smiled and drew the opaque roller shade down to the windowsill, slowly extinguishing the light.

When Blaze walked into Fourchette's, she recognized the back of his head. In school, she stared at it so many times. It looked the same now, except for a few grey hairs and slightly thinning density.

Buck sat alone at the bar while Clovis polished glassware standing on the other side.

"Hello partner, how is it going?" Blaze slid the stool next to him out, and rested her purse on the bar top.

"Blaze … what's hap … happening?" Buck said with hiccups.

"Clovis, can I have some sweet tea?"

"Have a real drink, for old time's sake," Buck said.

"It's 1:30 in the afternoon on a workday. Did you know today is Thursday?"

"Thursday, smursday. Why do I care?"

Clovis deposited a tall amber glass on a beverage napkin and frowned at her.

"So Buck, how long are you going to sit here?"

Buck shrugged, "Quit nagging me."

"I'm concerned about you. What about the championship title?" Blaze said.

"Doesn't matter, my wife's dead and my son hates me. What's left to live for?"

"I remember feeling that same way once. One minute I was on top of the world in love with the dream guy, then I laid on a surgical table cutting out my heart."

"Are you going to bring that up? I paid for it, didn't I? What more do you want?" Buck said.

"I want you to feel what I felt over the loss of our child."

"It was an accident. Who would have thought you'd get pregnant after one time? I must be very unlucky."

"I can't believe you're so insensitive. I guess it's the liquor. I just want to help you through your pain." Blaze tried to hug him.

Buck recoiled, "Get off me!"

"What about our affair? You called me that night and you called many nights after."

"You'll never be more than a piece of ass to me."

Blaze was horrified. "How can you be so heartless?"

"You'll never replace my Kacie either."

Blaze grabbed her purse and ran out crying.

"Barkeep, another round for everyone."

"There's no one here but us," Clovis said.

"All the more reason to celebrate," Buck said.

Clovis poured a shot of whiskey. "Aren't you going to Beau's graduation?"

Buck laughed, "Are you kidding?"

For six weeks, Buck repeated the same behavior, now a habit. He entered the bar around noon, drank all

321

day into the night and stumbled out to his truck after Clovis kicked him out.

Each day was the same. Clovis would inquire about Beau's upcoming graduation and Buck would consume enough alcohol to forget the question.

The day quickly arrived when the soon-to-be graduates stood single file in the hallway outside the gymnasium. Dressed in black gowns and caps, they waited for the ceremony to start.

Beau stood near the beginning of the line according to alphabetical last name, next to Meghan.

"I wish Saylor could be here," Meghan said.

"Me too," Beau said.

"How is she?"

"They won't let me see her, but I spoke with Mr. Landry this morning."

"Her parents must be a wreck."

"They canceled the rest of their road shows this season, so they could be at home."

"That's a shame. So what really happened? The paper says—,"

"The paper lies!"

"I've heard rumors that something attacked her and others are now afraid to go to the lake."

Ms. Chillingham stood at the front of the line. "Shhhh! Quiet everyone." She opened the double doors engaging the doorstops and spoke to the first student. "Take your seat, start at the first row." She motioned for the line to follow. When Beau walked by, she patted him on the back and smiled.

Short rows of white folding chairs facing the basketball hoop covered the gymnasium floor. Front and center the mayor stood behind a lectern draped in an American Flag. Families of the graduates sat in the bleachers on both sides of the court. Behind the mayor sat the school principal, Coach Ducet, Amber LeBlanc and an empty chair for Ms. Chillingham. A photographer from a school portrait company roamed around snapping pictures.

As Beau followed the others and took his seat, he felt hollow inside. This should have been a happy occasion, but instead both his parents were absent. His mother could not experience today, from her burial plot. His father could not experience today, from the bottom of a bottle. Saylor could not experience anything today or afterward, locked in a mental ward.

The only good thing was that school was finally over. Beau no longer had to spend his days bored, studying subjects he cared nothing about, while the rest of the world lived just beyond the fence. No longer did he have to socialize with people he disdained, Riley excluded.

Riley's friendship remained a constant. He was loyal, fun to be around and the only person who did not try to control him.

In kindergarten, Riley started the school year late. He had just moved from Florida. That first day he wore a rounded collar short-sleeve white shirt with denim Bermuda shorts. The elastic waistband and saddle-oxford shoes were far from trendy. His black silken pageboy haircut and slanted ebony eyes caused the other kids to tease him. He shied from the bullying unable to stand up for himself. Instead, he ran to the school nurse complaining of a stomachache. Lin left work to pick him up. After a number of recurrences, she ignored his calls.

Riley sat alone in the cafeteria pushing mashed potatoes around a compartmentalized fiberglass tray, immune to the noisy chatter and food-throwing going on around him.

Beau asked the server for an extra slice of chocolate cake, flashing his dimples. He approached Riley's table, sat across from him and offered the cake.

Riley at first looked at him puzzled, expecting something bad to happen.

Beau reached out to shake hands and introduced himself. They were best friends ever since.

As Beau walked down his row, he glanced at the bleachers and noticed Louis, who smiled back. Beau had not spoken to his grandfather since the funeral. He equally blamed Louis for terminating his mother's life-support without consulting him first.

The rest of the students took their seats and the mayor opened the convocation.

"Good afternoon. Welcome graduates, family and friends. Before we get started, I just want to thank you for helping me win reelection. Those of you who volunteered with the election campaign helped secure a bright future for Stray Oaks. Thanks again," Eugene said.

The crowd clapped.

"Pastor Foret, would you open the convocation with a prayer?"

Louis approached the lectern. "It is my honor to bless the Stray Oaks High School graduating class which includes my grandson. May the Almighty Father protect our young minds from temptation and guide them on the journey into adulthood, keep their hearts pure and reward them for righteousness. In his name we pray, Amen."

The crowd replied, "Amen."

"Now please help me in welcoming your Valedictorian, Amber LeBlanc."

Everyone clapped, while Amber's mother stood to take photographs, angering the professional photographer.

Amber approached the lectern moving the microphone down. "I dreamt of this day for a long time, carefully thinking about what words to say and writing many speeches over and over."

Amber removed the cordless microphone and walked toward the front row of students. "I could expound the virtues of hard work or tell you the world is rough out there." Amber walked around as she spoke looking at all the faces. She focused on Beau and stopped.

"In my time here, I learned the textbook material, aced the tests and have a bright future ahead of me, but the biggest most important lesson I learned came from just one person. He taught me to be true to myself, to be brave enough to stand in the face of adversity and to follow my passion. And that's what I encourage all of you to do, follow your passion no matter how many roadblocks are put before you. Keep trying to succeed and never give up." Amber replaced the microphone and took her seat.

One student clapped slowly pausing in between and the others joined in.

The mayor leaned into the microphone. "Thank you Amber for that most encouraging speech. Before we hand out the diplomas, Marvin would like to say a few words."

Marvin stood off to the side of the basketball court in the corner. He spoke loud with a tone of sadness. "As you all know, we are short one classmate today, however, she is here in memory. Saylor, I look around these walls and see you everywhere. Your school spirit, pep rally banners and friendship are everywhere in the hearts you touched. As football team captain, I honor you and pray for your speedy recovery. We all miss you."

Jennifer stood, then Walter. So did the rest of the cheer team. Then the entire class and everyone in the bleachers rose bowing their heads in a moment of silence.

"Thank you Marvin. Now, I will call the names of the graduates," Eugene said.

The photographer moved into position, kneeling.

Ms. Chillingham stood next to a small table covered in a stack of leather bound diploma certificates. She handed each one to the mayor, as he read the recipient's name aloud.

Beau was one of the first students to approach. He shook the mayor's hand and posed smiling at the camera. A small sense of accomplishment masked internal sorrow.

As he passed the bleachers, he heard a familiar voice say: *boy*. Vernon and Adele smiled at him. A light from a disposable camera flashed in Beau's face.

Beau took his seat filled with surprise that the Crenshaws were there.

Riley made his way hopping down the aisle on crutches.

Red, black and white bands of paint circled his leg cast. The top of his graduation cap had a smiley face made out of white tape.

Beau clapped and whistled, as Riley passed.

He opened the leather binder looking at the parchment document, which had his full name written in calligraphy. The raised gold metallic seal confirmed the last requirement needed to live his dream. Now nothing could stop him from going to art school.

Conveying the last diploma, the mayor congratulated the students. The air became thick with a gaggle of tossed caps. They tumbled down gently as tassels flopped. Cheers, hugs and screams of joy exalted the ceiling rafters.

Picking up his cap, Beau looked for Riley in the crowd. When he found him, they hugged.

"Congrats dude!" Riley said.

"Same to you."

"A bunch of us are heading to the lake, you coming?"

"I'll catch up. I need to do something first." Beau pushed through the crowd to find the Crenshaws.

Adele stood there in her blue dress smiling. She hugged Beau and patted him hard on the back.

Vernon reached his hand out to shake, but Beau hugged him instead.

"I'm really glad you're both here. Thanks for coming," Beau said.

"I'm proud of you and I know, so is your Maw," Vernon said.

Beau's eyes started to water. "Thanks, that means a lot to me." The moment seemed awkward yet comforting. "Are you going somewhere?"

"I need to get away for a while outdoors," Vernon said.

"Where to?" Beau said.

"A North Georgia river I've always wanted to fish," Vernon said.

"I've decided to leave early for Savannah."

"Won't you call us when you get settled there?" Adele said.

"I'll do that, for sure."

Adele hugged him again. "We are always here for you when you need someone to talk too."

A stack of plastic sleeved menus needed cleaning. Mabel wiped off the greasy fingerprints with glass cleaner. Standing by the hostess stand, she looked up from her task when the door opened.

"Welcome Beau, can I get you a table?" Mabel said.

"No thanks. Is my Dad here?" Beau said.

"Unfortunately, yes. Please get him to go home. He's wearing out his welcome."

"I totally understand, and apologize for his behavior."

"Oh and congratulations! Doesn't it feel good to have school behind you?"

"Yeah, you're right!"

Beau saw his father seated at the bar a few seats down from Mr. Stumpy. Beau tapped Buck on the shoulder.

Buck slowly turned his head to reveal a long beard and bloodshot eyes. "Whatz up?"

"I'm leaving for Savannah."

"Good for you."

"Thanks for coming to my graduation."

"Is it the weekend already?"

"Yes, you missed it," Beau said.

"Sorry, I'll fire my assistant."

"Adele and Vern made it."

"I'm sure your new family is proud," Buck said.

"You know about that?"

Buck chuckled, "I've always known you weren't my son."

"Forget it." Beau started to walk out and never look back.

Buck turned around pleading, "All I ever did was try to be a good father to you and give you a better life."

Beau felt a sudden empowerment to say how he felt. "I appreciate that, it's just not the life I want to live." And there it was, cold bitter honesty finally released.

Buck took a deep breath and turned around to the bar focusing on his glass. He did not argue or say anything snide.

The silent response surprised Beau, who had never shut him down before. "What about you and the championship?"

"My life ended the day your mother died."

"I'm sorry for that, as sorry as you are."

Beau ran into Dr. Comeau in the hospital hallway. "Excuse me, would you do me a favor?"

329

Looking tired with caffeine jitters, "What do you need kid?"

"I'm leaving for college, and I just want to say goodbye to her."

"I can't let you in there," Dr. Comeau said.

"Please, please, please." Beau made his saddest puppy-dog face.

"Oh, all right. But make it quick. I could get in a lot of trouble."

"Thank you!"

"Follow me and keep your mouth shut." She led him to the psychiatric wing. "She's in there." Dr. Comeau pointed to a small observation window.

The tiny room had cushioned walls. Saylor sat on the floor in pajamas with her legs crossed. An outline of a mirror made from black tape on the wall reflected her face in her mind. She raked her hair repeatedly in one spot pretending she held a brush causing a bald spot.

Beau placed his hand on the observation window, as he choked back tears. "I'm so sorry it had to end this way."

Saylor continued to stare at the wall unaware of his presence.

"You need to go now before someone sees you." Dr. Comeau escorted him out.

When Beau exited the elevator, Andre was pushing a medium sized stainless-steel box on a cart out the entry doors into the parking lot.

Beau hung back a minute in the lobby hoping not to be seen. He pulled out his cell phone and dialed Riley. "I've decided to get on the road, so I won't be coming by the lake."

"We're going to miss you, but I understand," Riley said as other students made a ruckus in the background.

"Have one for me," Beau said.

"I'll have more than one."

"I saw my Dad."

"How is he?" Riley said.

"Drunk. Then I saw Saylor."

"How is she?"

"Catatonic," Beau said.

"Bummer. Well, good luck and call me dude."

"Dude!"

They laughed for a moment at the inside joke.

"Later," Riley said.

Beau put the phone away and stepped into the entry vestibule with a smile on his face. Three men in black suits entered from the opposite direction in a hurry. One bumped into Beau without apologizing.

"Pardon me," Beau said.

The men did not stop or respond. They were looking for something.

As Beau walked out from under the covered drop-off area, he thought about the rest of his life, excited for a new adventure. He stepped off the curb and bright sunshine blinded him. Retrieving sunglasses from his shirt pocket, he looked up at the cloudless blue sky and smiled.

A backdrop of topaz cattails lined in rows marched down the subtle bank of Shallow Basin. Covered in short grass, flat marshy ground accepted the stainless-steel box, set down by a man in a white labcoat.

The box with a closed lid rattled, as something inside thrashed around violently, booming against the interior walls.

The man opened the lid, drawing it up to rest on top of the box.

The sound of Cicadas grew louder, building to a crescendo.

A medium sized dark-green creature with newly formed reptilian scales ran by in a flash. It screamed upon exit, set free from the cage. The sound grew fainter as the baby Creepler ran off into the swamp.

THE END